# The Legend of Augustus McBoone
## Prequel to Bear Hollow

### Rod Cochran

∞ INFINITY
PUBLISHING

ISBN 978-1-4958-1392-4
eISBN 978-1-4958-1393-1

Copyright © 2017 by Rod Cochran

All rights reserved, including the right of reproduction in any form, or by any mechanical or electronic means including photocopying or recording, or by any information storage or retrieval system, in whole or in part in any form, and in any case not without the written permission of the author and publisher.

This is a work of fiction. Names, characters, places, and incidents either are the product of the author's imagination or are used fictitiously. Any resemblance to actual events or locales or persons, living or dead, is entirely coincidental.

Published July 2017

INFINITY PUBLISHING
1094 New DeHaven Street, Suite 100
West Conshohocken, PA 19428-2713
Toll-free (877) BUY BOOK
Local Phone (610) 941-9999
Fax (610) 941-9959
Info@buybooksontheweb.com
www.buybooksontheweb.com

For Jim Lundgren A/K/A Mountain Man

James H. Lundgren
December 9, 1946 - July 8, 2016

The greatness of a man is in his integrity, and his ability to affect those around him positively. Jim had and did that.

# Author's Note

The **Legend of Augustus McBoone** is the first of several planned prequels to **Bear Hollow**. I plan on filling in the history to 1985. Also planned are sequels that take us to the present day. These characters are the children and grandchildren of Mac and Tom, Gus and Hayley. All interact with Stickwalker. Please note the recurrence of the word "plan." These are works of fiction and plans do change.

Comments about and recognition for **Bear Hollow** follow my note. I hope you find Gus' story as compelling as Mac and Tom's.

My 4-part epic fantasy **My Brother Methuselah** is also written. The first is published, the remainder will be released with the prequels of **Bear Hollow**. Although the action takes place 5,000 years ago you will find the present-day characters are throwbacks to the "First Earth" ones. In my humble opinion human nature has **not** changed.

# CONTRIBUTORS

The following contributed to the development of The Legend of Augustus McBoone. My heartfelt thanks to Cindy Cochran, Katie Gehman, Jason Gehman, Matt Cochran, Gary Cochran, Bob Cochran, Dick Colliver, Lindy Bower, Tom Bower, Randy Morgan, Brian Edgcomb, Gary Parker, Chuck Broughton, Ed Glover, Beth Hurler, Brenda Baker, Kasey Dunham, Harold Plank, Howard Fry, Rich Wilkinson, Mike Hale, Bob Cunningham, C. L. Franke, Dorothy Price, Francis Mitstifer, Mike Wagner, Ollie Litzelman, Luke Pierce, Mike Bollinger, Sandra Haupt, Jon Williams, Jim Lundgren and the Mase Estate.

Special thanks to Bill Robertson, college friend and author of the ten Bucktail novels (and many others) and Holly Lawrenson, typist.

# Sayings

Thou shalt have no other gods
    before me.

                               Moses
                               Exodus 20-3

Choose this day whom you will serve.
    But for me and my house,
We will serve the Lord.

                               Joshua, son of Nun
                               Joshua 24:15

The Lord is my shepherd; I shall not want.
He maketh me lie down in green pastures;
   He leadeth me beside the still waters.

                               David
                               Psalm 23:1-2

As the deer panteth for the water,
    So my soul panteth after thee…

                               David
                               Psalm 42:1

All authority in heaven and on earth has been given to me.

> Jesus, son of God
> Matthew 28:18

To accomplish great things We must not only act but also dream,Not only plan but also believe.

> Anatole France

Man is the only animal that blushes.

> Mark Twain

Neither a scrooge nor a patsy be.

> C. L. Franke

# CONTENTS

Dedication v
Author's Note vii
Contributors ix
Sayings xi
Chapters:
1. The Legend 1
2. Shave and Haircut, 4 Bits 11
3. Monday Drive 29
4. The Fighting 149th 41
5. A Have-Been 47
6. The Clan McBoone 55
7. A Forgiving Heart 73
8. The Hereafter and the Here 89
9. The Pine Era 95
10. Tinkering with my Dad 101
11. Pig's Ear Paddy 113
12. John Seagreaves 1817-1862 123
13. Bunkhouses, Outhouses and Hicks 131
14. Payday Loans and Such 145
15. Breakfast at Cookie's 151
16. Cookie 163
17. The Cadence of the Woods 171
18. Fighting in the Big Woods 179
19. Dying in the Big Woods 187
20. Lovin' Peggy Sue 191
21. 98 First Class Men 201

| | |
|---|---|
| 22. Heading Out | 213 |
| 23. J. E. P. Stickwalker | 231 |
| 24. Camp Curtin | 249 |
| 25. March to D.C. | 267 |
| 26. Red Reb | 289 |
| 27. Halloween | 301 |
| 28. Christmas Mail | 313 |
| 29. Fixin' Old Warhorse | 327 |
| 30. The Riverboat | 333 |
| 31. Hawks versus Heroes | 341 |
| 32. My First Rebel Yell | 347 |
| 33. A Bird's Eye View | 365 |
| 34. High Ground | 369 |
| 35. McPherson's Barn | 377 |
| 36. Huckleberry | 385 |
| 37. What Goes Around… | 397 |
| 38. Old Warhorse…Again | 403 |
| 39. Overnight at the Lady | 409 |
| 40. Whatcha' Cookin'? | 419 |
| Comments about and Recognition for Bear Hollow | 423 |
| Order Form | 427 |

## Chapter 1

# The Legend

**Steam Valley, October 1945**

The sun rose to a warm fall day. The gliding shadow crossed the north rim of Bear Hollow then banked east, directly into the Valley of Steam. At Big Curve it swung north, gliding over U. S. Route 15. Two miles later it turned east again, flying above a tree-lined gravel lane with a mowed strip of green up the center. Walnut husks lay scattered along the lane, a few still clung within brittle leaves whose branches intertwined above them. Sometimes the shadow would settle amidst these branches, firm up into its predator form and watch the groomed farmsteads below.

Sometimes. Not today.

When it neared the uppermost farmstead, the oldest at the head of the lane, the predator firmed up, lowered its talons, dipped down and screamed. The newborn lamb, the kind that followed Hayley to school, heard and blatted its fear.

But its mother was feeding too far away.

The predator screeched again, a cry of triumph. Momma's head perked up. She tensed when she realized the distance was too far. The predator closed on its prey, claws extended, reaching, reaching...

There came a shot, a puff of feathers, a screech of woe.

The big bird tumbled into the pasture.

"Grandpa!" admonished Hayley from outside the screen door. "One of these days, you're gonna get in trouble doing that!"

I chuckled. From the front porch I broke down the 10-gauge, a gift from my ballbat client The Babe, ejected the spent shell. The scent of Cordite wafted skyward, a scent from many times before.

"That may be...someday," I answered. The big bird shuddered and lay still. "Right now I'm sick and tired of these damn eagles stealing our lambs."

I reloaded, clacked my single-shot shut, retrieved the dead bird. The sheep had gathered in the closest corner of the pasture, spooked by their near-disaster.

I hoisted the eagle high. Her white head and curved yellow beak dripped red with blood. One dark brown wing dangled to the ground. A mature eagle she was, long wingspan, and I'm still ten inches over six feet.

Still. I've lost some heft the past couple of years but none of my height.

I've known only one man taller, and I've had eight tall sons. That man is J. E. P. Stickwalker. He stands a full head taller, a **real** giant. We fought together at Gettysburg, eighty-two years ago. Stickwalker was old then. He's still alive now. Hasn't lost any heft either.

I admire the bird. Kinda proud. Tell myself I made a good shot. All my kids were good shots but only three – Michael, Angus and Joshua, and my grandson Jacob – are close to being my equal.

Still. And I'm over one hundred years old.

Well, Michael and his son Jacob are better pistol shots, especially Jacob. But he's a Texas Ranger. Practices every week. I don't practice at all. Any more.

The lamb is suckling its momma. She is too kind. Little Mr. Troublemaker has no idea how close he came to being breakfast in the Big Woods.

*I called to Hayley: "You want any feathers?"*

*"Nah. I have lots."*

On the way past my barn I toss the carcass to our pigs who grunt their thanks.

Thanks! They don't thank anyone, pigs. Just grunt.

I lay the shotgun across my porch swing. In easy reach in case I need it. It's safe. A hammer gun needs cocked to shoot. I pat my pants pocket to make sure of my 32. A "train gun", I keep the top chamber empty for safety but one cock and that double-action can send four slugs faster than you can say…Spike Poorbaugh.

Mandi, I mean Hayley, went into my cabin, I mean house, to prepare my Corn Flakes with banana breakfast. We're creatures of habit. When she's not going to school or somewhere Hayley is here…in the mornings making my breakfast.

Hayley's a sturdy high-school senior, tall (although a foot shorter than me), left handed, buxom like her great-grandmother Mandi, right "pert" according to the locals. As her curls disappeared through the screen door she reminded me again of my first wife when she went through a door that I made, what, seventy-five years ago.

My 101ˢᵗ birthday approaches. Forgive me, I ramble. I pine for the first of my three wives. It amazes me how long you can love the love of your life.

The hogs have torn the eagle apart. The juiciest piece now hangs from the jaws of the meanest pig. Not the biggest. The most aggressive. We don't like each other. Somehow that boar knows I'm gonna have the last word. Like God and Satan. "I expect to smoke you soon," I yell to Mr. Mean Pig. He grunts and turns his curly tail toward me. Nice hams.

I enter my cabin, I mean house. Sit at the kitchen table. Several journals from the Pine Era and Civil War are stacked there. Alongside is a pile of today's stamped mail.

Hayley's mom, Brenda, sorts through other journals in the office. This large room is next to the kitchen and serves as the McBoone library. Has its own screened entrance from my wide wraparound porch. The double doors from the kitchen to the office are open – ostensibly for airflow and access but also to keep track of crusty old me banging around in my kitchen.

Brenda is the McBoone secretary, not quite as bossy as Hayley. She's "pert" too, married to Ralph, they also have an older daughter named Norma. Brenda keeps books, tracks orders, pays bills, answers the phone. She also types letters and invoices on McB stationery designed by her mom, and my third daughter with Mandi, Peggy Mae. Clickety-clacking is a female tradition handed down since Mandi. Brenda types on a new Underwood. Hayley's older model sits near. The original, worn out now, was a gift from Sam Clemens. It sets on the bookshelf flanked by signed first editions of **Tom Sawyer** and **Huckleberry Finn**.

Clemens delivered that machine, taught Mandi how to use it.

Encouraged her to teach me, damn him, but not everyone needs to type to survive, right? Clemens himself went back to handwriting his manuscripts. Seems he'd get frustrated and swear at that "infernal machine." Then his wife'd yell at him.

Back to those journals. Handwritten, of course.

They have recorded McBoone activities long before I was born.

Mandi, trying to get me to type on rainy days (after raiding the honey-pot, of course) would give up, exasperated with me as I read an old journal or caught up my own. My Dad's, Grand-dad's, great Grand-dad's are there and beyond. They're dog-eared and yellowed but still readable. Almanac stuff is detailed: Weather, moon phases, sunrises and sunsets, planting and harvesting dates, schedules for the day. Stuff of interest to a workingman. Prices too. Prices for what we charged and what we paid – stock, fur, metal, timber, stone, even groceries – all are there.

My year as a Bucktail is recounted, most stacked there on the table. Noted are marches, situations, places, promotions, battles and bitches (no one complains more than the soldier or has reason to). It's been eight decades since I soldiered. The two most vivid recollections I still have are the noises of battle and its smell.

I recall sitting back-to-back on a deer watch in Blackwolf with my grandson Jacob. He's getting squirmy. It's early December and cold and snowy. With the doubting anticipation of a kid he whispers, "When are they gonna come, Grandpa?" "They" being a herd of deer.

I whisper that patience is required of all hunters. Watching is hunting which means long cold periods of waiting, waiting and more waiting. When the quarry is sighted it's a short hot period of excitement followed by hours of bloody work, work and more work.

Jacob whispers back, "Oh."

A battle is a lot like that. The differences are noise and smell and the hope the blood you're stepping in is not all yours.

## The Legend of Augustus McBoone

*I start on my breakfast while Hayley goes to work with her mom. After a while she calls from her desk, "Grandpa, do you know you're a legend?"*

*I slurped from my cereal bowl to irritate the girls. They yelled in unison "Grandpa!"*

*Legends don't slurp.*

Hayley has been dwelling on this legend deal in school papers since her sixth grade. What I wrote as everyday occurrences intrigued her. And, because of the names I interacted with, her teachers. My journals include references to Huckleberry, Tom, Injun Joe, Sam Clemens, Louisa Longsdorf, Ulysses Grant, Teddy Roosevelt, Zane Grey, Jack London, Ty Cobb, Babe Ruth and others. I explained that it was a slower world than the 1940's. We were all getting started. Fame was not fleeting. Horses and wagons and trains brought us together. We had **time** so we talked. Got to know each other.

*Still, I was a natural, said Hayley.* "You mention the senses when you record. You don't just say cold. You say 'Colder than a witches tit in the Yukon'."

"Hayley!" *said her mom.*

*I smiled. London said that.*

Hayley stuck to her guns. "Mr. Bates says a good writer always includes the senses."

Bates is a no-nonsense teacher at the high school. No-nonsense, like me.

I finished my breakfast, stood and gathered the outgoing mail. It was Monday, us creatures of habit had an established routine on Monday. *"I'm going to town,"* I said. *"I'll bring our mail on my way back."*

*"Later, Grandpa."* This was Hayley. Her mom was busy clickety-clacking on the Underwood.

I left thinking, What the hell is this world coming to? Women are making the rules! I can't cuss, ogle or break wind like I'd like to. My wives kept me in line before. Well, maybe women have **always** made the rules. Modern girls like Hayley are more overt about it now.

Later! Is there always gonna be one? Us "legends" aren't here forever, ya know.

## Chapter 2

# SHAVE AND HAIRCUT, 4 BITS

Harold Fabel Senior and I discuss this legend business at my Monday shave and haircut. The girls make me shower and shave daily but allow me to skip shaving Sunday afternoon **if** I see Barber Hal Monday morning. *"You're treating me just like Mandi!"* I complain. The two give me their archy eyebrow sass and say, *"Yep!"* I grumble and clean up and one will nuzzle me and say, *"You smell good Grandpa!"*

I hum around, expecting another nuzzle. I like that part.

I go in early, before the line forms. Get in, get out and get on with my day. When no one else is around, we talk. Hal opines that I have lived long, experienced much, the tales told over the years aren't too tall.

"Kinda high those tales, but true," he reflects, grinning. "That's what makes a legend, Gus. Action and Truth."

"You mean a grain of truth, don't you?" Stories grew like a weed on fertilizer in Steam Valley.

Hal laughed. "Don't have to do much to get one started. There's a new one about you now. What happened between you and Spike last week?"

He was lathering me up for my shave so I couldn't answer right away. I read his sign instead. I made that sign when Hal got back from WWI. Back then I painted SHAVE and HAIRCUT, 2 Bits. When Junior was born eight years ago, Hal doubled his price, too cheap to hire me to repaint it! You could still see where he'd Xed out the 2. I'd tease him about it and he'd wait 'til he had me like today then respond with a smart comment.

Hal shaved my face, left my full cowboy mustache for the trim. After he toweled me off, I was able to speak. "So, who told?"

"Ford Irish. Saw Spike run across 15. Head all bloody. Came out of the woods below your lane."

I told Hal what happened.

"The way Ford tells it he saw it all."

"He didn't see a damn thing!"

"You're the biggest warrior around. Bigger now probably."

"I sent for the biggest warrior. Don't say anything though."

I could trust Hal.

"Administer some frontier justice maybe?"

"Maybe. Spike is headed over the edge. Can't control his urges."

"He's **always** been on the edge, Gus. There was an incident with our outfit in France. We needed him, so they buried it."

We were quiet while Hal started trimming my hair. I wore it longer than the style of the day. Wore it the way Mandi liked it. My hair was thick and wavy and pure white. Like drifted snow Hal would say, emphasizing the "drifted" part.

He knew me, Barber Hal.

I saw him frown in the mirror. "What?" I asked.

"Can you get in trouble, sending for the big man? What if Roby finds out?"

Hal worried about things a lot more than me. He wasn't much of a risk-taker. Doubling his price was probably the biggest risk he had taken in twenty-five years.

"Once he learns the truth the Sheriff will bury it like Squire and the Brass buried the thing in France. Besides, who would miss Spike Poorbaugh?"

"Mort maybe. When he needs cheap help at the junkyard."

"He's been using Charley and his horses for that," I said. I added, "Suppose Spike disappears and I'm implicated. What are they gonna do? Hang me?"

"Like when King's Arrow hung Elmer Sykes?"

Hal continued. "Administered frontier justice, didn't they? What, a hundred years ago? Started the feud?"

I nodded "yes" to all three questions. That hanging and Jacob Miller's death a year later were stories that endured in Steam Valley. Dad witnessed both. They were regrets that plagued him 'til the day he died.

I did **not** tell Hal that the feud mentioned had ended in June 1944, just after Betts died and the D-Day invasion. I ended it. I was fretting because I had not heard from Josh, a sergeant with the Big Red One who had stormed Omaha Beach. He did not know his mom had died and I did not know if he had lived. I was a bit testy. When the last of the Sykes Clan threatened me and mine in my shop, I threw caution to the four winds and throttled that 4-F son of a bitch. Hayley's Dad, Ralph, before shipping out with Mike Donachy, buried the body in a bog in Blackwolf. Weighted him down with truck chain, poled him deep.

He's a sturdy sort, Ralph. Quiet. He'll take our secret to his grave. At the time Brenda did not realize what a gem she had. Unpolished sure, but still a gem. She does now.

Feuds are best ended on the quiet. Think of it - "Frontier Justice" administered in 1944!

Even though I trusted Hal, it would do no good to fess up about the ending of young Elmer. Ralph and I shared a secret. In my long experience, a secret shared by more than two is no longer a secret. A good example is the incident with Spike. Ford had seen Spike's bloody head, made assumptions, and told. Made me a bigger legend when I was really lucky.

Which is why I sent for the big, old, silent, mean man.

"Let's talk about some real legends" I say to Hal who's taking his time, clipping slow. I wanted to switch the subject from hangings and feuds. He nodded his assent in the mirror.

"My first wife Mandi is a legend. Outside our family though folks don't know who she was. Amanda Patterson McBoone was a direct descendent of Daniel Boone, a Revolutionary War veteran. Her great-great grandmother was a sister. She married a Patterson, moved to the Williamsport area. Mandi's great-grandfather Benjamin scouted out the Williamson Trail, the main road from Williamsport north to Corning. In some cases the trees were so big they elected to go around the tree.

Benjamin Patterson built two inns in the 1790s – the first here in Fallbrook, the second in Corning. Mandi's direct ancestor was related to a Revolutionary War veteran and himself the founder of Fallbrook. Yet, ten years after moving here, her petition to the Founders Society was tabled by Mrs. Cole. Why? She sent Zeb a bill for me keeping his tannery running – a bill that skinflint refused to pay! I wanted to give those biddies a piece of my mind, but she forbade it. She had just lost our daughter Abby in childbirth and had keeping the rest of us fed and clothed on her mind. Too much pioneer for the politicians was all she said."

Hal nodded in the mirror. Fallbrook **was** a company town.

Hal knew a lot of this stuff. He also knew I ramble. On those rare occasions that I'd get on a roll he'd listen. There was always something new. I rambled …

"My oldest, Michael, is a legend. Born while I was away at war, his mother was Peggy Sue (Hal's eyebrows shot up. **This** was new). Michael lost his right hand in the Indian Wars while commanding a troop of Buffalo Soldiers. He is still one helluva shot. Especially with a pistol. His son Jacob is even better, a Texas Ranger, a dangerous gun fighter. They, and all my wives were hellacious scrappers while protecting their loved ones: Mandi shotgunned a bank robber, Sandy smacked an attacking bear in the nose and Betts started the gunfight that Jacob finished.

"You tell me, Hal, because I survived each of these fracases and others, why am I a legend and remembered and they're not?"

"It's the number of these fracases you've survived," said Hal, "And your visibility. You're the biggest man around, Gus."

"Here," I added as Hal nodded in the mirror. He mumbled though, said "And just about anywhere." I pretended I didn't hear and kept on.

"In my view legend and fame for me is folderol. Do we still use that word – folderol?"

Hal thought we did. He disagreed with my application of it.

"Fame is fleeting," I said. "I know that's a cliché but hear me out. It's dust to dust just like the Bible says. I have engraved enough tombstones to know. After 150 years, you are forgotten. No one decorates your grave. Well, the Boy Scouts may stick a flag if you're a veteran. But all the folks that really cared are dead. 150 years seems like a long time but two-thirds of that goes by fast, believe me. If you haven't endured nationally like Lincoln or explored like Boone, forget it. Be content. Or, if you're a long-lived giant like Stickwalker, become a hermit. Lay low.

"Stickwalker is the last of his kind. His tribe – gone. Same as the bison, panther, wolf. What difference had the Conestoga's made? Making a difference was a requirement in my day. "Weren't enough of us," explained Stickwalker. "We didn't breed like the damned Scots-Irish."

Stickwalker was more than a century old when we fought the Rebs at Gettysburg. He doesn't look any older now than he did in my prime in 1900. He once told me "My people lived long but…we all are a lot longer dead."

"It's almost two hundred years since the Scots-Irish Paxton Boys massacred his people. He is the only one that remembers his parents. My great-grandfather Devon was there, his recollection mentioned in his journal. A Paxton Boy, Devon's remembrance is identical to Stickwalker's who was twelve. If we did not have his journal Devon would be forgotten. (Barber Hal's eyebrows came up again. This reference to Devon was also new).

"After the massacre, Stickwalker began a quest to kill the Scots-Irish. He also vowed to protect those that had protected him at the mission. I was glad he owed my Moravian great-grandmother Mary his life as his protection extended to Dad and me and mine – even though we were one-half Scots-Irish.

"Devon might have had a part to play in the survival of Mary but as for Stickwalker – Devon was probably a racist sob.

"My second son Angus says legends just… happen. He's a writer. A happy one, which is rare for writers. Angus specializes in outdoor stories – hunting, fishing and trapping stuff. He was a quiet tagalong as a boy. He wrote a story about my guiding Teddy Roosevelt in 1900. Years later Zane Grey wanted details on a train ride west. What is it with writers and details? Sam Clemens wanted details a half century before! Anyway, we talked books and he asked my impression of Roosevelt.

"I told ZG (he insisted his friends call him ZG) that I liked Teddy. Overall. Likeable, candid, energetic, an early-riser, he was always wanting to help. Called it 'pulling his freight.' But…he got in my way! Worse, he was always looking for trouble.

"It will always find you, trouble. Especially when you cause it.

"ZG asked if I really wore buckskins as Angus had written. Sure, I said. All market hunters wore buckskins. I shot and skinned 'em. Mandi tanned and sewed 'em. Filled out her set too! You blended in with buckskins. Supple, comfortable, water repellent, they were. Wished I'd worn a set during the war. He then asked if I recognized myself as the tall buckskin- clad frontiersman in **The Spirit of the Border**? I thought ZG had used Mandi's great-great Uncle Daniel and told him so."

"You see, Dad" said Angus. "That's **how** you become a legend – when writers copy you."

I retorted. "Yeah, and on that hunt with your brother, TR (friends called him TR) wore buckskins too. Fancy, fringed things – clean compared to mine. Carried a new rifle, a 30-40 Krag bolt – action. We hunted Blackwolf. Shot a small bear and a nice buck. Had his picture taken. He wasn't a hunting legend yet but he sure wanted to be one. Big toothy grin, holdin' up that little bear."

"You stole his thunder, Dad! Without even trying. You towered over him. Your natural way is what Grey saw. TR called me later. Talked about my article." "I look like a child next to your dad," he said. "He wasn't whining, just accepting fact."

"That's alright though," he added, "Because in the woods, next to him, I am!"

"Looking back, I didn't journal much about Angus. He was Mandi's firstborn, named after Dad. He stayed in the background, was always there watching, noting. Seemed fine with him. He was the first to leave home, a pathbreaker so to speak. He'll be a legend himself...one of these days. He'll have to be dead first, otherwise he'd squelch it. Something he is very capable of doing..."

(Barber Hal had confirmation of the first new thing: Angus was Mandi's firstborn, not Michael).

I was still talking about Angus.

"You see, writing is Angus's **second** career. He is also General Angus McBoone, a U.S. Army three-star, retired, a quiet force **always** to be reckoned with. He left home for West Point, became an officer, saw action in the West, in the Philippines (some of TR's trouble) and in France in WWI. In France he employed Longstreet's tactics. (Longstreet was Lee's second -in-command during my war). Currently Angus advises FDR and his military boys on **both** theaters 'cause he's been there. Had to shoot and shoot again in the Philippines, used Saul Poorbaugh's battle tactics. Wrote his brother Michael to please-please-please hurry up his testing of that automatic 45! They needed the heavier bullet to stop these Maori Tribesmen, a few as big as he. His Navy Colt 36 wasn't slowing the sob's down and he'd had to throttle a couple. Good thing Dad taught us how!

"Mandi was gone by then. Second wife Sandra looked up while breastfeeding and said, "Just **what** are you teaching our boys?"

"Defense," I answered. "Defense."

"Secretly I was thrilled that she considered my children with Mandi **ours** – even though Angus was four years older than she.

"The evening after Michael got Angus' letter there were nine quick shots in a nearby field. Michael came in with a wagonload of wild boar. We were up most of that night butchering. That next morning, bright and early, a telegram reached the War Department saying The Automatic Colt 45 was more than adequate.

"Michael got awful good with that automatic. Taught Jacob too. Their skill came in handy later.

"He and Angus can be proud of their field-testing of that automatic. That sidearm has serviced our boys for the past two world wars. It's what Sergeant Josh and Captain Mac carry today.

"Again, Angus is too much a straight arrow to allow legend status while he is alive. Has one wife, three kids, a passel of grandkids, a pension, bills paid, money in the bank, nice home in D.C. He's eighty, doesn't look it. Angus is a humble, loyal, knowledgeable and dangerous man."

"Hal interrupted. "So how old is Michael?"

"Eighty-two".

(Hal shook his head. He cut Michael's hair too. Every McBoone looked at least a generation younger. Michael could bend a horseshoe with that left hand, and not show any strain).

I kept talking.

"I've noticed this about my family, my quiver as the Psalmist David describes. Our families, maybe all families, seem split between straight and crooked arrows. Michael bent then straightened out as did my granddaughter Brenda."

Hal did not look up. Didn't want to embarrass me, I think. Michael's thing was old news. Brenda's was hot and new. She probably thought no one knew. But everyone did. Hal got back to listening to me describe Steam Valley's number two character. I was number one, my son Esau, number two. This status conferred by the codgers across the way.

I said, "The most glaring example of a crooked arrow is my fourth son, Esau. Before Mandi had

Esau she had Caleb who was like Angus, a straight arrow. Caleb and Esau were Rough Riders. Caleb was an officer and a gentleman. I say 'was' as Caleb is dead now, gassed in WWI.

"Esau was not an officer and is working on the gentleman part. Lately. Maybe he's getting too old to bend back. He **is** a legend in the Big Timber Country of Michigan where he went in 1890. (Hal thinks Esau's a legend here too). A rugged, ruddy independent-minded man, much like his Biblical namesake, Esau was always popular with the ladies. Even the married ones, like Caleb's, if you get what I mean. (Hal looks up and nods. He gets it). Per third wife Betts, Esau made an honest woman out of Caleb's widow by marrying her. Finally. I told Betts regardless of the parentage of those kids, they're all McBoones!

"Esau was the armorer for the Rough Riders in Cuba. He also shooed TR's horses. His helper was Charley Bower. Esau and TR became close friends, drinking buddies. Went on hunting trips after they got home. He's a great singer and storyteller, the life of every party. When he comes for my 101st we'll have to get he and Bower together on Sawyer's Bench yonder. They'll tell some tales!"

Hal agreed. "You couldn't get these two together without stories."

Hal himself has stories. He ministered to Ernie Rollins after he got gassed and rescued by Spike Poorbaugh. This was a recurring WWI story.

Damn Krauts and their damn gas.

And damn you Samuel "Spike" Poorbaugh, son of Jesse! I patted my left pants pocket under Hal's sheet, felt Betts train gun there. I had carried that 32 since I'd whacked Spike off Hayley. Hadn't realized that loudmouth Ford Irish had witnessed Spike's escape. At least Esau controlled those primal urges. Spike couldn't.

Back to Esau.

"I brag too much about Esau. A more crooked version of me, I guess. He's led an adventurous life. Steady Angus, who I don't brag enough about, uses the word tumultuous. Economically, Esau has gone from logger to tycoon to logger and back to tycoon again. Domestically he's had several women, a bunch of kids (legitimate and otherwise), a bigger-than-Angus' passel of grandkids (his own quiver), a couple of wives (not at the same time, thank God). Today he's a young seventy-five, lives in the Pinelands with his second wife (Caleb's first). He owns a big new house, tens of thousands of acres and a log camp like this one. Everybody is paid off except me and I'm paid regular plus interest. He shot a huge buck there, a real Ebenezer. The buck's head is mounted above the fireplace. Angus thinks the monster is a world record and will measure it for Boone and Crockett on our next hunt."

Hal has finished my haircut, contemplated my "news". He splashes some toilet water on my face, yanks the sheet off and shakes it. I stand up, reach in my right pants pocket to pay Hal. He drapes the sheet over the chair, grabs a broom to sweep up my white hair. His cowbell announces another customer and newly minted game warden Jim Morningstar walks in.

Hal can't resist a tease. "How many deer you shot, Augustus?"

I answered. "According to Brenda, 2,351."

Jim laughed. "Not many market hunters left. By the way Mr. McBoone, I was getting gas at Evie's and heard a shot up your way."

Jim's deferential "Mr. McBoone" confirmed that the game commission also consider me a legend.

"An eagle," I explained. "After my lambs."

"Any feathers?" Jim knew us market hunters seldom missed.

"No clean ones - Pigs ate him."

Jim sat in the barber chair.

I handed Hal two silver dollars. The charge is four bits, fifty cents. I've been paying two dollars since before Hal raised his price. He knows better to offer change or respond. The money goes in the cash register. Ding!

"You ought to repair that ratty sign," I say and walk out before Hal can come up with a smart-alec answer. I look in the window and grin and wave. Hal's back is to me but he sees me in the mirror and waves back.

The codgers are gathering on Sawyer's Bench. Bower's not there. He and Mort are probably working at the junkyard. I climb into my Willys and drive off.

## Chapter 3

# MONDAY DRIVE

Route 15 was gravel in the thirties. I ran a grader and was foreman on the crew that built our section of it. Learned how by doing, I did. The fog has lifted, the road is paved and painted now. I'm driving the speed limit. The tires hum a tune. I travel south and think about my quiver ... and war.

The results are not all good for McBoone's in war. Caleb was not alone nor was he the first to ... die.

My youngest son with Mandi, Ira, ended up with Black Jack Pershing in the American Southwest. Good with horses, Ira was a hostler with Fred Shafer. (Fred now owns a sawmill below Miller's Landing). My grandson Jacob, good with guns, was an artilleryman for Black Jack as well. Jacob is the oldest of Michael's boys with Ophelia, the Cherokee woman, and lives near his mom in Texas. These men were U. S. Cavalry, Pony Soldiers chasing Pancho Villa, a Mexican bandit and Kraut ally in WWI. They never caught him (needed Dad I guess). Chased his dust. Shot at it, too. All survived but are forever scarred by this experience.

Sores heal, mostly. Allow you to live, work, breed. Look at Sawyer. At Michael. At me. Survivors of previous wars.

My two sons by Sandra, Adam and Peter, went to France. Same war as Ira and Jacob, Angus and Caleb. My grandson Joe went too. Adam became a flyboy, a squad leader. Quentin Roosevelt, TR's youngest, was a devil-may-care member of Adam's squadron. Adam came back. Quentin did not. Neither did Peter and Shelby's son Joe.

While the Devil may have cared he did not get Quentin, Peter or Joe. My letter to TR and Edith described my enduring faith that we would meet our boys in Heaven. I got a personal letter back saying they thought that too. That letter is in my WWI journals. Caleb was gassed, made it home, died later. The Devil did not get him either.

The Krauts deemed Quentin a prize. Sent photos of the boy's broken body to his parents and the papers. Big news! I'm glad Sandra and Shelby did not see photos of our dead boys. Adam and his squadron made the Krauts pay for their insolence. All enemy survivors were gunned down after that.

Peter and Joe are buried in the American Cemetery in Normandy. Their mothers visited their graves. Cabled me what they found – white wooden crosses with their names painted on. I set duplicates carved in stone here at the Brick Church.

But Sandra never saw Peter's stone marker. Or Joe's. She got sick with the flu on the voyage home. Died in my arms here in Steam Valley.

And here I am thirty-six years later - in Steam Valley.

There are McBoone's involved in a Second World War. The first war was supposed to end all wars. Didn't obviously. We're fighting where we fought before – Europe and the South Seas. Got Angus in D. C. telling the Brass how to win a two-front war. He's been there. I sure hope they listen.

I pull left onto the gravel lane and stop. Pick up my mail. My box is big, and like Hal's sign, needs repainted. Looks kinda ratty next to the six others - Michael, Shelby, Polly, Brenda, Ira, and Kelsey - keep boxes there. Our flags are down which means Watt has gotten and delivered our mail. I rifle through mine - three magazines, my lodge notice, checks and invoices pertaining to the McB Brand, personal letters and cards. I secure everything with a large rubber band, all but two letters. These I read right away. Good news! Josh and Sally have both arranged leave and will be at my 101$^{st}$ birthday celebration.

I climb back in my Willys, whistling. On a clear October morning in Steam Valley it feels good to be alive. Still. Roscoe the gander emerges from the pond-side ditch. Backside's kinda muddy. Eyes me warily, then waddles up the middle of the lane. Deliberately. I drive up behind him and "goose" him back into the ditch. A couple of tail feathers fly. He looks **so** offended. We have a competition, Roscoe and I.

I always win. I'd run over the impudent waddler but he's Hayley's...So is little Mr. Troublemaker, the lamb. Not so Mr. Mean Pig. He's mine. His hams'll be in the smokehouse before snow flies.

I try to sneak through my screen door. I'm anxious to get in my chair and read Angus's latest article in **Outdoor Life**. It had a tight new spring, that door, slamming behind and announcing my presence.

I scoot into the chair. The gals were in the library, both at their typewriters, clacking away. Maybe they didn't hear...

Have you noticed how tinkering runs in my family? This skill applies even to the bossy females. Brenda and Hayley fixed that screen door, and during the war with the men away, Norma serviced my Willys. Serviced all McB vehicles in fact, including our tractors. Norma and Hayley also shooed my horses. Bob 4 and Dick 5 were far more patient with them than with their dad and me. Those pretty sisters chattered while the horses rolled their eyes...Pretending they knew who and what they talked about.

Mike Donachy used to come but he got killed in Germany and his sons are either too old or young or uninterested to take over. His stepson Mac is a Captain in the Army Rangers. An engineer, he will probably make the service his career. Mike's son Tom is only eight, one of Mrs. Brown's students at the one-room school. He's a pisser, that Tom.

"Grandpa!" Hayley had heard. "You're remembering out loud again. Why is Tom a pisser, huh?"

"I'm gonna take a nap now." I say that to avoid her question. If I told **what** I saw Tom doing Hayley would tell her mom. Brenda would tell Betty Donachy and Tom would get in trouble - again.

It didn't work. She knew it wasn't time for my nap. So I tried another subject-change I knew would.

"I got letters from Josh and Sally today - They're comin'!"

"Yay!" Hayley was Sally's babysitter. My toddler grandson, would come with his mom.

Two of my children with Betts are in the service. Our third, Kelsey, lives down the lane. Sally is an ensign in the WAVES, a nurse on a hospital ship. When she's at sea her son lives with his grandparents in

Florida. Sally's husband Logan was a handsome black sailor killed by a kamikaze on Okinawa. Her letter also said she'd be bringing a "friend," a veteran with the 10th Mountain. Her high school chum Helen, who also married in the service, would be home too. Joshua is a combat soldier who could not relax until after the Battle of the Bulge. He met Ernie Pyle on Omaha Beach, who wrote him up for taking good care of his men.

Both gals return to their typewriters. Hayley knows I will not tell on Tom. She'll wait, content knowing whatever stunt I saw Tom pulling will come out eventually. Tom causes most of the trouble he's blamed for. It's not malicious, just fun. I think of the stuff Sawyer said he and Huck did way back in Hannibal and I pray that Tom never has that fun-loving spirit squashed by war.

I chose not to mention Sally's boyfriend to Brenda and Hayley. That should be fun - watching how they deal with him. When a daughter brings a fella to meet her dad, what's that tell you?

These are a few members of my family, my quiver. That's from Psalm 127 where David describes his family in archer terms. I'm sure he had a bigger quiver than mine but mine is approaching two hundred. David had fifteen wives to my three. There were also other women, a slew of them, to my five. (Five so far). But who's counting? David died at age seventy. I've lived thirty more years (So far) and had children with Betts into my eighties. And it was Betts who quit the honey-pot, not me.

I guess I am counting.

A favorite Sunday School refrain goes "Father Abraham had many sons" and preachers make a **big deal** about God blessing Abraham and his wife Sarah with their first and only child, Isaac, when they were **both very old** and beyond childbearing age. He was 100. She was 90. There **was** a miracle – Sarah **was** old. Not so Abraham! He lived 75 more years. Sarah died and Abraham married a lady named Keturah who bore him six more sons. He also had sons from other women. Sarah's servant bore Ishmael and Abe had concubines who had a bunch more. I don't know if he used honey or mandrakes or what…my point is the song is right but you gotta read your Bible to get the rest of the story. Now that's a quiver! Hayley would wonder why there is no mention of daughters. Maybe he didn't have any.

A thousand years later the Bible describes the life of my favorite quiver-maker, David. He's my favorite because he's so…human. David was… gentle and mean, happy and sad, musical and literate. He never quit, 'fessed up when he was wrong (And he was wrong a lot). A monster of a warrior, he couldn't keep his hands off the ladies (even a couple of married ones if you know what I mean). I doubt that all his women were "ladies" by the way. Not with what they did with David's rebel son Absalom on the roof of the Palace! Read your Old Testament, Second Samuel, Chapter Sixteen if you want saucy details.

A while back Hayley confided that her mom had not always been a "lady." I knew. Figured lots of folks knew. Brenda had become a crooked arrow while Ralph was away in the service. Norma caught them and told Hayley. My response was that their parents had some things to work out. When he got back Ralph did. Brenda, who thought her husband was a dolt and found out he wasn't, stayed and no longer strayed.

Ralph is a late-bloomer who gets better looking as he ages. He loves Brenda and their girls. He can keep a secret. He told me about Brenda but I never told him I knew.

These things happen in every quiver.

David did cause me some trouble while Brenda was having her fling. She came in one morning and asked what I wanted for Christmas. She was being nice. I was kinda cranky at being interrupted while reading a saucy anecdote about David. I told her I wanted a bedwarmer.

*"You have plenty of blankets, Augustus." She calls me that instead of Grandpa whenever she senses I'm being contrary, and she was right.*

*I got irritated, which also happens in every quiver, and shook my Scofield at her. "I said bedwarmer and I meant bedwarmer! Here, read Kings."*

*She did and colored up.*

*Sam Clemens observed in a lecture that man is the only animal that blushes. Or needs to.*

*At the time she was warming another man's bed. Was the scripture too close for comfort?*

*I let her off the hook. "I don't want a virgin, like Abishag," I said. "I mean a widow like Betts before we married. How about our neighbor, Mary Spencer? She's a widow and quite buxom. Bet she'd make a great bedwarmer."*

"Augustus!" she repeated. "Such thoughts! Betts has only been gone five months." She tut-tutted back to her typewriter, wasn't nice the rest of the day. She knew I ogled buxom women.

Kinda hypocritical, I thought. What's okay for the married goose is not okay for the widowed gander?

Anyway, after we won The Battle of the Bulge, the motor pool got mustered out and Ralph came home. Things between the married geese got better.

I took that nap. A bent arrow had straightened, fit secure in the safety of the family quiver.

I take two short naps a day. Midmorning and midafternoon. They keep you sharp, naps.

*I stirred when Hayley flopped beside me. She has my earliest Civil War journal. She nuzzles me.* "Mmmm, you smell good, Grandpa." *Who can get mad at a wake-up like that? Must be time for another writing project.*

"Aren't you supposed to be in school?" I ask.

*She gave me her "senior" look. This meant she was given flexibility underclassmen didn't have.* "Mr. Bates teaches at 11:20," *she answered.* "Ernie's picking me up."

*Ernie must be the new boyfriend. Of these, Hayley had lots. Like eagle feathers. She points to an open page of my journal.* "Grandpa, what's this word?"

*Someone, probably Brenda, possibly her mom, Peggy Mae, had lined it out. I hadn't looked at that particular journal in years.*

"Shitter," I said.

*She frowned.* "Shitter?" *she repeated the word as a question a little too loud.*

"Hayley!" *This came from her mom in the library.*

"Shitter," I emphasized loudly. "That word is important and should **not** have been lined out. No comment from the Peanut Gallery either."

*Silence. Good.*

*I explained.* "At camp we dug a long narrow ditch. A latrine it was, us soldiers called it the "shitter." We squatted, did our business and left. Some places the call was best done at night."

"Why?"

"Snipers."

"Oh."

"And K. P. wasn't peeling potatoes like Beatle Bailey. It was S. P. -Shitter Police. We limed the latrine at night. Our boots would get caked and we smelled."

"Eww!" *Hayley squealed just like Mandi. She took me way back, Hayley.* "Doesn't sound very glorious to me." *she added.*

"It's not. Especially in battle. You never saw so much blood and guts, shit and blowflies in your life. A battle, any battle, smells like a shitter, Hayley. With gunpowder."

*She shuddered. I went on. Silence in the Peanut Gallery.*

"For survivors the glory comes later. At parades, celebrations, holidays."

"Like Armistice?"

*I nodded, glad for the change of subject. "You gonna catch that baton, Hayley?"*

*Hayley was the band's lead majorette.*

*"I'll catch it Grandpa."*

*"Good, I'll be there."*

*"Grandpa?"*

*"Yes?"*

*She closed the journal. "You know you're the last one?"*

*I nodded. Company B's Private Joe Dale had lived to age 91. Like David, his latter days full of riches and honors.*

*"I know, Hayley. I'm the last Bucktail."*

## Chapter 4

# THE FIGHTING 149TH

I was a member of a band of Union sharpshooters in the Civil War. Formally we were a regiment - the 149th Pennsylvania Volunteers. Informally, after Gettysburg, we were the Fighting 149th.

Regiments were composed of Companies. The 149th had eleven companies – A through K. Each company had around one hundred men.

After Basics, the 149th totaled eleven hundred men. After Gettysburg, where we became the Fighting 149th, we didn't have near that many.

Not even close.

Company A, the one I was in, mustered out of Wellsboro. Company B, which had Joe Dale, mustered out of Curwensville. Companies C through K were all Pennsylvanians, most mustering out of the north-central region of our state.

We were outdoor boys, farm boys, boys (mostly). We were strong, did what we were told (mostly), knew how to shoot (mostly). A few, like me, could "bark" a squirrel at a hundred yards. We wore a buck tail sewn on our caps. Hence the name BUCKTAIL.

Old photos show us as rail thin. We foraged for good food, otherwise it was bad. Saul would say his bear dogs ate better. That included eating their own poop!

We noticed the Rebs were even skinnier and ran barefoot. Can you imagine shitter duty with no shoes?

*"Eww! Grandpa!"*

I smiled. I did love making Hayley squeal. It had been at least a decade since I reviewed that account. I was in my teens when I wrote it. The senses are there. Pretty good, huh?

Back to the war.

Historians tell us the bloodiest battle I fought in and the one that turned the tide in the war - Gettysburg - was a big coincidence. Bobby Lee and seventy thousand men were marching to nearby Hanover for shoes. Longstreet said the shoe need was **one** of several reasons they invaded. We met the Rebs at Gettysburg. With eighty thousand men.

We took the high ground. Longstreet did not want to fight there. Bobby Lee did. Gettysburg was a **huge** coincidence, maybe the biggest ever, because it involved one hundred fifty thousand men!

To Saul coincidences were unsettling, unpredictable. Saul Poorbaugh was a mean, crusty, carnal, observant man. When I met him he was in his thirties and in his prime. Saul was a hired killer, a bounty hunter. Not there he said for the glory promised us "boys" in the posters, there for the money promised when he brought in Reb scalps and ears. Looking back my presence brought unpredictability to Saul's service.

I owe my life to Saul Poorbaugh.

A veteran also of the Mexican War, Saul owed his life to Dad.

What goes around comes around, we still say.

A sharpshooter was supposed to shoot at a distance, which we did. However, during a charge, with no time to reload, the fight got **real** upclose and personal. You could smell Johnny's breath!

That's what happened in the last "coincidence" I was in.

I was wounded at Gettysburg, mustered out there, won The Medal there.

That first day was hot, the fighting fast, furious, close, smelly, loud. It's been eighty-two years and I still dream of it. My most vivid and recurring being a couple minutes spent with a dying soldier named...Huckleberry.

He wore the blue, an infantryman with the "First Missourah."

Gasping, gulping from my canteen, he asked me "Please find Tom!" Tom was around, somewhere.

Tom wore the gray, a cavalryman also from "Missourah."

That young officer lay behind me, his dead horse lay near. I had propped two of our wounded against its belly, told them both to stay down, the fight's almost over. I left and found...Huckleberry.

I was upright, not weaving, still capable. My tunic was slick with blood, some of it mine. I had taken a nasty saber slash earlier, the blade bouncing off my collarbone. Stickwalker saved my butt by bouncing his club off the Reb's head. Fortunately for us both, the Reb and me, the blows we took were glancing.

At The Medal ceremony, President Grant praised me for saving so many lives. That struck me as odd. I had probably killed five times as many as

I saved. Never mentioned that. The killing was expected I guess, the saving was not.

Two of the men I saved became politically influential. Helped my sons and me. Their careers were just getting started in 1870, as was mine.

I didn't tell Huckleberry about the Reb. There wasn't time anyway. Blood ran down my sleeve, covering the sergeant's chevrons there.

I wore lieutenant bars at Gettysburg, a sniper interrupting removal of the chevrons.

Blood bubbled out Huckleberry's gaping wounds. Front and back. He had taken a ball through his chest. Our fluids mixed as I propped his head to sip from my canteen - his blood, my water.

I lied to that dying soldier. Told him I couldn't find Tom when I suspected he was lying near. Later I learned they grew up together. Like brothers, even more so. Yet here they were, on opposite sides, fighting to the death on a field outside Gettysburg.

Over what?

Glory?

Tom was more idealistic than the practical Huck. Those ideals suffered a setback when Tom came to and learned the fate of Huckleberry.

Was it slavery?

Missouri never got its act together about that. A split state, it had Abolitionists and Yanks versus Racists and Rebs. Worst were the Guerillas, racist sob's more concerned with plunder and profit. Regarding slaves, Tom and Huck were fighting over the "right" to own one. Tom's family owned a slave, Huck's did not.

Saul Poorbaugh scoffed at the "right business." It's over "Who's Boss" was his opinion.

Stickwalker said the fight was between stubborn Scots-Irish Rebs and confused Trash Yanks. Trash, in this case, were the ethnics who got off a boat in an eastern port and found themselves soldiers in the Federal Army. These men talked strange, only Stickwalker could understand them.

Our army was a huge mix and mess. Those for the Union were Trash - Yanks, Federals, bluebellies. I met ethnics, volunteers, replacements, draftees, convicts and Bucktails.

The only good thing I can see out of war is that it mixes us up. Other than that - I hate it.

Hate it. Hate it. Hate it.

Those of us that have fought - hate war.

## Chapter 5

# A Have-Been

In the early 1870s I was interviewed by a reporter from Elmira about my role as a Bucktail and how I won The Medal. His name was Clemens.

He called the war our "previous conflict." He had spent three weeks in a Missouri Reb outfit. Never called, he got bored and left to join his brother in California. His eyes widened when I told him about Huckleberry. "What a unique name, Huckleberry!" He wrote a few of my stories down, embellished them, called me a "living legend."

Legend, hell! I wasn't even thirty.

Mandi posted these articles in a journal. I'll bet that's where Hayley got it.

Well, that moniker stuck. In due time, Teddy Roosevelt and Zane Grey both wrote about me in their books. Embellished their accounts too. I argued with all three – Clemens, Roosevelt, Grey – 'til they died. Not one recanted, ever. Poked fun at me. Claimed I was too sensitive. Their letters are also posted in my journals. Our daughter, Peggy Mae, pled guilty to that after Mandi died.

I enjoyed the exchanges with these strong-willed characters, as much intrigued by them as them by me. When it came to critics, though, I was much thicker-skinned. Angus once told me I was immune to criticism "Cause, Dad, you just don't give a shit." Not so those three!

They battled their critics, and each other, all their lives, and always in writing. Sometimes their opinions were gentle, sometimes caustic. TR and ZG teased each other. ZG complained (gently) that TR never listened…to him. TR responded (also gently) that he did so! When he was out west he never heard "hyar" so much…Until **after** he read Grey's westerns.

The exchanges between Clemens and Roosevelt were not gentle. They were nasty, downright caustic.

Clemens started it by describing Roosevelt as "A glory-seeking cowboy." TR responded that Clemens was "A coward who fled to California to write about frogs." To that Clemens wrote "Roosevelt was so self-centered he wanted to be the bride at every wedding, the corpse at every funeral."

As I said earlier, 1860s Missouri was a state of and in the state of conflict. If you wanted to hear agitators - go to Missouri.

Judge Sawyer wrote me that maybe Clemens was smarter than all us veterans. He avoided the "conflict" and still remained popular - folks clamored for his wit and wisdom.

I've pondered the issue for decades. Tom died after our 1930 Reunion. The knot on his head finally burst. According to the Good Book, we all die and are judged. Is Clemens going to be judged as a great writer, a coward, or a loving husband and dad? Is TR going to be judged as a good writer, a self-centered glory-seeker, or a loving husband and dad? Only God knows. I think the latter outweighs the former for both, but who in His universe am I?

There's a great scene in **Tom Sawyer** where Huck isn't sure he **wants** to go to the Victorian heaven the Widow Watson ascribes to. Too tight for him. The writer of that passage used to boast (who's self-centered now?) he was favored by The Almighty (intellectuals just can't say God) because he was brought into this world in 1835 by Halley's comet. Clemens (or Twain, you pick) did not expect to ride its tail out in 1910, but he did.

So, where'd he go? Heaven or Hell? TR had his own caustic answer. It doesn't take a Ford engineer to figure that out.

Ten years later Roosevelt found out himself, dying from breathing problems. Widow Edith suspected the flu. 'Teddy would never admit to suffering from a malady as everyday as the flu," she wrote. "Hadn't I lost my second wife Sandra and third son Caleb to breathing problems brought on by the flu?"

Yep.

ZG died from a stroke in 1939. Widow Dolly wrote asking if I recalled making two hickory items that adorned their trophy wall? I replied that I had lathed a thirty-four inch bat for her husband when he was more famous as a ballplayer than a writer. A decade later I made him an eight-foot fishing pole. By then he wanted to be known as a famous fisherman **and** a famous writer. By chance we met on a train going west in the early 1920s. After supper (and a few whiskeys) he promised that the McB brand would forever be prominently displayed by the Grey's. Dolly answered that I was always prominent in their life. She was curious. Did I still resemble the tall frontiersman in **The Spirit of the Border**?

If I hadn't been married, I would have hopped on a train. She was buxom, that Dolly. Instead, I called her. "Dolly, I'm ninety-five years old. I might have looked like Lew Wetzel sixty years ago. I hunted and trapped in buckskin. I could run down a deer. While I've killed dozens of panthers I could never scream like one. And, there's no way on God's Green Earth I would ever pollute a spring with a body like Wetzel done."

She chuckled. "ZG showed me your note about the spring. He appreciated your honesty, Gus. He could take it - if it came from you."

We hung up. Write on occasion. Haven't spoken to her since. I may want to take that train ride. Better call first.

Seems all my non-family correspondence is with widows and ball-players now. This happens when you pass the century mark and have outlived your acquaintances.

I am a hypocrite though. Fessing up would divulge a secret and involve Ralph. He buried Sykes in Blackwolf. Poled him deep in Three Oaks Spring. So, I'm a polluter, too, even though I told Dolly Grey I could never do that.

I have lived an adventurous life...compared to... everybody. I really don't like the word "have" – it's too past tense. I dislike the word "has" as in "has-been" even more. It means you're done. It's all over but the shouting. But I'm not done...

# The Legend of Augustus McBoone

shouting. So, I put the best of the two phrases together. I'm a have-been now. Leaves room for more doing.

Looking back though, my century went by fast. I know codgers who can't remember. Just can't. If that happens to me anyone that wants can refer to my journals. I swear the stuff in there is true. Also, I've told Ralph where my secret stuff is kept. When the time comes, he'll know.

Another thing about this legend business – I don't recall thinking my life, at the time, was adventurous. It was just...life.

Over my one-hundred year lifespan I have been (there's that "have" again) a hungry child, an orphan, a tinkerer, a logger, a real orphan, a hungry soldier, a writer, an armorer, a lieutenant, a hungry hunter, a trapper, a teamster, an engraver, a raftsman, a farmer, a medal winner, a boxer, a gunfighter, an inventor, a builder, a landowner, a Mason, a lover, a husband, a father-grandfather-great grandfather, a widower, a killer, a hungry believer, a Free-thinker (if Abe Lincoln can write that as his religious affiliation, so can I). Whew! Wonder what I left out?

I have outlived three wives, fathered sixteen children that I know of, have or had at least eighty grandchildren, one hundred great-grandchildren. That's a full quiver.

If any of those great-grandchildren are as frisky as Mandi and I were when we were teens, I should be seeing some great-greats pretty soon.

"Grandpa!"

*That's Hayley. One of the teens and the bossiest of them all. She left my chair a half chapter ago to help her mom in the library.*

*She went on, "You're talking out loud again."*

"Too loud." *I mumble this knowing she is listening close and will hear. She practically lives here, you know.*

*Hayley tells me all. Knows me best. I guess she's earned the right to be bossy.*

## Chapter 6

# THE CLAN MCBOONE

I was born in a cabin east of Knoxville on October 31st 1844. Halloween. Aunt Flo would tell that I was so big and ugly I scared my mom to death. I grew up thinking I killed her. I have since concluded that Flo was the ugly one.

Since the memory of Mary's death was "so painful" we never celebrated my birthday.

The McBoone's did celebrate Harvest at Halloween. All but me.

After burying Mom in the Pioneer Cemetery out back my dad Angus grew sad, hit the bottle, then the road. He was gone almost ten years.

Flo had sixteen children, fourteen by her husband, two by a neighbor man. You could tell the difference but all took the name McBoone. She and Fergus had seven while I lived there. With me and the two adults that meant ten mouths to feed. Back then big families were required to tend the farm. An extra hand should have been welcome, especially when feeding that one extra was part of the agreement transferring ownership to Fergus and Flo.

Alas, Dad should have been more explicit. Taking care of me was **not** in the deed. Dad told me later - they had a handshake deal. Flo said Dad was too drunk to remember, Fergus couldn't (or wouldn't). Dad claimed his memory was clear. If Flo ever wondered why I refused to shake their hands, the deal they broke with Dad was why.

Anyway, while I was a newborn, Dad left. Fergus named me.

Babies are hard to abuse. Easy to ignore. Cheap if you share a teat with a cousin. As soon as I could walk I did chores. Still, Flo thought I cost too much to keep in "her" house. So, as soon as I could milk the cow, I slept in the barn. On cold nights I'd wrap myself in a horse blanket and sleep next to the cow. She loved me, didn't kick or roll. I smelled. Once a day I'd eat leftovers on an empty molasses barrel turned up in the barn. If Flo brought the food, she'd cuff me for not doing a chore a cousin was supposed to do or if she caught me with milk she claimed I stole.

We did not like each other, Flo and I.

Flo was prone to "fits" and while having one would chase Fergus and the kids out of "her" house. Fergus would grab a jug and a plug of home-grown and seek refuge in the barn. The kids would follow. We were too young to share the whiskey or tobacco but on the way they'd grab food from the kitchen and share with me - as long as I milked the cow and shared with them.

I counted on Flo's fits and would do my best to make one happen. I was smart-aleck enough to realize a fit meant sweet meat from the kitchen. She had her faults, Flo, but was really good at cooking, baking and canning. Also making and having babies. Until number sixteen.

Fergus would tell the same story knowing that when he was done, they could return to the house as Flo's fit was over. His story would get better as he drank from the jug. Details may differ, but the theme stayed the same. Fergus's story was how the McBoone's got their name.

Here's how:

"Way back in the 1500's a prosperous Englishman named Boone moved to Scotland. There he bought an inn and a farm. To fit in he added "Mc" to his name and became a Presbyterian. The Scots tolerated him because he made good whiskey and was a great fixer. He also was crosseyed so they might have felt sorry for him too. They liked him better when he didn't turn them in after they stole his cows. He claimed he couldn't see who done it. Somehow he held on, saved more coin, married, kept the inn and sold the farm."

(I never knew a crosseyed McBoone. How'd he see to fix things? I kept silent. This was Fergus' story).

"In the early 1600s a racist British King offered free land to any Scot willing to move to Northern Ireland and fight for it. Now Scots love free stuff, like land, and don't mind a good fight now and again. So a bunch of Scots, including the clan McBoone, sold out, moved to Northern Ireland. Became the Scots-Irish. Wore orange kilts. No underpants."

Here Fergus would pause, arch an eyebrow, allow us cousins to giggle about the image of a proud Scot without underpants, then continue.

"It bein' nice farmland folks were already there, the Catholic Irish. They wore green kilts. Again, no underpants."

He'd pause again, we'd giggle again and he'd go on. "They dinna get along those two. Still don't. The population there did not deter the Scottish invaders. They justified their invasion by saying those that wore the green were Papists, not of the 'true faith,' hence deserving displacement. This, of course, was the British objective all along."

"Seventy-five years later another racist British King..."

"Ain't we all racists, Papa?" The interrupter was Constance, their second child and first girl. Connie was always adopting critters, the latest a raccoon family that scampered around the barn like ringtailed kittens until her mongrel dog Queenie sniffed them out and shook them dead. Connie accused me of letting Queenie in the barn. I lied and shook my head. I did dislike sharing my milk with them coon kits, so...

Connie's question indicated her brain was catching up to her heart, a troubling development. Fergus who needed time for Flo to cool off and fix supper, feigned innocence: "Whatever do you mean, Constance?"

"Well, you're always saying things like 'slippery like a g-d Nigger, sneaky like a g-d Injun, oily like a g-d Eyetalian.' Ain't that racism, Papa?"

It was considered improper for girls to swear so Connie spelled out the first letters of the bad words. Church Lady Flo kept a bar of soap handy for the mouths of her daughters. Her sons could swear like sailors and did. Well, they swore like Fergus.

I remember munching on a coveted cookie and wondering "What's an Eyetalian?" The first two I had seen in Knoxville. But it seemed to me

## The Legend of Augustus McBoone

that anybody Fergus didn't like was damned by Gawd, by God!

Fergus squirmed around the situation by sending Connie to "peep through the knothole, see what your mom's doin'."

She came back. "Still in her fit Papa, still rockin'."

Content that he had time to finish, Fergus got back to it. That is, the story. He never answered Connie's question.

"The Crown reasoned that since they provided free land and support to four generations of Scots-Irish, the new prosperous generation should not object to reimbursing England for their investment."

This meant taxes.

Then Fergus launched into his diatribe against the Crown and the King's penchant for imposing his will. The good Brits never knew the difference between could-would-should.

Could they pay? Yes.

Would they? Depends...

Should they? Don'cha be tellin' us what to do you g-d Shite!

So they dithered and delayed.

Fergus spoke the initials of bad words to show some sensitivity to his daughter's situation. Back to the story:

"The King needing cash and seeing he couldn't depend on the Scots-Irish, borrowed from his English subjects. He ended up owing sixteen thousand pounds to his wealthy naval headman, Admiral William Penn. Now Elder was an Anglican like the king and of the 'true faith.' His son, Younger, had become a Quaker and was not. Elder died, Younger inherited and pestered the king for his money."

Remember this is Fergus telling his story. This may not be history. He was repeating what was handed down by storytellers. And I'm repeating the story to you.

"Maybe Younger wore his sword, probably he didn't, bein' by then a peace promotin' Quaker. The king knew Younger to be a formidable warrior since while a member of the 'true faith' he had commanded one of his father's ships, was battle-hardened, reputed the best swordsman in Europe."

Fergus said England the last time. It really didn't matter. Younger could handle himself and the Court knew it.

"The King paid Younger off with a deed to 45,000 square miles of land in the New World. Imagine, square **miles**! The Crown was still cash-strapped so William didn't have much choice but to take it. Probably thought somethin' is better than nothin', right?

"The land, his land, became Penn's Sylvania, Penn's woods. Explorers told him a squirrel could cross his land and **never** touch the ground!"

I loved this part of Fergus's story! I imagined that squirrel traveling the boundary of Penn's land, leaping from branch to branch three hundred miles east to west then turning and leaping another one hundred fifty south to north. Those were **miles**! He'd be a gray gray by the time he got to Knoxville, too old and out of breath to finish the rectangle. He'd only gone halfway! I prayed he'd find comfort from other squirrels on his journey. He must have stopped on his northern trek from west to east, met a girl squirrel, started having babies. There were now thousands of grays around Knoxville, plaguing us farmers, eating our corn, descendants of one traveller one hundred fifty years before...

That's the way my imagination worked in the early 1850s.

"*It's still working, Grandpa!*"

"*Hayley are you still listening?*"

"Yep. Continue please."

"Ok, Boss."

Fergus spat on the dirt floor, took a long sip from his jug, stuck a fresh wad in his jaw, got it where it didn't interfere, kept on with his version of how we got our name.

"Those that have money can turn their holdin's into more money and that's what Penn did with his Woods. Bein' from a maritime background he knew the Navy needed timber. Bein' a persecuted Quaker he knew his people needed sanctuary. So, he planned a twofer: After he sold his timber he would sell the cleared land. It was a long voyage to the New World, distance itself a protection. The Navy couldn't use it all - his woods were too big. The resources were still there to build farms and towns and meetin' houses. Religious liberty would prevail and milk and honey (and money) would bless the Penn's in the New World. Thank you Gawd!"

"And Admiral Penn," added Connie.

"Him too," agreed Fergus, who **never** gave the king credit for anything.

"Younger waited for the land to be cleared, a town started, a house built, and overseers hired to manage his estates in the British Isles before moving lock, stock and molasses barrel to his City of Brotherly Love - from where the squirrel began his trek, as the crow flies, two hundred fifty miles south and east of here, to Philadelphia.

"Now Younger was not only a good swordsman and a devoted Quaker, he was also a foine businessman and that ken is what brought us to the New World. Knowin' his holdin' was too big for just the Quakers his factors advertised for settlers in the British Isles and Europe. They looked for those that were persecuted, offered payment plans for land purchases, even loans for ship's fare.

"From Europe came Lutherans and Anabaptists, from England Quakers and a few nosy Anglicans, from Ireland the Presbyterians. All claimed membership in the 'true faith', but were willing to compromise for religious liberty, freedom from governmental interference, cheap land and low taxes.

"For the Presbyterians, the last three items were more important than the first. Their "Reformed" branch had been led in Scotland by the fierce tightass John Knox and migrated to Ireland. They hated Papists more than they hated government, eradicated the one and tolerated the other. In Penn's Sylvania they were forced to tolerate other Protestants, which they did...barely. The Reformed Presbyterians were the Scots-Irish. We quit ditherin' and delayin' and moved, whole boatloads of us.

"The Clan McBoone was invited along. We came too - lock, stock and whiskey barrel. Included in the lock and stock were tools as fixers required tools."

Connie interrupted again! "We got tools, Papa, and lots of jugs. Don't we need more casks, Papa?"

Connie was looking around, overthinking stuff, scratching mean Queenie's ears. I wished I could look as innocent and get forgiven as fast as her dog!

Fergus harrumphed, stood, told us he needed a break, strode over to the knothole and looked out. He swore: "You and your g-d fits, woman!"

He returned to his stool and sat. We settled around. This included Connie whose question was again ignored. She seemed nonplussed, still scratching Queenie's ears. Having told us how we got our name, and how we got to Penn's Sylvania, if there was time he would tell how we got to Knoxville.

Today there was time.

Fergus continued:

"From Philadelphia the Scots-Irish trekked west and north, meltin' into the Big Woods. They carved out settlements and caused woe to any

## The Legend of Augustus McBoone

Brother who demanded they pay for what they took. If that Brother wasn't a tough sob, he might not make it home."

Remember, this is Fergus' side of the story.

"This was **their** land they told the Brother, before tarring and feathering or killing him. What right did a g-d Penn have to charge for land he had never seen? And the Injun? Bare-butt heathens, just like the green-kilt Irish, not of the 'true faith,' remove 'em, kill 'em all! Didn't the Lord give Joshua free reign three thousand years ago? So Gawd, yes God, gave them this land. They had a responsibility to make milk and honey (and whiskey) in it.

"It wasn't easy keepin' this land. Like Joshua, they encountered resistance, caused battles and wars. Their trails were littered with burnt bodies and homes. Still, as in Northern Ireland, they hung on. Bred like…squirrels. Took 'em a hunert years. They said the early Scots-Irish believed in the Three Johns: John Calvin, John Knox and John Barleycorn. And, kept the Ten Commandments and anything else they got their hands on."

I liked the truth of the Three Johns too.

At this point Connie stamped her foot, wanting to know (finally) who John Barleycorn was. This time Fergus answered by pointing to his jug. "Oh," she said.

She could be dense sometimes, his Constance.

My uncle converted the bulk of his own corn to whiskey. Aged it in four large white oak barrels set on wood blocks tall enough to enable drawing off into smaller barrels called casks. But Fergus drew his off into earthenware jugs. As Connie noted, he had a lot more jugs than casks. Mr. Glover, the banker, looked after Fergus. In 1865 he paid me for a wagonload of casks. I still keep a couple in my workshop.

*"You keep 'em filled don'cha Grandpa?"*

*"Yep. Aged and filled."*

He lived long, my uncle. And all his long life he made wonderful whiskey. Drank up his profits though.

Back to his story:

"During that hunert years, the Penn's, their Quaker buddies, and their allies in the Tory government thought it best to buy off the heathens. Why fight when they could pay? They had more money than the Scots-Irish, so they paid. They too felt the white race had a destiny to populate Penn's Sylvania with Christians, uh, Protestants only. They chose to spend money, not lives.

## The Legend of Augustus McBoone

"In the 1780s a great thing happened! The Revolution sent the Tory Penn's scurrying back to their British Isle estates. Us Scots-Irish helped send them and a Tory-free Pennsylvania government took over. The new General Assembly established state boundaries and within them settled disputes of ownership and title. The disputes involving earlier finagling by the Scots-Irish were found in their favor so the hunert years of fightin' paid off.

"The Pennsylvania boundaries followed the squirrel. The area between the $40^{th}$ and $42^{nd}$ parallels North Latitude and the $74^{th}$ to $81^{st}$ West Longitude became our state." Seeing our eyes glaze with this detail, Fergus, good storyteller that he was, added: "Yep, the Assembly established what that old gray dinna do - the rectangle-all on paper. But that squirrel did something the politicians did not. Know what that was?"

We answered in unison; "Come to Knoxville!" One voice added "Find a girl squirrel!" Fergus' eyes twinkled. "You're all right, especially you Connie."

Constance beamed. She got one right.

"The Assembly looked at their new map, decided that this northwest section needed settlement... by whites. The politicians auctioned off this land to speculators, encouraged them to resell. Those were moneyed folks in Philadelphia. Folks like Bingham, Strawbridge, even the Trustees of the

Episcopal Academy showed up. The Episcopalians were former Anglicans and Tories who pledged allegiance to the Assembly and spurned the King. Must be they had some coin, huh? The speculators hired agents to sell this land, the agents hired surveyors to measure lots off and road builders to open it up. Me and Angus came here via the Williamson Road. Started in Williamsport it did. Crossed the border and ended at Painted Post. We turned west at the junction of the Cowanesque and Tioga Rivers. Followed the Cowanesque twenty miles and…here we are!

"At least the hirelings who came here knew what we dealt with. Mountains, rivers, trees, critters, Injuns and such. The agents devised payment plans, took coin or goods that could be converted to coin as payment. The goods were mostly livestock, poultry, produce or whiskey. It's a lot easier to ship casks of whiskey than shocks of corn. Pays better too."

I'm thinking: How do **you** know if you're drinking it all up?

"We came, built farms and homes and towns, established townships and counties. Paid taxes, too." He spat. He didn't like taxes, Fergus. "Ten dollars a year is too g-d high, I think. The surrounding land was huge. Our hamlets were tiny compared to the Big Woods. In those woods the squirrel could still cross miles of land and never touch the ground. The speculators kept that land, paid taxes too." He spit out the rest of his chaw, kept talking.

"Me and Angus bought two hunert acres from the Strawbridge Estate, paid coin plus one cask of whiskey for twenty years."

Fergus never told who paid the coin. I never saw any casks leave the farm, ever. More on that, later.

"We brought our wives, worked hard, built what we got here. Our land runs north to south, hilltop to hilltop, the river near the center. Half is fertile valley land. Topsoil is deep, runs along the water. Grows the tallest corn. The hillsides are timbered with hardwoods - maple, oak, chestnut. The hilltops run to softwoods - evergreens, pine and hemlock rule there.

"We partners worked the land till Ugly here was born and Mary died. Then Angus left, I named Augustus and Flo and I are left to work the land, send the whiskey and pay the g-d taxes."

Thus ended the story. Remember this is from Fergus, not me. Fergus had the oldest boy check on Flo. Couldn't send Connie off anymore. She had more to say:

"Papa, I don't think Augustus is ugly."

Bless you, Connie!

"You're all born long and ugly," he said. "A McBoone stays long, not ugly."

"Could I have crosseyed kids, Papa?"

"Only if your g-d husband is crosseyed, Connie."

This satisfied Constance. I always thought she was the prettiest McBoone. Her sisters ran long and lean, the youngest kinda horse-faced. Connie married a local named Edgcomb. None of their seven were crosseyed.

My oldest cousin yelled from the knothole. "She's off her rocker Pa! Fixin' supper. Smoke comin' from the chimney."

Everyone rose to go, except me. I had to stay in the barn. Fergus let his six troop out. He turned to me and said, "Don't you be makin' her mad again so soon, ya hear?"

I nodded. But her cookies smelt so good...

I resolved to be more careful around my uncle - he was smarter than he looked. But not smart enough to keep the mortgage and taxes paid.

Or Flo home when he should.

*"Grandpa!"* Haley brought me back to 1945. *"You are being sarcastic."*

*"Can't help it."*

*"Didn't her fling with the headmaster happen after you left the farm?"*

*I nodded.*

*"And doesn't McB own the farm today?"*

*"Yes, Hayley. Mandi and I bought it in 1888. Fergus, then a cousin have run it for us ever since. Squire transferred the deed after WWI."*

*What goes around comes around I guess.*

## Chapter 7

# A Forgiving Heart

Flo was a fertile woman who squirted out a babe every two years. I ended up with nine more McBoone cousins. I guess feeding me became too much of a burden as she dropped me off one afternoon at the Boy's Home.

It might have had something to do with Philadelphia... She'd had a fit a couple days back. During Fergus' story I asked him where Philadelphia was. I hadn't seen any casks shipped there, ever. One of my older cousins told me Constance mentioned my question to her mom. It didn't put her into another fit but it did tick her off. None of us knew why.

Then.

It was a hot midsummer day. Our chores done, four cousins and I went swimming in the deep hole below the Academy Corner's Bridge. Connie wasn't there. Flo made her stay and watch the two youngest since she had "cannin' to finish."

Then Flo hitched up their wagon. Her fit and my questions were in the past.

I thought.

Flo arrived with their wagon, yelled for me to get out of the pool. Had I been a teen I'd a told her where to go but I was seven goin' on eleven. I went instead...into the bushes and changed into the dry pants and shirt she threw down at me. Hand-me-downs they were, patched and repatched. I never had new clothes until Dad came three summers later. There were no underpants or shoes. No youngster wore them in the summer. No poor youngster anyway.

An aside: That bridge and I share a history. In one incident in 1865 I blew a bank robber and his horse off that bridge. Mandi had peppered his backside with double aughts. He thought he'd gotten away with the money, a workin' girl could remove the buck. It was a thousand-yard moving shot. My bullet deflected down through his saddle. It's been eighty years. I still feel bad about that horse. Not him. He had been with Bill Sykes.

"Grandpa!"

"*It was a great shot, Hayley. I shoulda' aimed a little higher. Mighta' saved the horse...*"

"You're digressing. Back to the swimming hole."

"*Yes, Boss.*"

I climbed into the box. Noticed a tied flour sack and sat on it.

After a few minutes of silence, she tied up at the Boy's Home.

The Home, or Academy to the educated folks, was a place for orphans and wayward boys. Flo told the headmaster I was an orphan they couldn't control any more. It seemed the "Christian thing" to put me where I could get regular discipline. She handed him the tied sack. It was my extra set of clothes and barn shoes. No unders.

What a liar! I wasn't an orphan. I had a dad… somewhere. What kind of "Christian" kicks their kin out…even of their barn?

It didn't matter. I was done. In the Home. Flo had credibility, a farm, a jug and herself.

She handed the headmaster some of Fergus' "foinest" and he invited her to his room. Flo became a regular visitor for a while and two of my boy-cousins grew up short and stocky like the headmaster.

Actually, I liked the Academy better than the barn. I slept in a top bunk, ate two squares a day. When I got smacked, it was for being a smart-alec. Once

I got two smacks and no supper. I had wondered aloud why the only Alec I knew was dumb, not smart.

Alec and I were piling brush on a stone row. Heard an unmistakable rattle. He reached under a flat stone and…got nailed for being curious. That's dumb, right? His arm swelled, he got stupid, they said delirious, the Doc came and sawed off his arm. I still think losing an arm when that loss could have been avoided is dumb. Getting smacked twice by the headmaster was mild compared to the cuffings I got from Flo.

The Home operated a farm a mile west of the McBoone place. My chores were tolerable. Once they found I was good with stock I spent half my days tending them. The other half was spent at school. School was never out at the Academy. They had to create stuff for us to do. I learned to read and write there.

Dad taught me to journal, to write what I felt, to use my senses.

He came for me when I was ten. There was no mistaking him for a McBoone. He was tall and lean, and left-handed. I told the headmaster "See? I told you I wasn't an orphan!"

Dad said he needed help with the tinkering trade. He'd been to Philadelphia and paid off the

Strawbridges, his coin replacing the casks Fergus did not send. He caught up the back taxes, made arrangements to be contacted in the inevitability Fergus would fall behind again. Dad was wise, softhearted I thought then, wise I think now. He knew Fergus always had a coulda-woulda-shoulda excuse for not paying Caesar. So he made sure he was contacted. Squire says Dad had conveyed the deed, he had no legal right to interfere. But things were different back then. Caesar didn't care who paid the coin.

This worked while Dad lived. Not so much with me.

Dad visited Fergus and Flo and my cousins. Told them hi and bye. He was on his way to the Big Woods with me in a covered wagon. He gave the headmaster the coin equal to my tuition. It didn't go to the school. Flo was expecting and Fergus forbade any future visits. So no more jugs for the headmaster. No more trysts with Flo. Once Mr. Glover and his Board learned that he siphoned off coin there was no room left for the headmaster.

My two cousins never knew their real daddy.

"Grandpa!"

"I know. I'm being sarcastic again. I'll quit."

"That's gonna be hard for you Grandpa."

*"Still a smart-alec, you think?"*

*"Yep."*

Dad stopped at the general store and bought me some new clothes and shoes, even two pairs of underwear. When he stopped at the bank I realized folks knew and respected Angus McBoone, the tinkerer. Fergus, though flawed, was liked too. But not Flo. Dad introduced me to Mr. Glover, the young bank president. He shook my hand! Dad left money there, too.

On the road is where my **real** education began, The sober Angus was a handy and learned man. Said I was a natural, a quick study. He taught me mechanics and mathematics. How to shoot and fight. He bought books and we read together. He encouraged journaling and when our books and journals took up too much room we'd stop at the Knoxville Bank and deposit our load there. He had a room full of our stuff, Mr. Glover. We also left money. Tinkerers made money. Competent tinkerers were welcome everywhere.

It was an adjustment being welcomed. I had gone from a blanket next to a cow to a bunk above a dumb-alec to a bedroll inside a covered wagon. I had also gone from being ignored to tolerated to loved. I smelled different too. I now smelled of leather and woodsmoke and outdoor air and soap and water. I wore underpants. I was cared for. I was loved.

I grew older and taller. Every time we neared Knoxville, I yearned to teach Fergus and Flo a lesson.

"Forgive them", said Dad.

"Why? After all they've done?"

"Fergus is my older brother. Your only uncle. He protected me when we were growing up. He was a great partner until your mom died and I went away. He's got a drinking problem, worse than mine. Worse than that - he married a heartless bitch."

I agreed with that!

Dad added. "I have forgiven Fergus. I'm working on forgiving Flo."

I'm still working on forgiving Flo. It's 1945 and she died in 1869.

Her sixteenth babe did not squirt out. It got hung up inside, had to be removed with a scalpel, and Flo died of complications. The babe, a long girl, lived. By then Mandi and I were living in Steam Valley, had two babes of our own and a third on the way. Fergus sent a letter requesting sixty dollars and a tombstone. Told me, after requesting the loan, about Flo and how he buried her next to my mother. Oh, he said, the newborn is foine. I wanted to go back and inscribe the word BITCH on her tombstone. Mandi advised restraint. "What's the point?" she said.

I didn't go back. Sent seventy dollars, sixty for the back taxes and ten for the stone. I knew we'd never get paid back. I didn't say I was sorry for your loss 'cause I wasn't.

That sixteenth cousin? That girl? Grew up tall and horsefacey. She married, had a big family, looked after her dad there on the farm. She's been runnin' it for us since 1888.

Doing a good job. Makes fine whiskey. Gotta be sneaky about that now though.

"*Grandpa!*"

"*Just for me Hayley. Just for me.*"

Dad might have forgiven Flo. I haven't…yet. Probably never will. Kinda harsh that way, I know. It's hard to forgive Johnnie Rebs or the Sykes Gang. As time marches on I find it easier to forgive those who killed my buddies in war than those who murdered my dad in peace.

Notice I said "easier." This means I'm not entirely over war and not at all over murder, yet. That might have to do with when and who and where I fought. The Civil War was eight decades ago and involved Americans fighting Americans. In America. World War II may be winding down, but it's still right now, we had to go there again and Americans died fighting Krauts and Japs. Josh and Sally are on leave only, which means we may have to go back. I've not heard of forgiveness from them. Nor will they hear it from me.

They say it helps to talk with those you trust - your kin, a close friend, a clergyman. I've found my kin and close friends to be wounded and unforgiving like me. Barber Hal does not like Krauts, for example. And, I've only had one preacher long enough to get to know him.

It was ten years before Barber Hal and I opened up to each other. I went to him every week, same as I went to our preachers. Note the plural.

I've had more preachers than horses and dogs. I'm on Bob 4, Dick 5, B 9 and Preacher 12. This means two things: One, horses live longer than dogs and two, preachers don't stay around long.

I'd be hitching up Bob and Dick or scratching B's ears and telling them private stuff. Sandra or Betts would overhear. They have big ears, women.

"Grandpa!"

*I knew they were listenin':*

Anyway, they'd overhear. Then they'd blab to the preacher's wife and she'd blab to him. Mandi never blabbed like that. I've always talked to my horses and dogs, Mandi too. Together we'd talk to that one preacher. I could never talk private to Sandra or Betts.

Maybe that's why I love Mandi so.

"Augustus," Sandra or Betts' preacher would say, "You must forgive!" This also means two things: One, preachers give advice that's not asked for and two, time for a sit-down with my current missus.

I would respond though. "You forgive! After you've been abused or lost loved ones to violence or war."

The one preacher that did lose, understood. Those that haven't, won't. Never will.

Dad's favorite book was his Bible. That book never got left off. Every night he'd read aloud a passage. The best parts for me were the battles described in the Old Testament. Huge hand-to-hand conflicts they were, larger than the Civil War. Hundreds of thousands of men died, left valleys full of dry bones and houses full of widows and children. No wonder marriages were plural, there weren't enough men! Did those wives forgive the men who killed their husbands? Did they snuggle up with the victors later? Ezekiel said they snuggled. I think they snuggled to survive. Surviving and forgiving are not the same thing. I never thought women were spoils of war. Back then they did. Had slaves too.

*"Could I be a spoil of war, Grandpa?"*

*"They'd have to beat us, I think."*

*"Me too."*

Before Ezekiel was Moses' Chieftain, Joshua. An absolute annihilator he was. He killed the men and their families . Burned their farms with their livestock inside. The only thing he took was the land. Did what he was told by God. The enemies were pagans, unbelievers, so kill 'em all! And he did, mostly. They weren't of the 'true faith'.

I could see it back then. Am troubled by it now. Today "true faith" seems an excuse for thievery to me.

The Paxton boys used this argument for wiping out Stickwalker's tribe in 1762. Even though the Conestogas were pagans they were leaning the Moravian way, were probably more Christian than the Scots-Irish Presbyterians.

Is God ever on the loser's side? How do we discern? What happens when both sides pray to the same

## The Legend of Augustus McBoone

god? Like the Civil War. After a battle, the ground was littered with blue and gray, a truce declared, survivors of both sides would shake hands, sing together "Glory Hallelujah, His Truth is Marching on," bury their dead.

Whose truth went marching on?

It was hard for me to do that - shake hands after a battle. Only did it once. In a Union hospital tent at Gettysburg.

How can I forgive the Sykes Gang for killing Dad? Or the Rebs that blew my Bucktails to pieces? Or the Choctaw buck that lopped off Michael's hand? Or that Spanish sniper that drilled Esau's Captain? Or that officer that ordered Jacob to shoot at dust? Or the Krauts that gassed Caleb and shot Peter and Joe? Or the drunk that hit Peggy Mae? Or that Jap that kamikazeed Logan?

Regarding Flo there's a coulda-woulda-shoulda conundrum for me. I could forgive her and I would forgive her but I do not believe I should.

They also say time heals all wounds. I say time patches wounds, scabs them, never really heals.

I buried Dad's Bible with him. He valued it. At the time I didn't think it protected him like it should. Kinda resentful I guess. I didn't read from The Book for a while. Didn't have one at D.C. Heard the 23rd recited a couple of times. I got one off a dead Reb at Chancellorsville. It didn't protect him either but soldiers told of incidents where one had. Better to be safe than…dead, I thought.

There was an inscription inside. I looked closer. I had seen this man! In D. C. at church.

The inscription read: "Gerald, remember to talk to the Lord like you're talking to a friend."

Dated 24th Oct. 1862. Gerald wore black that day. I wore blue. The only Union soldier there.

They had a tolerance for Yankee occupiers, those Copperheads. Also, my size and it being Sunday protected me. Later I discovered Pastor Brands also wore the gray, a Reb Chaplain. I never saw him again.

But Teddy Collins had. Collins owned vast tracts of timberland in western Pennsylvania. Dad helped him get started. Collins Pine has never missed a dividend payment. A cradle-to-grave empire he created, entirely out of the Big Woods. We spoke a similar language, he more Irish and eloquent than me. He had a bigger heart than me too. He was the real-deal do-gooder, Teddy Collins was. He spoke at a Methodist Convention that Sandra dragged me to. We took our Bibles. After speaking he offered to sign them. Signed with a scripture - Job 22:22, you can look it up. When he got to my

Bible and saw the inscription his eyes widened, just like Clemens. Wanted my story. Brands was a great theologian, a founder of Methodism, he told Sandra and me. If I was ever to get rid of that Bible, please let him know.

That Bible sets near the old Underwood, alongside **Tom Sawyer** and **Huckleberry Finn**. It's an heirloom, that Bible.

The one I read now is an edition written by a lawyer named Scofield in 1909. Got that from a Reb too. A live one. Also a lawyer. Signed with his favorite scripture - Joshua 24:15. You can look that up as well. Judge Thomas Sawyer mailed that from Hannibal, Missouri. Pronounced Missourah.

Tom's a good sort, for a Reb. He's a better forgiver than me, for sure. For example he has forgiven Stickwalker for that everlasting knot on his head. But I still swear at him whenever his saber slash on my collarbone acts up. It has taken a while, several reunions and a visit to Hannibal, but we've become friends.

Speaking of friends, the first and last time I saw the haunt of Huckleberry was at the 1900 Reunion. That was where Huck learned that Tom still lived and that Tom and I were friends. I asked Tom one time — Did I replace Huck as Tom's friend? Partly. Only partly, he said.

As I grow older I read my Scofield more. I emphasize the New Testament now. It's more comforting than the Old. The comfort is in knowing there is a reunion coming with my loved ones. Especially Mandi and Dad and my kids. And yes, Uncle Fergus.

But not Aunt Flo. Too damned mean. Yep. Flo was damned because she was mean. I think.

That Scofield is kinda ratty now. Needs rebound. I hate to send it away. There are decades of reflections penned inside. It has survived all kinds of neglect - from being stuffed inside a saddlebag to being exposed on the roof of my car. It's another Journal.

The man that sent it to me made two more Reunions before he died. He was a good sort, for a Reb.

Scofield, a lawyer like Sawyer and Hayes, claimed to take a different look at things. But I find more similarity when compared with Pastor Brand's King James. Oh, Scofield's is more modern, easier to read. Both differ with the Bible I buried with Dad. His has more books, was written in French, was a Papist Bible. (I never told Fergus). Scofield's and Brand's are Protestant Bibles. The Papist and Protestant Bibles read alike as far as the New Testament goes, which is what I emphasize today.

I sit down now and ponder. The worry-warts have gone home. I sit in my chair, stoke the fire, smoke my pipe, keep my Scofield and a tumbler near. I never drink a third whiskey. Not like Fergus. It's smooth, that whiskey. Oak aged. From Fergus' recipe.

I can forgive Fergus. He had a heart.

I can't forgive Flo. She didn't.

# Chapter 8

# THE HEREAFTER AND THE HERE

Finally! Free to smoke, drink, indulge my fantasies. I love those gals and they love me. Still, I'm sure they look forward to the daily time, as I do, when we're shut of each other. I'm only talking about the here, now. Not the hereafter.

I made a long poker to stoke that fire. Do that from my chair. Smart, huh?

Does a 101(almost) year-old have fantasies?

Yep.

Remembrances?

Yep.

More pertaining to the hereafter than the here you might think...except right now I'm considering... pews. Yep, pews. The next church I build is gonna have cushions on its pews. That oak wood sure looks nice but is too hard on my skinny butt. Or Widow Flaherty's fat butt. Or Mary Spencer's nice butt. She brings her two pretty daughters, Julie and Nan. That Julie is shapin' up like her mom... and Hayley. She and Brenda would disapprove of my noticing any female butts, but I still do. It's only church, only an hour per week, but, pun intended...

We shouldn't suffer so.

Those that believe you go to church to squirm, to be uncomfortable, are only considering their hereafter and not the here. Well, they might be considering mine too. If they consider anything at all.

I've built a number of churches. My name is even etched on one window. Gold lettering on stained glass. Says I was the ARCHITECT. Hell! I'm a builder, not an architect. That church has the same high framing as the barn down the road. I built both. At the same time. When I started, you couldn't tell one from the other. Only the rows of pretty tombstones around the one and the barbed wire fence around the other described our intent. Then the belltower, stone, windows and siding set the church apart from the barn. I recall the Church Board threatening to withhold payment because I hired Eyetalians to put on the finish. Imagine, Papists making money from their pretty Protestant church! If they had known their stained glass came from a colored artisan, they'd a'pitched a hissy I'll tell you. I paid all those craftsmen ahead of time, they were that good. That black man and his Eyetalian buddies were responsible for that architect panel. He built it, they installed it. They knew I'd fuss but couldn't do much since winter was coming and I wanted to close up that structure before Sunday Service. They were honorable men, hanging that window and installing those hard oak pews **after** I'd paid them.

I stuck to my guns. They wanted a pretty church, didn't they? I was under budget and ahead of time. The Board paid me, a couple of months after the farmer did.

They never had my name removed as architect. Nor have they installed cushions on those pews. My work drawings for both are in the journal for that year. You will find I like inches and feet and fours as my units of measure. Those may be the only drawings in existence for those structures. The church bell clangs and the faithful fill those hard pews every Sunday. The cowbell clangs and the cows file in every day, including Sunday.

Whether builder or architect - I finished the job.

Those structures were built when I was a lot younger - a spry seventy. Back then I reflected less and did more. I set their rafters! Had more adventures. Today, shooting that eagle was a big adventure. Thirty years ago, not at all. Back then you were rewarded if you shot a pesky predator. In a few years they may want to shoot me...

And really get offended when I shoot back!

I'm here now and at 101(almost) I yearn for earlier days when my sap ran strong. I've been married and faithful seventy-eight of those years. I've had three wives, each a quarter century or so. All were good women. But it's my child bride, my first love, my Mandi, I pine for most and she's been gone fifty-five years!

Codgers tell me they remember yesteryear better than yesterday. I used to think that was nonsense... until I lost Mandi. I remember her first words - "Whatcha' cookin'?" That was 1863, yesteryear. Yet to me it happened yesterday.

Of all the McBoone stones at the Brick Church, it's Mandi's I visit the most. Her stone reads:

**AMANDA PATTERSON MCBOONE**
**1849-1890**
**Aged 41 years, 1 month, 2 days**
**The Best Wife This Man Ever Had**

I've caught grief over that last inscription. But **never** from wives Sandra or Betts or **any** member of the clan McBoone. All know I miss Mandi. All know I inscribed her stone soon after she died. And all know I still mean it. Even after fifty-five years.

My stone sets in the middle of the McBoone row, next to Mandi's. My stone reads:

**AUGUSTUS MCBOONE**
**1844 -**
**Aged          Years**

Since I'm still "here" the rest is up to Hayley to inscribe. I've taught her. She has the skill and patience required of a great engraver. There's room to add any comment she would like. Her choice.

The Squire and I were talking in his office the other day. About my estate. My will. I said, "I refuse to rule from the grave! Not like Louisa."

His response was, "Good!"

He's got a lot of sense, Squire. For a young man.

I've been reading Clemens (Twain) lately. I hope I don't end up as crotchety as he did. Speaking of ending - I was watching Halley's comet before I learned he died. Big ball of a star it was, whitish, trailing smaller stars. In the northeast. It'll be back in 1985. I'll be 141 (almost). That might be in my hereafter, I think.

## The Legend of Augustus McBoone

Well, my tumbler is empty. I'll not have three. I've contemplated the hereafter and the here and I'm still not sleepy. Don't want to read. I have that bat order from Boston. Think I'll go to the shop, tie on an apron, and start lathing. I have some high quality ash blanks there. He's very specific about length, width, barrel circumference, weight. Like Grey, Ruth, Cochran, Cobb. Ten dozen bats they want. For a returning flyboy named Williams. Ted Williams.

Ever hear of him?

## Chapter 9

# THE PINE ERA

Early Tuesday morning I got up, cleaned up, dressed and did my chores(I don't dress up for chores.) This was usual. Then I went to the library, and a hiding spot, pulled out a dozen volumes total, stacked them in date order next to my chair and started to read aloud. This was unusual.

Usually the worry-warts would find me in the barn or shop. This morning they rushed into the house expecting to find me...dead.

I wasn't.

*"Whatcha' readin', Grandpa?"*

Hayley's "greeting" took me back to July 4th, 1863, when Mandi approached, curious to know what I was cookin'. I swear to God Hayley is the reincarnation of Mandi and thank Him for making her that way.

A man would be a sapless eunuch to not notice Hayley or her mom, Brenda. Or Brenda's mom, Peggy Mae. Oh, Peggy Mae was sure no one would want her after she got clawed by the bear. But those scars only disfigured one side of her face. Genuine suitors didn't care. Those that dared mention her face I sent packing. She had such a big heart, Peggy Mae! B8 would wait for her every morning, his tail wagging. Then one day she didn't come. I'd find him stretched out between the graves of her and her husband. It was only a few months before I got B9.

*Grandpa!*

*I answered. She could be impatient, Hayley. "I'm reading our journals from the time I tinkered with Dad."*

They were "ours" because the earliest ones were penned by Dad. Later ones were written by me. We tinkered in north-central Pennsylvania during its Pine Era.

The Pine Era lasted from our pioneer beginnings through the end of the Civil War. For two centuries, from 1670-1870, the money tree was the stately white pine. After 1870, the money tree was the hemlock.

Remember Fergus' story about the squirrel? He could jump from treetop to treetop, traverse an immense evergreen forest, and never touch the ground. Below he could see the occasional glade or stream or canopy of hardwood trees. In 1670 the break was occasional and still below, usually a hundred feet below.

Pennsylvania pines were sturdy and tall. There were a few bare branches up its bare trunk which flared out to a limby evergreen top. This is where the squirrel stayed, high up. The pines grew close together. Being a softwood it was relatively easy to fall with a crosscut and shape with an adze. Floated higher too.

The tallest and hardiest pines grew in the high plateau region of the state. Mountaineers said it was so cold the snow would leave as late as June and return in September. This north-central area had two names: Germans called it the Black Forest. The rest called it the Big Woods.

We had stretches here and there where "civilization" was making an inroad. Knoxville was one. Fallbrook was one. Harrisonville another. I have survived all three.

Every pioneer farmer became a logger in the winter and a raftsman in the spring. Glades were used to store the logs, streams to transport them. Camps and towns sprung up to meet an increasing demand - pine before the Civil War, hemlock after. This demand met its zenith in Williamsport where something was needed to slow and organize the volume of logs. That something was the "Boom," built along the swollen Susquehanna.

Built by Major James Perkins in the early 1850s the Boom was a series of juts creating diversion ponds called "cribs." (Loggers have colorful names for stuff). A mill could yank its "branded" log from its crib, saw and sell its boards that day. No one cared about "green" (undried) lumber in the 1850s. The carpenter just made do. The Boom was huge - six miles long. Then Peter Herdic bought it from Major Perkins and expanded the length to seven.

In a decade, hundreds of mills sawed and sold millions of feet of lumber. Each year. They ran around the clock. Williamsport, with its railroad and telegraph hubs, became the "Lumber Capital of the World." Had more millionaires per thousand folks than any other place on earth. More fortunes were made (and lost) in the Eastern Timber Rush than the Western Gold and Silver Rushes combined. You didn't know that did you?

But (always a but), Pines were not quickly replaced. Demand outstripped supply. Those requiring huge volumes moved to the "Pinelands" of Michigan and Wisconsin . Did it over. Their pine wasn't as hardy as ours, but it was pine.

Those that stayed went back and cut hemlock. It became the money tree. Know why? The bark. Used in the tanning process. Tanneries replaced sawmills, the mills adapted, the timber rush continued until 1920.

Tanner's made leather. Our population required shoes and belts, saddles and holsters. Soldiers especially required these. Our society required soldiers...until 1920. According to the Powers That Be...

Then demand outstripped supply again. The hemlock was gone. The squirrel could no longer cross Penn's Land. Those dependent on hemlock had to create a different process to tan. They did but (there's that but again) this created another era, one not nearly as prosperous as the one before.

For **me** the Pine Era lasted from my time with my dad in 1855 to my enlistment in 1862. Most of our tinkering was done at Pine Era log camps. We were like preachers, traveling a circuit. I saw the Era peak and end and never realized it was happening. Too young I guess. The same held true for the Hemlock Era which began after I mustered out in 1863 and endured until the last doughboy came home in 1920. Although I technically was not a young man I was still full of sap and busy and didn't notice then either. I think now any era is defined **after** it occurs. Those that lived in it describe it...later. I've lived through the Gilded Age, the Farm and Mechanical Eras, the Flu Season, the Roaring Twenties, the Great Depression. I'd have to look at my journals to tell when one ended and the other began. I can tell you this: If our experiences aren't recorded and those memories allowed to fade or die, then that Era will waft away like a Steam Valley fog.

I grew up in the Pine Era, grew out of the Hemlock, grew old watching the hills come back. Slow. As for me, I ask you - Is one hundred years of life old? Not for a tree or a turtle or a Conestoga. But I'm a regular man. So why me? Abraham's sap was flowing strong when he was one hundred. His dad lived to be two hundred five. I doubt they were "regular."

Even if I lived that long, I really doubt I'd see the Pine Era, the Big Woods, again. Patches maybe.

# Chapter 10

# TINKERING WITH MY DAD

You know my history until I was ten. You know Dad left soon after I was born and Mom died. You know he had a drinking problem. What you don't know is where he was those years and why I never heard from him.

You've had glimpses is all.

Dad sent letters. Flo never shared a one. I blame Flo as she got the mail. Must've destroyed them. They knew Dad was alive, knew I wasn't an orphan. She never said one good thing about him. I think Flo was hoping Dad would not return as that put off the Day of Reckoning. Fergus always cared, but lived in a clamorous, foggy, female-whipped world of too many kids, too much whiskey, allowed Flo too much control over our lives. As far as the Day of Reckoning, well, Fergus always put off today anything that could be done tomorrow. And the day after...

## The Legend of Augustus McBoone

He was flawed, Fergus. Still, he loved Dad and Dad loved him. At the Day of Reckoning, Dad forgave Fergus.

He ignored Flo.

After that day, Dad and I traveled and tinkered. On that day I took my McGuffey Reader and what I wore. All I had. Hopped aboard "our" wagon, a boy almost ten, going on fourteen. Going on an adventure!

On that day my "real" education began. From that day, Dad told me where he'd been, things he'd done, things he wished he hadn't. His biggest regret was leaving me with Flo.

I now think that bitch hardened and smartened me, honed my sense of injustice. That's the most credit she's ever gonna get from me.

Here are what Dad's journals and stories reveal about the years 1844 to 1854:

During those years Dad was drinking, tinkering and logging; drinking, soldiering and wandering. He made his way to California, lost count of the jugs consumed there and back.

That first winter Dad cut pine for Silas Billings. The lumberman operated a sawmill in Knoxville (later bought by the Edgcomb's). That spring Dad rafted pine logs and spars east down the Cowanesque, Tioga and Chemung Rivers to the North Branch of the Susquehanna. From Wilkes-Barre he and Billing's crew rafted southwest to the Main Branch at Selinsgrove. Billings had sawlog buyers there and further south at Harrisburg. The rafts of spars they floated further and sold to shipbuilders in the Chesapeake Bay.

This was the roundabout way and fraught with danger. Disaster lurked around every bend. If they got to the Chesapeake and made money, they bought horses and rode the three hundred miles home. If they didn't, they walked...from wherever they got. Billings tired of the long and unpredictable raft trips east and moved west, cutting tracts of pine in the Big Woods, rafting that down the more predictable Pine Creek drainage to the West Branch of the Susquehanna to Williamsport. If he chose to go on it was a straighter, safer run all the way to the Chesapeake. Note I did not say it was without danger, rafting is **always** dangerous. I said the west was **safer**. Dad did not work for Billings when he cut the west but he did credit him for opening up the Cowanesque and Pine Creek drainages to rafting. (Dad did raft down the Pine Creek drainage. Later, but not for Billings).

One spring Dad rode a horse to Harrisburg. Got drunk and lost his money and horse in a poker game. He then joined the Army and went west with General Zachary Taylor. Got drunk in the cities of Pittsburgh, Cincinnati, St. Louis, New Orleans, San Antonio. Met Saul Poorbaugh and J. E. P. Stickwalker at the Alamo. Poorbaugh was a kid, Stickwalker a **real** giant. Seeing that bullet-riddled mission made them **REMEMBER**. On this journey Dad fixed anything that broke - axles, cannons, cookpots, guns, bayonets, knives. In one battle Dad shoved Saul out of the way of a bayonet thrust, throttled that Mexican himself. He became Taylor's chief armorer, Sergeant Angus McBoone.

He had a likable, competent way about him, Dad.

Dad mustered out in San Antonio. He and a wandering sailor named Seagreaves then trekked on to the Gold Fields of California. They didn't strike gold so they split up, Seagreaves heading west to the Port of San Francisco, Dad heading back east to the Woods of Pennsylvania.

When sober Dad reasoned there was more gold in trees and was right. In Harrisburg Dad met Jacob Miller of the King's Arrow Timber Company. Miller was a principled man, too principled at times, Dad thought. Miller's crew needed a "handy" man so Dad teamed up with King's Arrow and its practical foreman, Ike Mcfee. They made money and Dad invested in the King's Arrow, becoming both an owner and junior partner. He also encountered Seagreaves embarking from a whaler in the Chesapeake and convinced Miller to hire him for their log crew.

In the spring of 1850, on a log drive down Little Pine Creek, King's Arrow tangled with Bill and Elmer Sykes. The Sykes brothers were "Algierines," log thieves who sawed off the ends of "branded" logs, rebranded and sold the timber as their own. Miller's brand was a King's arrow, Dad's was McB, Sykes was double S. One in ten of every log and spar was branded McB. Miller's and Dad's brands were registered with the State. The Sykes brothers could not be bothered with that "shit."

Ike heard a saw up a side stream. He investigated and caught Elmer sawing the end off a King's Arrow log. He made the mistake of dragging the smaller man to their campfire for a "discussion." Elmer was a "smart aleck" who offended King's Arrow. He never thought they would administer "frontier justice" - until it was too late. The discussion turned deadly and into a vote. Dad and Ike argued that "frontier justice" was too harsh a penalty for the theft of a ten-dollar log. But the rest of the crew, including a wavering Jacob Miller, argued for an example to be set. They hanged Elmer from a bare sycamore on a knoll north of English Center. Elmer screamed and swore and kicked like hell, without avail. Orlando provided the rope and Seagreaves tied the knot. They left him hanging for all raftsmen to see.

Dad and Ike hung back, refused to help. But the majority had spoken and majorities were a big deal in 1850.

Wherever they stopped they built a fire. Orlando, believing more of a message was necessary, still hot about being called a g-d Papist, stuck a timber brand in the coals and branded Elmer through his jeans with it. Elmer, already dead, could not cry out. But the brand did - for vengeance. Orlando had grabbed the wrong iron. Elmer Syke's buttock was branded McB.

Bill Sykes came back, cut his brother down and threw his body in the rain-swollen creek. Elmer floated amidst thousands of logs down the watershed to Williamsport. There "hicks" from Cochran-Wolverton fished him out and buried the body in an unmarked grave near the mill. They saw that he had been hanged and branded. They also knew his brother, Big Bill, to be a pigheaded and dangerous man.

Hicks (loggers) talk. Word spread that Angus McBoone hanged and branded Elmer. So, although frontier justice was realized, McB got most of the blame.

The Sykes-McBoone feud lasted ninety-four years. Before it ended thirteen men had died - two good ones and eleven bad ones. I ended it by throttling the last Sykes in my shop. Ralph poled the body into the bog at Three oaks. As I said earlier, I feel kinda hypocritical about that since I told Dolly Grey I'd never pollute a spring like Lew Wetzel did.

The next snowy winter was spent logging off the Longsdorf Tract near Buttonwood. Dad and Miller marked trees across Bear to Great Swamp. He and Miller cut and squared the timbers for the Covered Bridge. He helped the crew bury Orlando who had been killed by a huge cat.

And, he helped King's Arrow bury Jacob Miller after their logs crushed him.

Years later, I freshened Dad's engraving on Miller's stone. Added a King's Arrow.

I did this at the request of Lady Louisa.

Saul and Jesse witnessed my chisel work. I had since come to know my Dad's distrust of Jesse was frontier prejudice. Saul was more outgoing than his standoffish twin. Dad had served with Saul in Mexico, knew the breeds were dangerous men.

"You were always handy, Gus," said Saul, admiring the King's Arrow I had chiseled below Jacob Miller's name. Saul limped badly now. The minnie embedded in his hip was really bothering. Jesse and Songbird had both confided their concerns. I too was concerned.

I owed my life to Saul. He owed his to Dad. That may be the vagaries of battle - what goes around comes around - is what we believed.

Jacob Miller's untimely death sent change in motion. Dad and Ike finished the drive, paid everybody off, the crew scattered to the four winds. Ike and Dad returned to Buttonwood, never finished the Longsdorf cut. Ike became Louisa's lifelong foreman. The Poorbaughs built a permanent cabin on the back side of Potash. Bear Hollow remained pristine, a big patch of Big Woods, a haven for big cats.

Dad had eyes for Louisa. She was only twenty. Dad in his early thirties. But she was still in love with Jacob Miller and told Dad so. Miller's memory remained strong all her long life. An example is when she asked me to freshen his stone. And, place one for her alongside his. This was 1877, twenty-six years after Miller's passing. Twenty-six years! The lady pined like the widow she never really was.

"You are a talented man, Angus," Louisa said, adding "with a son to raise. It's irresponsible to expect your brother and sister-in-law to do that."

Jacob or Ike must have told her about me.

Dad heard this from her after he and Ike paid her for her share of King's Arrow that she had inherited from Miller. She then distributed ten percent back to Dad and offered to buy his share. He demurred saying one day that share would go to me. She said "whenever" and that's the way it's been for ninety plus years.

King's Arrow had purchased a timber deed from her father, which Louisa also inherited. That deed was never recorded. Nor was the debt for fifteen hundred that Miller couldn't repay because the trees remained and he was dead. So the trees of King's Arrow came under the farm. Louisa owned ninety percent of one and one hundred percent of the other. She controlled both. I never made an issue of it. What goes around comes around, right?

Dad quit drinking. Worked on the Boom, began his tinkering trade, saved some coin. After getting me he never visited the Lady, never told what he found in Knoxville. Deep down he might have harbored the notion to return someday and impress Louisa. This dream of Dad's never came true. He might have died too soon.

I came in Dad's stead.

On Reckoning Day Dad met with Fergus and Flo. Told them he'd paid off the mortgage, caught up the back taxes, gave cash to the headmaster for my tuition. Flo's visits were never mentioned. Mr. Glover, a director of the Academy, said they never saw a cent of McBoone money. The headmaster was fired for that and other chicanery. By then I was almost ten, going on fourteen. (I want to repeat that part).

"Augustus," said Dad, "you're coming with me."

We tinkered and travelled from 1854 to 1862. I grew tall, strong, capable. I learned from Angus, a natural teacher. I was a natural, too, with tinkering, timbering, teamstering - just about anything. Ours was an outdoor life but I never wanted for the basics - clothing, food, warmth, love. We hunted and fished, read and journaled. I graduated from McGuffey to Scott; lost myself in the novels of Cooper, Hawthorne, Dickens, Austin, Stowe and others. We'd buy the local papers, discuss the events of the day. Wellsborough's **Agitator,** was it always that yellow? Does "agitating" sell papers? Is that stuff all true? Are all papers that way? Why? Why are sides so polarized, so stubborn?

Is there going to be a war?

When the wagon grew heavy with journals and books cramped our sleeping, competed with our trade, we'd unload at the bank. Dad would visit Fergus while I stayed in town. He'd leave coin with Fergus and books and coin with Mr. Glover.

Money left with Mr. Glover was always a good investment. Money left with Fergus was not. When pressed about this silly allegiance to his older brother - what goes around comes around - is what Dad would usually say.

The one book that Dad would **not** leave was his Bible. He'd carried it since the Mexican War and read it daily. Had to translate it for me as it was a Douay Version, written in French. Only Stickwalker could read it at the time. Dad's Bible was a gift from a Mexican officer, actually a French mercenary who they executed for leading a firing squad at the Alamo. The mercenary would not be needing his Bible any more.

Saul volunteered for that squad. Dad could not. They all "remembered". But the officer was only carrying out Santa Anna's orders! Dad had a soft spot when it came to "frontier justice." He really did.

"Dad!" I said. "That sob lined up a bunch of Texican survivors against an adobe wall. Left no one standing. One was Davy Crockett!" I did not share Dad's attitude toward forgiveness. Still don't.

We'd discuss that Bible. The Douay was different from the Bible the circuit preachers carried. Dad had learned French from Stickwalker. His had more Jesus stories, more history, a mystical book called Tobit. Dad said, and I agree, that belief was in your heart. God didn't care what Bible you carried. Maybe you didn't carry one at all. Did you go to Hell if you couldn't read?

I buried that Bible with Dad. I've told you a bit of my feelings at the time. I'll go into more detail later.

## The Legend of Augustus McBoone

Our covered wagon was our home. We had one team all the years we tinkered together. Both were big draft horses. Our left-side horse was Moe, the right-side was Dan. Moe was brown. Dan was black. Both were stallions. Stallions could be trouble. Moe and Dan were not. You had to be strong and earn their respect. They respected Dad and learned to respect me. We never whipped them, never had to. The wagon was heavy, the grades sometimes very steep. We never had to get off and help. They could pull, Moe and Dan.

It sounds like we were vagabonds, but we weren't. Folks expected us, welcomed us, would feed us. They waited for us to shoe their horses, fix machinery, sharpen and file tools, weld cookpots, share the news. We followed the Pine Era log camps mostly. They always had lots of work, good cooks and cash on hand. While the camps paid better, there still were farmsteads along the road. Dad always took what came. "What goes around comes around," he'd say.

## Chapter 11

# PIG'S-EAR PADDY

In late July 1862 we pulled into a log camp west of Galeton. I was seventeen going on twenty-one. Dad was forty, going on forty. This was a large camp, on its way to becoming a town. It had a tavern, a mess hall with a bunkhouse above it, a general store, a smithy, a barber shop, company offices with telegraph, several two-story wood houses for the bosses and their families, a bigger two-story with wraparound porch for the working-girls, a church, a wide dirt Main Street with hitching posts, dug wells, outhouses, and barns with corrals in front and pasture out back. It did not yet have a school, post office, band, ball team, sawmill or bank but the wives were working on the school and post, the husbands on the band and ball team. Demand itself would supply the mill and bank if the camp survived. A wooden walkway was built along the fronts. This was paid for by the working-girls who didn't mind pulling their skirts up for money but objected loudly when they were forced to do so for mud.

The railroad hadn't gotten there yet either but scuttlebutt said it wouldn't be long. The same demand that created the telegraph and stage would soon bring the railroad.

We got there at twilight, just as the evening was getting noisier. Their workday and supper over, most of the men were streaming into the batwing doors of the tavern. All windows were open, to catch the evening breeze. Inside, someone played a piano, another an accordian.

A description of terms here: Workmen were "hicks", the tavern a "pig's ear", the camp boss was the "jobber," the barmaids and prostitutes were "working-girls".

A "steady" teamster cared for his horses first, resisted the temptations of a cold glass of cider, a pretzel, the news. Dad drove us back of Smitty's barn, unharnessed and cared for our team, parked our wagon, left a note for the hostler saying we would settle with him later.

We left the wagon outside. It had a canvas cover, contained our tools, clothes, books, journals, ammo, bedding and stuff. We relied on the "Hick's Code." No one bothered our stuff.

We weren't stupid though. These were dangerous times with rough men. Not so much in camp because of the families but the road was perilous.

It was easy to lose yourself in the Big Woods. We wore money belts, knives, pistols. Fastened a rifle and shotgun under the seat. A false bottom hid our valuables - a brace of pearl-handled pistols, bags of gold and silver coin.

We came through the back door. Eased our way up to the bar. We couldn't sneak in. We were a head taller than anyone else. Seagreaves was playing the piano. The accordion player had left. Men were standing around Seagreaves, drinks in their hands. Another group was huddled over a card game by a corner window. Two barmaids were delivering trays of drinks. They wore bright dresses, low in the front. One neared me. I saw a hick stuff a dollar bill down her front. That lady smiled. She had pretty teeth. I then heard another hick admonish the stuffer: "You be careful. She's Cookie's woman."

The Cook really ran a Pine Era log camp. No one wanted to get on the bad side of Cookie.

Seagreaves saw Dad and called for a song. Dad had a great baritone. Soon they were singing a jolly "Yellow Rose of Texas." I stood sipping a cold glass of sweet cider at the bar. The Irish barkeep, Paddy, stood opposite. "You know the story behind that song, Augustus?"

I nodded. The song, a favorite of Mexican War Veterans. Yellow Rose **was not** the name of a Texas flower. Rose was the name of a mulatto (yellow) working-girl who kept General Santa Anna busy before The Battle of San Jacinto. The Mexicans were unaware of Texicans creeping near - until it was too late. The Texicans won that battle and the war. Americans helped later.

Saul said Rose raised her price a dollar after that.

Paddy, the Irish barkeep, was more of a listener than a talker, a far-thinking man. Maybe ten years older than Dad, Paddy was a balding, brawny man. He wore a blue scalp bandana, tufts of red-gray hair grew around his ears, a gold ring dangled from one. That gold earring told us he had been a sailor (Seagreaves wore one too). It cried out for someone to pull it. The sap in his belt discouraged trying. His thick right bicep displayed the tattoo of a busty redhead, his left forearm said he "loved his mother." Cookie's woman came up with an empty tray. Paddy filled it with mugs of beer and a shot glass of rye. I noticed a similarity between the busty redhead and the barmaid. It wasn't the hair. She was blonde. The dollar bill was gone.

Paddy also kept loaded sawed-offs on each end of the bar. Dad and I had strapped them in. He preferred peace to violence, Paddy, but was always prepared. His pig's-ear was the site where frontier justice was adjudicated. Done on Sunday, after church, justice was dispensed quickly. The men more interested in drinking than judging.

Paddy and I talked: "We noticed a pile of squared hardwoods by the river. Short for pilings, Dad thought. Saw some poles too."

"Ties and telegraph poles," Paddy said. Armies of both sides are tearin' up tracks and tearin' down poles." He whispered as sympathies were mixed in log camps. "Lots of money cuttin' for the Army - the right one. Union is paying in specie. Confederates in scrip. Word is their scrip is scrap. Got nothin' to back it up."

"So, all this is going to the Union?"

"Yep. Already paid half. Other half on delivery. In coin."

He added. "The South can win every battle, can't win the war. Ain't got the money."

It took money to win a war. A new lesson for me. From a far-thinking man.

"Still shippin' spars?" I asked.

He nodded. "And buildin' and bridge timbers. Anything we got the Union is sucking up. Owner's gettin' rich."

He said this as if he wasn't. I knew better. Dad told me Paddy owned the bar. He was a silent partner in the camp. Always was. Paddy's allegiance followed money, not the cause.

Another lesson.

"Dad said a soldier spends more time with a shovel than a gun."

Paddy agreed. "But there's a poster at the store. The Union is recruitin' 'First Class Men,' Sharpshooters. Pays a decent bonus but..," he whispered again. "Only thirteen dollars a month."

"That's all?" Even a beginning hick, a "gopher", made thirteen dollars **a week** in camp.

Paddy nodded. "That poster is bait. Those that come back say thirteen dollars a month. Until they draft, no hicks will join. How old are you Gus?"

I said "Seven..." and never finished. A loud **Blang** came from the piano. All eyes turned there.

Dad and Seagreaves were surrounded by the group of card players. Their leader was Bill Sykes. He held his knife, edge up, was stalking Dad.

He was good with a blade, Sykes.

I slipped the thong off my Colt. Loosened my Bowie in its sheath.

Paddy ducked down, came up with his Express. That's two barrels, cut off. With double-aught buck, at close range, it would blow a man, even a thick man like Sykes, in two.

It got so quiet! Tick, tick went the wall clock. Clack, clack went the hammers on the shotgun.

Paddy couldn't miss. He broke the silence. "Unless you want to die now Bill, I'd back the hell away from there."

Bill straightened up. Looked around. Dad had drawn his pistol, so had I. Bill saw me. Saw Paddy with his sawed-off pointed at his belly. Seagreaves also stood, held a cocked sleeve gun, probably a 41. He outnumbered them eight to four but...they had guns, he had knives. He shook his head. Damn fool had brought a knife to a gunfight.

I already knew this lesson. Basic lumber camp lore.

While Sykes was surely damned, he was no fool. He backed away, sheathed his knife, sat at the card table, shuffled cards. He wanted all to see his hands. The rest followed. The last, a thick, defiant young man, kept looking at me.

Bill, Jr.

Thus began a long history between Junior and I.

Dad and Seagreaves came up to the bar. Business and the barmaids bustled as usual. Dad came shaking his head. He did not want to shoot Senior. Had enough of shooting men in the war, his war.

I still think Dad should have put a hole between Senior's eyes, right there.

"You can't reason with a pig, Angus," said Paddy, pouring a glass of cold cider. "You want a whiskey?"

Dad shook his head.

Paddy continued, "We know you didn't hang Elmer, Angus." Paddy emphasized the **we** and **you**.

Seagreaves said nothing. His sleeve gun remained in his hand, uncocked. It was a 41. Had two barrels.

Paddy kept talking, diffusing the situation, adding stuff we already knew. "Bill can fight. He's fast, like Jesse, and strong. He's not scared, he's canny. Likes a sure thing. Watch his card play! He'll kill from ambush, cause it's safer."

I listened. Dad and Seagreaves did not.

Dad was stuck on Elmer: "I didn't hang him. But I didn't stop it either."

Seagreaves shoved his derringer back up his sleeve. "Elmer was a smartass and a backstabber, Angus." he said.

What had Elmer called him, a "limey prick?"

Dad was adamant. "We caught him stealing a log, John. We hanged him over a log!"

First time I ever heard Dad call Seagreaves by his Christian first name of John.

"He deserved to die, Angus." This was Seagraves response, stubbornly justifying "frontier justice." I saw the hate Dad and Ike dealt with in English Center.

Dad remained adamant. "Not for a log! I didn't like Elmer either. But I can't abide what we did because of one log."

"Well, it's over now," said Seagreaves.

"I don't think it's over," said Paddy, a far-thinking man.

Dad and I downed our ciders, walked to the pasture, grabbed our wagon by the tongue and pulled it into the barn. We barricaded its doors, slept inside our wagon inside that barn. Took turns riding shotgun, we did.

## The Legend of Augustus McBoone

It was a fitful night for Dad and me.

A busy night for the Sykes' crew.

The last night for Seagreaves.

## Chapter 12

# JOHN SEAGREAVES, 1817-1862

This is how Seagreaves died:

He and two friends were weaving their way to the working-girls house when the Syke's crew materialized out of the shadows. The two with Seagreaves were shoved aside and held. They saw it all, told Dad and me later.

It was over soon. A knife fight it was, except Seagreaves never had a chance to pull his. Bill Senior, reputed as fast as Jesse Poorbaugh and maybe stronger, held Seagreaves' wrists while three of his crew stabbed him. The remaining four stood guard over the two friends.

Senior rationalized since Elmer never had a chance, why should Seagreaves? Or any member of the Miller-McBoone crew for that matter? Or their families? Still, Senior preferred a sure thing. Probably why he didn't try to save his brother.

Seagreaves, gasping, dying, told his killers he wasn't sorry for hanging Elmer. He was a thieving backstabber which is what the lot of you are now. You can expect to be crow bait when you die! That's how Bill here treated his own brother. We left, he cut Elmer down, dumped him in the creek. A crew of hicks pulled him out in Williamsport. Miller and McBoone paid for his burial. He wasn't worth much, Elmer.

Then Seagreaves died. They robbed him, those scoundrels.

Seagreaves always kept enough on him to pay for his own burial with some left over for a working-girl. They cut his weapon and money belt off his body, sliced the lobe containing his ear ring. They left a bloody pile of rents and tears. Disappeared into the shadows. His friends hallowed some passersby, they shoveled him into a wagon, rolled him in canvas and buried him by lamplight in the woods.

One of the gravediggers sold Dad his boots. We stuffed them in his sailor's bag. He had a "toothpick" but that and its sheath were gone. Had the gravedigger kept that? We decided not to ask. Seagreaves left no kith or kin. Dad recalled being told he was five years older and his Christian name was John. So Dad painted **John Seagreaves**, **1817-1862** on his cross. His was a shallow grave, above frostline. All they had was lamplight under the trees.

The hicks would miss his playing, Paddy his trade, the working-girls his tricks, the jobber his skill with the adze.

I remember thinking: Is this all there is?

There was no law. The Sykes crew were too valuable to the jobber, too dangerous to confront. By the time the hicks headed to the Big Woods, Seagreaves had been replaced as a hewer, his four dollars a day promised the new man.

Sailor Seagreaves told Dad he wanted to be buried at sea. In his case, a sea of trees. Dad could have his stuff. He wouldn't be needing it anyway. "Just see me buried, Angus." So, we buried him better, piling rocks from the stream atop his grave.

*"You found him, didn't you Grandpa? When you went looking for your dad?"*

*"I found the rocks, Hayley. They were buried too shallow, no coffins. I found the rusted grommets from the tarps. I couldn't find Dad's Bible or his wedding band. The crosses had rotted away. I carved two stones. Placed them at their heads. They're surrounded by other graves now. It's a nice spot for a graveyard. Shady. Townsfolk left a couple of pine trees."*

## The Legend of Augustus McBoone

The sea was known by the cold-country Europeans as the Black Forest. They were immigrants. For those born there it was the Big Woods. Didn't matter the name, we all thought it would never end.

But a sea of water is more constant than a sea of trees. The sea of water just keeps filling its hole. Not so the sea of trees. Every day we'd fall a "patch." The patch was normally one hundred acres of a "warrant" comprising a thousand. The jobber was given one hundred of these warrants by the owner. Before the Civil War we took all the pine and some of the hardwoods. After the War, we took all the hemlock and the rest of the hardwoods. Two more wars later there was no expanse left to cut. Only patches remained.

The patches were surrounded by "slashings." Piles of branches and briars and berries. Became a haven for snakes, bugs and bears. Fires too burned the slashings. Thousands of acres burned.

During the heyday of the Pine Era, the jobber would negotiate a timber purchase with a mill. He'd hire his crew, build his camp, deliver the timber, distribute the proceeds. He would pay his bills by the day, his crew by the week, his investors by the month, his owner by the quarter. His contract required strict accounting. Any net profit would be paid by the year. The jobber took a draw every week, prayed in church for a profit that year. He could end up a millionaire or a pauper, the jobber.

My son Esau experienced both.

The secret was being a far-thinking man, like Paddy. Don't get greedy! Don't stay too long! Cash can build up like a pile of logs. Can burn up too. The building is slow. The burn - up is fast. Don't stay too long!

If Fergus' squirrel lived as long as Stickwalker, he would see change in Penn's Woods. In 1670 he could have traveled anywhere - and never touched the ground. A century later towns in southeast Pennsylvania needed barn and bridge timbers, shipbuilders were hollering for spars and framing lumber. It still had to be rafted to them. By then Mr. Squirrel had emigrated to Harrisburg.

Wars create new hungers. The Revolution was no different. The Penns, by then more English than American, more Anglican than Quaker, were sent packing. This was a "glorious thing" according to Fergus. The Pennsylvania General Assembly took over this land. The new breed of independents did not feel sorry for the Penns. The "poor lads" had scampered back to safe havens in England and Ireland. Think of George Washington on a thousand pensions. Whenever a pesky title problem arose, the Penns were sent a little money. Their property was worth a lot more but, like their ancestor William, they didn't have much choice. They had to take it.

By 1790 Mr. Squirrel could start his trek north of Harrisburg and never touch the ground. To encourage development the General Assembly decided to sell "their" land. A bunch of Revolutionary War soldiers who were paid in property decided to sell too. In his last legislative act, Benjamin Franklin sponsored a bill to sell warrants at auction, to start the bidding at ten cents per acre. In the City of Brotherly Love, speculators like Bingham, Keating, Strawbridge, even the Trustees of the Episcopal Society bought and resold their warrants. The trustees were Tories who stayed. They took their medicine, changed from Anglican to Episcopalian, hoarded their coin, became loyal Pennsylvanians, I mean, Americans.

*Coin has a way of changing enemies into friends doesn't it?*

"Grandpa! You're being sarcastic...again."

"Almost done, Hayley. Almost..."

Prices went up. By 1800 the going rate per acre was one dollar. By 1825 it was two. By 1850 it was four. By 1875 it was eight. By 1900 it was sixteen. Until the end of World War One the price for land and timber doubled every twenty-five years. However, with the timber gone, the owners did not pay their taxes, the land reverted, the state auctioned it off again.

*"A later account says you bought the southeast warrant for three dollars per acre."*

*"It was pretty ravaged, Hayley".*

*"What about this year's? The southwest warrant?"*

*The State accepted twenty-five. Squire's transferred both deeds. It's got timber. Michael, your Dad and I have been all over it."*

*"Twenty-five thousand dollars!" She shook her head, thinking of what she could do with that much money. She sighed and said, "Whatever."*

*Females have a hard time with land and timber. They really do. They have to be convinced.*

*Back to Mr. Squirrel:*

By 1860 he would have to start his trek at Lock Haven to never touch the ground. If he looked north he would see the Black Forest. If he looked south and east he could see the Boom, cities, towns and railroads. And war. **WAR** was chasing him.

Another word back then was **PROGRESS**. It started with one hundred acre patches. Progress and war was chasing him.

In 1862, when he had gotten as far as our lumber camp, he could see below a fresh dug grave. In the early morning, the mist rising, he could hear pigs rooting in the dirt. He would hear a shot, see one fall, the rest run squealing away. He'd see Dad and I coming with a wagonload of rocks, see the rifle barrel smoking in my hand. He'd sit very still, and watch. He'd watch us pile the rocks, see me plant a cross, hear Dad recite the 23rd. He'd see us gut that pig, load the carcass in the wagon, take it to camp for butchering.

If he was a smart squirrel, he'd trek deep into that expanse and hide. We knew how to bark a squirrel. If he stayed close to camp he could end up in a pot of stew.

## Chapter 13

# BUNKHOUSES, OUTHOUSES AND HICKS

At sunrise Dad and I drove back to camp, hung the pig, washed in the creek, stabled our horses, packed Seagreave's duffle, washed again, breakfasted with the men.

We clambered up the outside steps to the empty bunkhouse, found Seagreaves sailor's bag, stuffed his boots, looked around. Five of the beds were filthy, five were made, the other fifteen in various stages of in-between.

Seagreaves had been one of the in-betweens. Likewise, his partner had helped bury him, might have gotten in too late to change and up too late to make the bed. He'd have a new "sidekick" in a night or two. No choice either.

The windows were open. Flies were streaming in with the morning breeze. The metal pails were full of piss and puke. Flies had found them, many struggling in the sticky ribbons hung over each pail. "Gopher" was still at breakfast. Hadn't bothered to dump their smelly contents in the outhouse, yet. He'd have to hurry today. He'd be on Seagreave's wagon, on its way to their patch. The jobber would have to hire another gopher by nightfall.

Gopher would be promoted to "bucker" today.

After that experience I swore to God I'd **never** sleep in a bunkhouse again. Oh, the swearing of youth! I don't think God heeded my prayer. He had other things in mind for Yours Truly. I have had enough dormitory life to know I don't want any more. Academy, log camp, army, jail - no more for me.

*"Wait a minute, Grandpa! You were in jail? I never read anything about that!"*

*"Happened in Johnstown after Mandi died." I regretted mentioning jail. I wasn't proud of that. I diaried about it then hid it.*

*Back to the bunkhouse:*

I prefer my own bed and bedmate now. For most of my life that mate has been a wife. Today, at almost one-hundred-one, I'd settle for a bedwarmer, like Mary Spencer.

"Grandpa! You stop!"

"I'm workin' at that, Hayley."

*I noticed Brenda was listening but keeping her head down. She suspected I confided in Ralph, resented that I had not shared with her. You gotta earn that trust, girl:*

I've observed while sleeping with bunches of men that ten percent are neatniks, ten percent are slobs, the remainder depend on the circumstances. If close to home and inspection they were neat. If more than a half day's ride they weren't. Still, none of us bothered to bathe or shave until after payday, Saturday evening. What was the point? If the hick cleaned up and applied "smellum-good" on Saturday and stuck around - it was for a working-girl, not the wife.

Sunday was for the wife.

I always had trouble with a hick cleaning up on Saturday then paying two dollars for Molly. And get in line. That gal was used to smelly men. Charged the same, too.

I never left money with Mandi. Never denied her either. Once a week we would picnic in the woods. I'd be sweaty. She'd bring a towel. After our picnic and honey we'd both need the towel.

"Grandpa! I can't put that in my report!"

*"I know Hayley. Someday. Maybe someday."*

*"Stay on subject, Grandpa. You're rambling."*

*"Okay. Okay. But they are great memories. True too."*

A hick bunkhouse needed burnt down after fifty years. Too buggy. That's why Dad and I slept in barns. We'd gotten caught in a storm a couple of years before, were forced to sleep with the men. It was a cold September and all the bugs were coming in. We needed hot baths and our heads shaved after that. The first and last time I ever saw Dad bald and no handlebar. We burnt our clothes including our shoes. Made the storekeeper happy, as I recall.

About all that could be salvaged from a bunkhouse were the metal parts - the stove and piping, the metal frames of the double beds. Still it was best to dunk them in a river then repaint them.

I once fished a four-holer out of a stream after a flash flood. A white oak plank it was, polished, with its underside branded 1824. Been sat on for thirty-five years. No amount of sandpaper could smooth around those holes better than butt action. I sold that plank to a jobber for ten dollars. Never got so much for a five foot length of oak. On impulse I looked at Hayley.

*"Know why those holes were the same size?"*

*She frowned. This perplexed her, I could tell. It was common for a family to have small to big holes. Finally she gave up. "No."*

*"Ever hear of Communism?"*

*"Yeah...But what's politics got to do with the shitter?"*

*"Hayley!" This came from her mom who was too near.*

*I smiled. "Communal use. We had to share. If you weren't big enough to sit with the boys you weren't big enough to work in the woods."*

*"Really?"*

*Hayley sometimes had difficulty believing my tales (If, as Hal said, they weren't too tall). This time she humored me: "Like knights wearing armor, Grandpa?"*

*"We didn't have squires, Hayley, but there were roles... starting with the gopher. He had to be big enough to sit in the outhouse before going out with a crew. A male grew from a boy to a man real fast in the woods, Hayley."*

*"Oh," she said, coloring. I loved to make her blush! She was seeing the male side and not the communal image of four hicks sitting doing their business at the same time. Time to bail her out. Before her mom bawled her out.*

*These tales are not tall, I swear:*

## The Legend of Augustus McBoone

One time I sat alone. Three dark holes yawned open beside me. The hicks had all gone to the woods and Dad was busy with the smith. I snuck off to answer a call. Sitting there, I was tall and done and bored. Didn't want to go back to shoeing nasty horses right away. I kicked my heel in the packed dirt and unearthed some coins. Four big cents, two nickels and a quarter had fallen from some unsteady hick's britches. I cleaned the dirt off. All were dated in the 1840s. Finders, keepers, right? I bought some shells with the money.

Beds were communal too. Like I said, hicks slept two to a bed and did not get to choose their partner. Provided his own blanket, rolled another if he wanted a pillow. If a hick was an "unsteady" like the one who lost his coins and came to bed late, he'd roll his pard over to make room. He slept in his clothes. If he wasn't too drunk he might remember to take off his shoes.

His "shitkickers" were usually caked with woods junk - mud, needles, leaves, clumps of dung. Every fifth bunk had a tin bucket beside it - for nighttime urges and such.

Gopher's job was to empty those buckets every morning.

There was music to a filled bunkhouse late at night. Fifty men laid there - snoring, farting, belching, scratching, talking in their sleep. Oh Molly! Sweet

Molly, they'd say. They pissed and puked in the same bucket they spat in. Woe to the unsteady who came in late and "kicked the bucket." The clatter and slosh would waken the nearby hicks and the "kicker" would be called names he didn't know he had: Stupid, Polack, Greenhorn, Turd, Asshole...

"*Grandpa!*"

*See? Told ya I couldn't swear:*

Blankets usually smelled like the horse it came from.

It was a noisome, pungent place, the bunkhouse.

But it always had a good roof. Like the camp cook, a good roof was required.

For "steadies" their underwear served as pajamas - short johns for the summer, long in the winter. Faded red they were with buttoned dropdown in the back. Clothes worn that day were hung over the bottom bed frame. A duffel was shoved under the bed. There was the hick's Sunday best.

When the market was good there was no time for washing clothes. Hicks, steadies and unsteadies both, went to the company store, changed and charged, emerged all bright and shiny. The dirty outfit went in the fire. Hopefully the hick had cleaned up (some) before entering the store.

On Sunday, if the hick was a "fearing" man (as in God, wife or Molly), he'd go to Service. Usually, two services - church and nooner.

"What's a nooner?" asked Hayley.

Brenda knew, "That's when we lock the bedroom door, Dear."

"Oh".

*I'm glad she and Ralph were back to that!*

I continued. Also glad Hayley didn't know what a nooner was. Until now:

First the hick had to take a sit bath in the creek. What a sight! From spring breakup to winter ice-over, on Sunday morning there'd be a row of shivering hicks, in their pink johns if they were steadies, in the pink if they weren't, bathing in the creek. The young men splashing, the older ones watching. Kind of an old bull-young bull thing.

"What's that?" asked Hayley.

I grinned.

"Augustus..." Brenda also knew the bull story.

"Okay," she relented, "you tell her. But no salty language!"

*Hayley still looked confused. She knows I'm being naughty.*

*The story goes like this: The young bull says lets run down and breed one of them cows. The old bull says lets walk down and breed them all.*

*"Oh" said Hayley again coloring, thinking.*

*I loved it when she did that! Blush, I mean.*

*I wasn't sure about the thinking part. Then she hit us with it.*

*"Why is it you have to have a pecker to be boss?"*

*Hayley!*

*Now who's being naughty?*

*Brenda looks at me accusingly. You started this.*

*I scratched my head. This was turning into a birds and bees discussion:*

*Nooners, bulls, women's rights...Back to the creek. It's safer. I pulled a Fergus and did not answer her question:*

*After the bath the hick would dry off, put on some clean pants, go to the kitchen for a pan of hot water, bring that and a bar of soap to the mirror on a porch post, pull out his toothpick and shave.*

"A toothpick was a boot knife, right?" asked Hayley.

"Yep. And the best sharpener was Dad." I showed her my hand. "When that knife could shave hair off the back of his hand it was ready." Then the hick would take bootblack, shine his "go-to-meetin'" shoes, cover any spots in his broadcloth, pat down his cowlick...

Hayley interrupted. "With bootblack? What if he had light hair?"

"There would be a smear."

"Eww!"

I loved it when she did that. I continued:

"Then he'd don a white shirt, add a string tie, whistle on his way to get Molly, sweet demure Molly!"

"Mom! Grandpa's eyes are twinkling. He's being naughty again!"

"Augustus..You stop!"

I grinned at Hayley. She grinned back. Wicked girl! (I'll forgive her tattling):

At first service he'd sing lustily, with Molly lookin' he'd drop a shiny silver dollar in the collection. Cling! That proved he had money to spend. At second service he'd pay Molly two and add a dollar if they got ardent and she gave him a hickey.

He would show his buddies his hickey.

I looked at Hayley. Expecting another question. This time I was disappointed.

*"I know what a hickey is, Grandpa. Norma brought one home the other day."*

*"She did?" asked Brenda.*

*"Make-up covers 'em, Mom."*

*"Oh", said Brenda. This time she blushed, which reminded me of the older Mandi.*

*Time to bail out Norma. I went on:*

If he woke up late and without four dollars the hick would forgo the Sunday church routine, stand up Molly and head for the mess hall for coffee and stew. No hickey meant no money. He'd be unsteady until after a gallon of coffee and a couple of bowls of stew. Then it was porch and pipe...in his work clothes. If he was still unsteady he would peek at the post mirror to see if he had lost a fight and if any damage was done. He should have eleven dollars left after paying seven for his loan yesterday. But his pants pocket only held one dollar. The mirror said "No fight" but his pocket said "No money," so what happened? His bloodshot eyes and achy head told him he had spent five dollars on booze which meant the

## The Legend of Augustus McBoone

rest he lost at Chuck-a-luck. He talked to himself: Rube, you can't get drunk and then play Chuck-a-luck! He resolved to mend his ways – play **before** he got drunk - next time. For Rube, it was always "next time."

Then he'd go back into the mess for more coffee and stew. He should grab some soap, head for the "crick" and "warsh" himself and his clothes. He didn't.

*"Eww!" squealed Hayley. "What happened to Molly? She'd be all dressed for church..."*

*"Another hick would take her. She never missed first or second service, Molly."*

*"Grandpa!"*

*"Augustus!"*

*I couldn't help it, added "Sweet, demure Molly." Then went on with my story:*

On Sunday, Cookie kept a cauldron of stew bubbling. Some sliced bread and a jar of jam near. Don't look too close at the meat nestled there amongst the beans, taters and carrots. Cookie grabbed what was hanging in his smokehouse, sliced and diced it, threw it in. The hick didn't care. With salt and pepper it was always good. (He served snake in August). The hick would down it all, wipe his bowl clean with the "jam-bread," stack the bowl. Gopher would wash the bowl. Or not. Had to hold oatmeal on Monday.

With that dollar burning a hole the hick'd head for the pig's-ear for more carousing...you could always charge at the pig's-ear. Maybe he could turn that one into five at Chuck-a-luck. If not he'd borrow five from the Tinkerman. He couldn't run a chit at Chuck-a-luck or at the working-girls. They didn't have hearts, those people.

"*Oh, poor hick!*" *exclaimed Hayley, looking all pouty.*

*She didn't have a heart either, Hayley:*

You know, the only sickness I can recall is typhoid which could wipe out the entire camp - unless one or two were immune. Not like during the war. Or any wars. There were hangovers and injuries aplenty. But darn little sickness. You got up, went to work, steady or unsteady. The air was clear and clean in the woods.

Once a hick broke a sweat, he felt better.

Some of those hicks lived a long time. Most of the long-livers were reformed unsteadies. They smoked their pipes, drank their hooch, raised their families(with Molly) and broke a sweat. Six days a week they broke a sweat. One back and forth with the saw, all it took.

## The Legend of Augustus McBoone

*"You were a hick, weren't you Grandpa?"*

*I nodded.*

We were a tough lot, us hicks.

## Chapter 14

# PAYDAY LOANS AND SUCH

Just because a hick **made** money does not mean he **had** money. Big difference. After Sunday there was a whispered trade between those that **needed** money and those that **saved** it. A loan until payday cost the borrower fifty cents per day. The hick borrowing five on Wednesday paid seven on Saturday. The charge began the evening he borrowed the money.

I never heard of any quibbling. The borrower did not want to dry up his money pot. Like gossip, word travelled faster than an echo in a timber camp. Those that borrowed were usually paying for the bad habits of the day - booze, gambling, working-girls...

*"Those habits are still bad, Grandpa." This was Hayley. She and her mom were in the next room. Supposedly working. This meant what they heard was more interesting than the bills they were paying.*

I kept on:

## The Legend of Augustus McBoone

A "steady" kept an account book in his shirt pocket. When that pocket was unbuttoned, he had money to lend. After supper, the steadies settled on the porch, smoked their pipes, drank coffee, wrote letters home, unbuttoned their shirt pockets. Unsteadies came and went. At sunset the steady hit the outhouse and then his bed.

The unsteadies weaved in hours later, some forgetting to hit the outhouse, others forgetting to remove their clothes. Drunk or sober it didn't matter, you had the same wake-up call. Monday through Saturday, at five, Sunday at seven. Except for Cookie. He got up every day at four.

Dad was a steady. Actually a reformed unsteady. In my experience, the reformed person has more credibility. For example: The boozehound adulterer who's put two wives in early graves, comes home and pours a bottle of whiskey in the outhouse. He then takes care of his third wife and family, saves some coin, puts a dollar in the collection every Sunday. Only visits the pig's-ear and working-girls once a month, on Saturday. That "reformed" sob has more credibility than the teatotalling family man who never strayed.

"You've had three wives, Grandpa. You've strayed."

"Not while I was married, Hayley."

"They wouldn't let you."

"I'm not married now."

"Now, **we** won't let you."

Back to Dad, he's safer:

Dad only exhibited one "vice", a vice I share - we smoked a pipe! We didn't know it was a vice. In fact, Dad never did. Back then pipe smoking was part of the culture, especially the work culture - it kept skeeters away.

Smoking became a vice during the Temperance Days. Those ladies lumped any of man's pleasures under the mantle of vices. I'm glad none of my ladies ever joined a crusade; we would never have had any babies!

"Babies are God's gift, Grandpa."

"It was the making of the baby, Hayley."

"How could they make a baby and **not** enjoy the process?"

"By claiming they had to do it. Claimed they were forced!" Meanwhile, I'm thinking, what does Hayley know about the process? I knew her mom was listening. So did she. Was she sending a message? She was smart that way, Hayley.

"Did you smoke cigarettes, Grandpa?"

"Just a pipe."

"Mom smokes. My teacher smokes. Dad said cigarettes were part of their rations in the Army. But Norma got expelled for three days when she was a senior. And I'm not allowed. How come?"

I'm thinking, Hayley is switching here. From baby-making, a pleasure she **may** know about, to smoking which she **wanted** to know about. These modern women! Had Norma, now working at the milk plant, who had a steady who gave her a hickey and who smokes occasionally, had she told?

"Cigarette smoking came about because of fashion and flappers, Hayley."

She looked at me quizzically. I continued:

"Flappers made it fashionable for ladies to be seen with a cigarette. Now it seems all adults have one hanging from their lips." I emphasized the word "adults." "Before the 1920s it was men who smoked cigarettes. Before the war, it was pipes."

"Your war, Grandpa?"

"Mine, Hayley. I started smoking a pipe with Dad. I've tried cigarettes. Find them blah, bland."

"Norma thinks they're bland, too Grandpa."

*So, the older sister had told. Brenda and Ralph might want to keep an eye. Their youngest was curious about sex and smoking.*

*Keep out of this, Gus! It's natural, she's normal, thank God! Oh, Hayley is saucy, over-confident, forthright - too much at times. She's only seventeen. She'll have to make her own way.*

*I went back to reading. Aloud. Back to Dad and loans and such:*

Raising me kept Dad away from the ladies. He politely refused all offers, even free ones. He never got over Mary. Just like Mandi and me. Also, Dad never got over being **turned down** by Louisa. Only twenty, she correctly sensed she would be a replacement. Just like Sandra and Betts with me. Unlike them, Louisa had a choice. I thought she made a bad one, loving a dead man, but she was strong- willed and loyal.

Dad was loyal too. Stayed loyal to Mom and Fergus and Ike and Seagreaves and me. A great example. A great dad.

After he quit drinking, Dad became a steady. He made money. He loaned money. Taught me simple rules: Pay your bills, spend less than you make, keep a portion of savings working, always. He invested in King's Arrow and two other timber projects. One went bust. But that jobber, Walter

## The Legend of Augustus McBoone

Wright, became my Colonel, survived Gettysburg, and sent me twenty dollars a month until he paid Dad off. I told him he didn't have to do that, but he felt bad and did. I never got a return out of King's Arrow and may not. Don't care. Louisa never cut any more timber so no percentage is due.

Dad always said - what goes around comes around. That is proving so true.

## Chapter 15

# BREAKFAST AT COOKIE'S

We were the last for breakfast. The mess consisted of two long tables with chairs for sixty men. There were forty-nine hicks so there was room for two more.

Actually, no matter the size of camp, there was **always** room for a couple more. We sat at the end nearest the open door; Dad on the right, me at the end. We didn't want our long-armed left-handedness to get in anyone's way.

The concept of "boarding-house reach" came from the log camps, I think.

The mess was hazy this morning. More pipe smoking. Contemplating the death of a hick did that. The smell of stale sweat and fresh bread mixed with the "backy" smoke. We contributed to the gaminess of that smell. While we rinsed off in the creek, washed with soap in the camp basin, there was still the smell of pig offal about us. It would wear off. Hunters brought that scent into camp all the time.

I heaped my plates with food. A fly fell from the paper above my shoulder. Landed in my oatmeal. I covered it with brown sugar. Pretended it was a raisin.

"Eww, Grandpa!"

"You like raisins, don't you Hayley?"

"I don't like flies."

"These were big. Horse flies."

"Augustus"...warned Brenda. "You stop!"

Yep, they're listening. I read on:

Seagreaves killing had cast it's pall - over mood, not appetites. These men had a strenuous twelve-hour day ahead. They required fuel... I thought of the Biblical David, breaking his fast after the death of his first son by Bathsheba. Like him, we had to look forward to our day, not mope about the night before.

Bill Senior sat with his crew at the opposite end of the table. The hicks in between were quiet, leery of what happened to Seagreaves happening to them. Like the war, there were mixed feelings. Half felt Elmer got what he deserved, too bad about

Seagreaves. The other half felt frontier justice too harsh for the theft of a log, Seagreaves got what he deserved. I disagreed with the second half. Thought frontier justice was required again. There should be eight men hanging from the naked chestnut at the east of the camp.

At the Sykes end of the table all were subdued except one - Junior. It was his first knifing. He exulted, told all his part in it. He had been a guard. Held back a man grown, he did!

When Dad and I came in Senior growled at Junior to shut up.

He did.

But those eight still blamed King's Arrow including McFee, including Dad. That enmity spilled over to include our families. This meant Ike when he had children and me and mine when I had them. They were pigheaded feudists, the Sykes crew. You couldn't reason with them.

The hicks were rugged men of varied heights and ages. I was the tallest and the youngest. Only Senior and Junior carried extra pounds, very little fat. It was the middle of the week so none of the men were shaved. Mustaches, especially handlebars ruled. The best handlebar was Dad's. Mine was growing, still wispy and thin. We were all dressed in yesterday's stained work clothes with longsleeved underwear shirts and denim jeans. Some were belted, some wore suspenders, some wore both. I was belted, Dad wore both. The more prosperous older men wore bibs. We all wore high leather boots with hobnailed soles. Today especially Bowies were evident, toothpick and switchblades unseen. Caps of all kinds hung from our chairs. Dad and I wore 1848 campaign hats. Slouches and derbies were the most popular.

The hicks were dressed for protection and the woods. Long sleeves protected skin from whipping branches and bloodsucking bugs. High-top shoes blunted striking snakes, hobnails squashed them. Hobnails were also great for steep sides and kicking out. The kicking was aggressive. A stomper was always a threat. The hick's faces wore scars to prove it. A small man with big feet could do more damage than a big man with small feet. Dad and I were blessed with both. Senior and Junior had average size feet. Cookie was the exception - a big man with small feet.

Regardless of his inability to stomp, no one messed with Cookie. He was good with a blade and deceptively fast. He also had at least fifty allies. Any hick stupid enough to fight Cookie risked being carried out on a board.

Our necks and hands were bronzed from long hours in the sun. There were no black or yellow men in Pennsylvania's Pine Era. The "inferior" races came later, after the war. (War mixes races during the conflict, sets them adrift after it).

I have mixed-race grandchildren. Haven't seen an inferior one yet!

*"How many we got, Grandpa?"*

*"Not sure exactly. From Michael and Ophelia to Sally and Logan. We're spread far and wide Hayley."* Hayley's *"we"* indicated she was inclusive. Brenda knew; she sent the Christmas cards and money. The fact that she was generous to all indicated while she knew she never complained. There were racist sob's out there but none in my clan McBoone:

The hicks were skilled as well. It was no accident they scoffed at thirteen dollars a month. Back when a dollar a day was a decent wage for a laborer, a Pine Era timberman made a lot more… and earned it. On a normal crew the **axe man** and his **hewer** were paid four dollars, the **two sawyers** were paid three and the **bucker** was paid two. The sixth member of the crew was a "special." The **teamster**, who provided horses and tack but no food, was paid five. It cost twenty-one dollars a day, minimum, to pay one Pine Era work crew.

There were seven crews working at this log camp, six normal and one abnormal. That one abnormal crew required "frontier justice," which didn't happen.

### The Legend of Augustus McBoone

Then came the hierarchy. These men usually had money invested in the operation. I've told the role of the **owner**. The **jobber** was the superintendent. The **woods boss** served as foreman. **The paymaster** kept the books and paid the men and bills. The last three took draws which usually cost another twenty-one dollars a day.

**Cookie** was in a class by himself. He was the highest paid…and worked the longest hours to earn his coin. Three "squares" a day for six days were his responsibility. These squares were a hot breakfast and supper, a cold lunch. The hot meals were eaten at camp. The cold lunch was delivered to the patch. Cookie ordered the food, butchered it, prepared it. He was the quintessential baker and candlestick maker. No camp survived without a cook.

Other specialists were the **storekeep**, the **bar-owner**, the **smith**, the **barber** and the **working-girls**. Some, not all, had skin in the game. These folks charged by the item or the job.

*"How much could a working-girl make, Grandpa? Was it hard?" Hayley's eyes were twinkling. Wicked girl!*

*I answered. "A buxom working-girl could make paymaster's wages six days a week and half again on Sunday. A skinny-minnie just starting, could do better than a gopher."*

"Augustus, Hayley…you both stop!" This came from buxom Brenda who did her best to stifle saucy talk after she had been the subject of it.

"Just trying to figure out a girl's worth, Mom," said Hayley.

I'm thinking that Brenda is trying, in her way, to be a decent mom. She (might) suspect that a few people know about her affair, does not know that all do. She and Ralph are back together. That's all that matters, now. Time to bail Brenda out. "It was hard bein' a working-girl," I said. "They earned their coin. Every dollar of it. Most hicks got their wives from that house, ya know."

"Really?" asked Hayley.

I nodded. Went back to my reading. It was safer:

Jobbers also hired **teams**. The Sykes crew was one, Dad and I another. We were specialists of a sort. Sykes and Company were hired for volume, Dad and I for being fixers.

Bill Senior was reputed the best axe-man in the Big Woods. A natural with a blade, he once won a hundred-dollar bet by dropping a pine tree on a nail keg. He then bucked and hewed it into a one-hundred-foot spar in less than an hour. Dad could too, just never showed off that skill. Dad wouldn't have to beat his horse to skid that spar.

## The Legend of Augustus McBoone

Bill did. They were "bulls of the woods," each having a son to raise.

While Bill's seven relatives weren't as strong or as fast or as canny as he they weren't slackers either. The jobber paid Bill thirty dollars a day, six days a week. What Bill paid his men was his business. He allowed no alcohol while working, made up for this hardass discipline after hours and on Sunday. They had four locales and the eight kept together: their patch, the pig's ear, the working-girls home and the bunkhouse.

"You mean they all showed up together? All eight?"

"Like I said, Hayley, those girls earned their coin."

"Oh", she said, adding "I guess it's better to have one than eight waiting in line."

*I didn't say anything. Her mom said, "Yes, Dear."*

*I went on with my reading:*

Apparently one-eighty a week wasn't enough because in August 1862 Senior became a head outlaw and his crew a gang. They were a murderous, racist, rapist bunch of sob's, the Sykes Gang. Guns, knives and masks became their tools in trade. A hunter could make a good living off their bounties. But he'd have to be **really** careful, really good and really smart. Take them one at a time, like in the outhouse. Even then he had to be sure there wasn't someone else in there. And, what was the point of bringing one in alive? Bounty paid the same. Poster said Dead or Alive.

I never hunted men for a living. Critters, yes. Men, no. Men were too much trouble.

*"But you've killed men, Grandpa!"*

*"Yes, I have. To live, not to make a living. Big difference."*

I went on:

Dad and I were a team. We got seven dollars each for tinkering. Dad got another five if teamstering needed done. On the camp circuit we could gross one hundred per week easy and still go to church on Sunday, be at the next camp for breakfast bright and early Monday morning. Dad taught me to never wear out our welcome, to finish our work and not argue. That way the camp we were leaving looked forward to our return. Dad cultivated relationships with every cook, barkeep and boss in the Big Woods. Dad said the cook was the peak of every wood's hierarchy. He always had work: We'd weld pots and pans, sweep stovepipes, sharpen blades, listen to his stories. The cook always told good stories.

*A cook was more attractive than buxom Gladys, worth more than her weight in gold.*

*"Gladys, Grandpa?"*

*"I meant Molly, sorry."* Still listening those two. *(I never knew a working-girl named Gladys):*

Competition was fierce. There weren't enough cooks to go around. Few cared like Cookie. It was hard work preparing those squares. Mess hall meals were served family style. Lunches were delivered to the woods. Lunch was called "dinner." Breakfast was hot with eggs, bacon, ham, sausage, scrapple, pancakes with syrup or jam, toast with butter, jam or both, oatmeal with brown sugar all downed with gallons of milk, sweet cider or coffee. Evening supper was more of the same plus meat and 'taters. You never knew what kind of meat and never asked. Whether domestic - cow, sheep, pig or goat; or fowl - chicken, turkey, duck or geese; or wild - deer, bear, squab, snake or squirrel. It all depended on the season and what Cookie could prepare to scale. Spring brought ham and leeks, summer snake and cabbage, fall squirrel and 'taters, winter something's liver and onions.

*"Something, Grandpa?"*

*I nodded.*

*"Eww!"*

*I loved hearing that:*

A smart jobber made sure Cookie had facilities and stock. Besides a mess hall with a large kitchen, he had a stocked larder. Here were fifty-pound sacks of flour, sugar, salt and coffee along with shelves stocked with jarred and canned goods. He had a barn with slaughterhouse attached and separate smoke, ice and out houses. He had a two-story home, two dug wells, a cold spring and clear run gurgled near. You never did anything to roil that spring! That really roiled Cookie! When you worked for Cookie (as I did) you kept his outhouse limed, his smokehouse hickoried, his icehouse sawdusted. Fish kept the water clean, dogs chased critters away, cats ate the vermin, pigs ate everything else, flypaper caught the bugs.

Like I said, this was a good camp. But it was Cookie who cared, who kept the men there. Cookie and his kind stayed, turned a good timber camp into a town.

## Chapter 16

# COOKIE

Dad loved Cookie stories. He loved hearing him tell them. He loved hearing about him. He was a real character, Cookie - a true-blue advocate of the Big Woods, and me. So, in honor of Dad and Cookie, here are a couple remembrances of Erasmus Alexander:

Cookie's specialty was pie. Year after year his pie won the blue ribbon at the County Fair. This became a matter of serious (yes, serious) concern to the local Lady Lutherans.

One year a delegation showed up, all bonneted and parasoled, and demanded (yes, demanded) his recipe for pie. They shared (yes, shared) their recipes and so should he!

Remember, this is Cookie's side of the story. I'm telling it the way he told it to us. Trying anyway.

In response Cookie showed their latest **Recipes for the Home** on his bookshelf. If they had bothered they would have noted the book had never been opened. It sat there as bright and shiny as the day it was printed. Although he could cipher, Cookie could barely read or write. The ladies did not know that. Nor did they know Cookie supported every cause, which so far included the Working-Girls Christmas, their Sidewalk Committee, the Lady Lutherans Recipe Book and the County Fair. Cookie felt it was his responsibility to give back... and he did. Generously.

So, when the Ladies demanded (yes, demanded) he share, he swallowed his great pride...and shared.

Remember, this is Cookie's story. Told Cookies way...

Cookie, a brawny man with dainty feet, was a chewer. Big plug of "backy" always (yes, always) stuck out his unshaven cheek. He wiped his hands on his stained apron, tied around coveralls with no undershirt, black body hair peeking out front and back, and motioned the church ladies to follow. They did.

He described the scene as proud papa black duck leading his entourage (yes, entourage) of the pink faithful to the lilies.

"Where he's the old bull, Grandpa?" She gave me her "wicked girl" smile.

"Hayley!"

*I elaborated. Again, in Cookie's words:*

All gray and plump they were, this entourage.

Wore sachets where Molly didn't.

"So, they were all grammas, older than Cookie?" asked Hayley.

"Yes, Dear." replied Brenda.

*That resolved, I went on:*

Can you imagine, getting all dressed up to visit a cook at a timber camp? Cookie himself seemed incredulous.

He took them to his dessert table. They gathered around, saw the makings of that day's berry pie spread out there. Blueberry, he recalled. Big greased rollin' pin set beside some dough already flattened out. His shoulder scraped a length of flypaper and a couple of captives fell, struggled in the dough. Until then he hadn't said anything, just motioned for the ducklings to follow.

"My secret is" - he had their attention now - "tobacco juice!" And he spit that plug into a bucket beside the table. It splashed and discolored the hem of the plumpest biddie's dress.

## The Legend of Augustus McBoone

*"Eww, Grandpa!"*

*Brenda gave me a hairy eyeball. Why? They both knew the story:*

Dad loved that part. Would slap a knee and laugh and laugh. I can still hear his laugh.

As Cookie told us, the flustered Lady Lutherans fluttered, flounced and fled.

It's a great storyteller that uses all those action "f" words, right? No one ever seemed to tire of hearing Cookie's stories. No one's eyes glazed over, like at church. Hayley's observation about the "old bull" and her mom's quick reaction assured me I had a rapt audience. I knew the next story would garner the same reaction from Brenda, wasn't sure about Hayley's. I thought, I'm almost 101 years. I can read what I want. Here goes:

Cookie's pies **were** good. Pie baking followed his cooking - whatever was in season. He would buy fresh from his army of pickers. This included the Lady Lutherans and their grandkids. Those wise old gals knew Cookie paid cash. He'd buy rhubarb, strawberries, blueberries (high bush, low and huckle), raspberries, blackberries, elderberries, currants, bushels of apples and pears. He'd also buy their jars of jellies and jams, and cans of veggies, peaches and horseradish.

Our first year in the Big Woods, Mandi decided to take Cookie on at the Fair. Her mom had trained her well - at the Inn. Mandi was used to baking for groups. So, a couple of days before the Fair I got treated to extra stuff: more food, a third bucket of hot water for my bath, a long long back rub and two dollops of honey. Then she pried Cookie's secret out of me. We made love twice that night...

"Augustus!"

"Shh Mom. I wanna hear."

Anyway she went to sleep mumbling "Maybe I can mush some up."

I smoked a pipe. Never chewed. That next day she went to the store.

At the Fair Mandi's pie brought the red ribbon. Second place to Cookie, who won the blue. Again.

Mandi was competitive. Didn't like coming in second. I probably made her madder when I asked if she had put any spit in.

That night I got a cold bath and a cold shoulder. The harrumph! routine. No honey therefore, no nooky.

"Augustus!"

"I know what nooky is, Mom."

*I kept reading:*

Mandi got over her mad when I told her I honestly did not know Cookie's recipe. I only knew his story. Did you really put mushed tobacco juice in? No. I used Mom's recipe.

That night things were back to normal. Mandi didn't like being denied either.

"Augustus!"

*Wicked Girl just smiled.*

*Told ya they were listening:*

Cookie won at the Fair every year and retired at seventy-five. The year Mandi died. She came in second until then.

Never beat him.

I now believe Cookie had no recipe to divulge. His success was all due to experience and scale. He baked every day. He measured different. While the Ladies and Mandi measured in "tads and pinches," Cookie used "scoops and shovels."

He was the best storyteller, Cookie. If alive today (he died in 1905, at ninety) he, not Bower, would command the Codger's Bench at Sawyer's Hardware. I swear to God that Will Rodgers grew up hearing Cookie stories.

The jobber knew that satisfying Cookie was his number one priority. Know who was Number Two? Not Mr. Jobber. He was Number Three.

Number Two was Mrs. Jobber. This bugged Dad so he'd send me. I'd shoe her horse, Pansy, weld a pot or two, have a cookie or two or four. She liked me, Mrs. Jobber.

Then I'd return to Dad. While loading our wagon with lunches Dad would add some sharpening tools. The jobber always had work for us in the woods and Dad did his best not to tick Number Three off.

Still, Cookie was Number One. He enhanced his status after he married Mrs. Jobber. Mr. Jobber died in his forties and Cookie's woman ran off with a hick. Took her teenage daughter with her. So, Mrs. Jobber and Cookie hooked up. She squirted out two babies of his. Together they raised seven children and were married thirty years. They never had to move. The railroad came. Cookie organized the band, ball team, and hose company. Together they built the school and formed the mill.

The grateful town fathers named the town after Cookie. Too often, they wait until you're dead, but Cookie was still alive. His wife kept the secret, sprung it on him. He teared up.

## The Legend of Augustus McBoone

They grew the camp into a town, those two. Heck of a name for a town - Erasmus, Potter County, Pennsylvania.

## Chapter 17

# THE CADENCE OF THE WOODS

Arnie Sorenson was the new hewer on crew number Five. Before he had been a sawyer on the same crew. He knew the men, the drill. He was a popular man, Arnie. The jobber had promoted him, promising Seagreave's wage of four dollars a day. He liked Seagreaves but he was dead. There was this opening and it paid one dollar more a day.

Arnie was a tall, strong man closing on thirty. A hick for ten years, Arnie had been trained by his dad Soren in all the functions of a "forester" in Sweden. Soren had followed his dad who had followed his dad. This forester chain had remained unbroken since the Twelfth Century. Arnie, who would have kept the chain going through the nineteenth if he could, could not. He was Soren's sixth son. All his older brothers were foresters and worked with their dad - in Sweden. There was no future there so Arnie borrowed the fare from Soren and emigrated to America.

## The Legend of Augustus McBoone

They manicured their woods in Sweden. Not so in America! The only manicure Arnie experienced stateside was when Peggy Sue worked on her mom's nails and Molly applied these nails to Arnie's back. That had happened this past Sunday while Cookie was away at the Fair. But Cookie could afford to pay Sweet Molly more so Arnie really needed that extra dollar a day. And, if the crew processed more than twenty spars a day, they were each paid a "premium" of twenty cents apiece per spar. Working like hell Arnie had the potential of rivaling Cookie. In earnings anyway. Which was all that mattered to Molly. Well, not all.

It was in the Big Woods that Arnie first became aware of his foreign limitations. These men were good! They took their time in Sweden. In America, time was money. So Arnie picked up his pace and not his chips. He stuck it out, progressing from gopher to bucker to sawyer in ten years. Now he was a hewer. On a great day, a fifty spar day, with his premium, he could make ten dollars a day. Now he could send money back to his dad. Now he could afford Molly.

Arnie still lived for today, had not yet become a far-thinking man like Paddy, Cookie or the Tinkerman. But they were in their forties, he had at least ten years to go. His main attractions were he was clean and young and virile, an "eager beaver" to Molly.

Arnie was a "good man" according to his unsteady buddies, a rugged hick who could work sunup to sundown and still have energy left for drinking, gambling, carousing and Molly. The order of the last three depended on the availability of Molly.

Today crew Number Five was cutting a patch of white pine, spar timbers. It would take the crew a while to get "up to speed" but the jobber wanted the spars so the woods boss agreed to help so number Five would earn their premium.

There was a process to the cut and a cadence, a rhythm, that assured productivity and safety in the Big Woods. The process went like this: The **axe-man** with his "double bit" cut the deep notch that determined the direction of the pine's fall. Two **sawyers** seesawing at each end of a "crosscut" would cut into the notch from the opposite side and leave a four-inch connector called a "hinge." This connector was all that held the tree up. The tree would sway, quiver, the hinge would crack! and the tree would fall. The pine did not realize it was dying until it raised dust from the wood's floor. With needles sprinkling down the **bucker** would "top" the tree with a "one-man crosscut" and "limb" the remaining pole with his "single-bit." He would not remove all the limbs, but leave the pole supported by spearlike sticks called "risers" for the **hewer** (Arnie's new job). This craftsman would shape the pole into a squared timber with his "adze." This job took the most time. It was here the woods boss helped Arnie. Longer than ninety-two feet the timber became a "spar." Shorter than that it became a "beam." The **teamster** then hooked his "grabs" to the log and "chained" all to the team's "harness." After the bucker broke the risers, the teamster and team "skidded" the timber to the "landing."

The most dangerous and unpredictable part of this process was the "falling" of the tree. Here the "cadence" was required. Singing loud and clear was more important than carrying a tune. Even then, there was a rhythm to it. Arnie would have to repeat the hewers call, the most important part of the process. It went like this: Undercut, top cut, back cut, down!

The axe-man shouted Undercut, sawyer one shouted Topcut, sawyer two Backcut, the hinge would crack! and the hewer sang out Down!

Loud and clear, Arnie had to shout out Down!

The cadence was like marching in war. It had a meaning. When you heard Down, you got the hell out of the way. There was no respect either - everyone was busy getting the hell out of the way.

If you didn't, according to hick lore, Hell was **not** far away.

The best crew, the one that produced consistently more, was the eight-man crew of specialists run by Bill Sykes Senior.

Senior and Company were standoffish; made it clear they didn't like anybody. Which was probably why nobody liked them. You kept the hell out of their way. Seagreaves had not, the reason Arnie was promoted today.

Arnie admitted grudgingly they were workers. With a crew of eight they processed fifty percent more timber with thirty-three percent more men. And they took their assigned patches as they came, no "plumb" jobs.

Senior, the fastest axe-man around, was also the best sawyer, bucker, hewer, even teamster. Why would horses mind such a mean spirit? 'Cause he'd whip them, that's why! Senior was the top hick. An absolute son of a bitch he was and smart like a boar pig.

They were all related, that crew. Senior, the biggest was the oldest at forty-five. Some of the others were in-laws or cousins. The youngest was Bill's son, Junior, bull-strong and pigheaded like his Dad. Of the middle six, three were "foreigners." Swede was from Sweden, Bama from Alabama, and Missourah from Missouri.

## The Legend of Augustus McBoone

Swede knew of Arnie's dad. He never said why he came to the Big Woods. Probably wanted back home. A runner, he was not like Arnie who had left to see the world. Arnie had wanderlust, until he met Molly. Then his lust changed.

While working as a sawyer, Arnie had witnessed Senior in action. Bama, their hewer, had forgotten to shout Down! and laughed. For this Senior had slammed Bama to the ground. Pointing a beefy finger, he raged at Bama."You always yell Down! Always, ya hear?"

Bama nodded, meekly.

Senior added, "You're gonna see a man killed, you don't."

Senior's speed and intensity affected Arnie. He wondered why it mattered so to Senior. He always kept that bigmouth Missourah and another man looking. On watch they were. Like ravens in a tree, cawing at any danger. Why?

The cadence was a law of the woods and Senior followed it. Probably the only law he respected.

Arnie did not like the way Senior bulled his way to be first in line to draw his pay. He also didn't like it that the other hicks let him.

Men talk. Arnie knew there was only one hick with the logging skills of Sykes. Angus McBoone. But he made too much tinkering. Tall, rangy, competent and strong, Angus McBoone, a reformed unsteady, was the best at everything.

And, all the hicks liked him.

The hicks that weren't feudists anyway.

## Chapter 18

# FIGHTING IN THE BIG WOODS

I finished my oatmeal as the hicks stood. Forty-one slid their chairs under the table. Eight did not. The Sykes's crew figured Cookie or Gopher should do that. As if on cue the workmen filed out the front door to the wide walkway, there to await the wagons to take them to their work sites. Junior, last out, jostled my chair.

Smitty, sitting opposite Dad said, "He had plenty of room."

Junior hadn't done any harm. "Just hungover I guess." I said this loudly so Junior would hear.

Dad and Smitty went to clean our wagon before loading that day's lunch deliveries. I got assigned to help Cookie who wanted the wood stove in the corner swept out. I groaned. Stove cleaning was a dirty job. Normally this was Gopher's task but he was learning to buck timber today. "Summer's the best time to do it," explained Cookie. "Draft needs fixed too." Cookie was sweeping under the Sykes end of the table, then pushing those eight chairs in.

The wall calendar read July 31, 1862. There was a large-busted redhead on it. July must be the month for redheads, I thought.

I wondered if Seagreaves had died on Wednesday or Thursday. Then shrugged. An inconsequential detail, now. He was just another dead hick to replace. No constable had been telegraphed. No one actually claimed to see him die. Junior had bragged he'd seen it before his dad shushed him. But Junior was a Sykes. It made me mad - them getting away with murder.

I dismantled the stove, set the elbow and faulty draft aside when I heard the wagon pull up. The loudest mouth of camp complained, "That's not the way we do it in Missourah!" His voice carried, Missourah. I'm thinking, "I don't give a damn how they do it there, you ass."

I peered upward into the straight section of pipe that perforated the ceiling, the bunkhouse, the roof. Saw a meager crescent of light. The pipe was caked with soot.

Needed chained from the top down. No wonder the draft wouldn't work! I cocked my head to see better, thought of the progression of tasks to clean that pipe, looked closer when...I was grabbed, lifted and shoved headfirst into that sooty pipe. He let go and I fell out choking and sputtering, my hair and face matted with soot. I shook my head. Wiped my eyes.

There stood Junior doubled over with laughter, pointing at my blackened face. "Made a nigger out of me," he crowed. Proud of his joke.

It took a strong man to lift one hundred eighty pounds two feet into a stove pipe. Junior was a bull, three years older and one hundred pounds heavier than me. A strapping lad, he stood six feet two and fleshy, unlike most hicks, more like his dad.

I was four inches taller with long arms and hard hands. My reach was a foot more than Junior's.

He straightened up, still laughing, his guard down.

I stood and slugged him square in the nose. Felt it squish.

My blow staggered and bloodied him, sent his Bowler flying. It did not knock him down. I readied another but Cookie rushed us with his broom. "Not in my mess," he growled. "Take it outside!"

"It" being a fight.

The word spread like wildfire. "Fight! Fight!"

I led the way into the street. The hicks jumped off their wagons, circled around. A fight was a distraction to be discussed a long time. They could be late to work today. They had seen this one coming, since Junior jostled my chair.

I had witnessed logger fights. Fast, wicked, brutal conflicts they were. Dad and I had worked on my skills but this was my first real fight. I waded into Junior, blackfaced, mad clean through.

But not killing mad. That happened, later.

Junior wanted to kill me. That had been the intent if I fought back.

Bama handed Junior a piece of stove wood. He swung it at me. A glancing blow, it still rung my bell. Knocked me down.

While down, Missourah kicked me, scraped his hobnails across my back. Tore my shirt and skin. I yelled. That hurt!

Missourah had forgotten himself. It wasn't dark. There were scores of witnesses. In helping his nephew he forgot the cardinal rule in a logger's fight - one against one.

A tall rangy hick grabbed Missourah and shoved him aside. "One on one," he said.

Missourah grabbed for his knife. Other hicks crowded him, convinced him that was a bad idea. My head cleared. Another hick threw me a long piece of stove wood. I now had a two-foot advantage. I circled Junior, waiting my chance.

Missourah's kick spurred the hicks. The enmity toward the Sykes crew spilled out. It was one thing to kill in the dark. Quite another to kick a kid when he's down in broad daylight. Their knives came out, pointed at the surprised crew. It was still one on one. I started hearing pointers. Break his head! Bust his knee!

Junior's eyes widened, looked confused. Blood streamed out his nose. In buckets it seemed. I measured him. My scalp was cut, my back was scraped, but I was upright and I glared. This was getting serious. They told him I was easy.

I wasn't.

I rushed him, swung my stick for his head. He raised his thick forearm to block my blow. I heard a crack, knew I had missed his head.

Junior yelled out in pain, dropped his stick, grabbed hold of his broken forearm. Seeing my opening I held my stick like a ballbat, aimed for splitting his head like a melon, stepped forward...

Got grabbed and driven into a pile of hicks.

Dad.

We got up together. I was restrained by my stronger heavier Dad. He yelled at Senior. "A fight's one thing, Bill! A killing's another!"

Senior growled: "You ganged up on Elmer."

Arnie Sorenson chipped in. He had been the rangy hick who shoved Missourah away. He didn't approve of their ganging up on me, obviously. "And you didn't on Seagreaves? Or Gus here? What was your intent, Sykes?"

The hicks recognized this as another set-up. The one who threw me the stick yelled, "You want what Elmer got? There's a tree yonder!"

Senior looked around. Saw dozens of angry hicks, knives drawn. He and his crew would be rent like Seagreaves then hung. He knew. Odds were real bad. He shrugged off his holders. Best to separate, spread folks out, improve the odds. He drew out a blue kerchief for his son's bloody nose, walked toward. Using the hanky as a cover he drew his own blade.

Dad wheeled on Senior. I never saw a man move so fast! His Bowie was out, pointed end snugged against Bill's throat.

"Cut his throat, Angus! Just one swipe," said the hick that had thrown me the wood.

Senior's own blade was low. Two feet from Dad's ribs. Two feet too far.

Another voice drawled, "Careful, Bill." All eyes turned to Missourah, whose gravelly voice carried. Arnie's knife was pressed against his shirt. It would slide under his rib cage, then into his heart. None of us knew Arnie was a knife fighter. Somewhere he had been.

All knew Dad was.

Slowly, very slowly, Senior sheathed his blade. To this day I wish Dad had cut his throat, or shot him the evening before. Ah me, he didn't.

Junior was holding his broken right forearm with his left. Blood mixing with tears. Poor thing!

Senior grabbed him by the left elbow and dragged him sobbing to the barber shop. There to get that bone set. We could hear him chastising Junior. "Don't you ever give time! Ever!"

A group of hicks followed behind. To be sure.

Arnie shoved Missourah to Dad, said I should hobnail his back, at least. Dad shook his head. Missourah ran to his wagon. The disappointed

Arnie walked toward Number Five's still holding his Bowie. His stock had increased among the hicks.

Together, Dad and I walked to Smitty's. I pulled off my torn shirt, washed off in his trough. While rummaging around in our wagon for another shirt, I realized I had so much to learn. I was tucking it in and said to Smitty, "So this was all a set-up. To kill me?"

Smitty nodded. "That stick Bama gave Junior was the sign. Hicks use fists or feet, never a club. And the scrap is always one on one." He added. "They didn't expect Junior to laugh nor the men to back you when you got kicked. They got too cocky, that crew."

"So instead of poking fun Junior should have kept poking me."

Smitty laughed at my bad joke. Then he got serious. "Those men are killers, Augustus. Senior wants evens which means he hates all associated with the hanging of Elmer. Junior has grown up with that hate. This ain't over. They're not a crew. They're a gang."

That said, Smitty convinced me he was also a far-thinking man.

## Chapter 19

# DYING IN THE BIG WOODS

Later that day Senior got his "evens."

Dad and I were delivering lunches. Should have driven out of camp but didn't. Felt we had a job to do. Also felt that giving up was giving in and the Sykes crew had been subdued. If only temporarily. "It's your funeral," said the far-thinking Smitty.

The Sykes patch was the farthest out. Dad, knowing we were outnumbered in the woods, thought it best to leave their lunches on a stump. "Just holler and get out," he said. Saw no sense in stirring up more trouble.

Dad was driving. I sat alongside. The trail was rutted. Our wagon lurched slow along. Our team's harness jangled. We skirted a meadow and started in the Big Woods. I watched a woodchuck chew some grass, then duck into his hole. What spooked him? I thought this, didn't alert Dad.

There was no crack!, no cadence, no warning at all. A tall tree fell from behind us and enveloped our wagon in green. I smelled pine. Dad was speared through the chest by a sharp branch. Another hit me on the head and knocked me under the wagon. The tree trunk followed and crushed Dad, our wagon and the horse, Moe, on the left side. The right front wheel and axle saved me. I heard a death rattle and a drawl before passing out. "You got a twofer, Bill," was the sentence I heard.

The crew we had just left heard a horse scream and their teamster came to investigate. Our right-side horse, Dan, smelled blood and was straining and screaming. While tying him to a tree the teamster found Dad crushed in its branches. Then my foot moved and he called for help. His crew came. The closest crew melted into the Big Woods.

Crew Five took us in, Dad to a grave beside Seagreaves, me to Cookie's. I must have been delirious. I kept mumbling, "We had no warning, we had no warning." Cookie said it could have been an accident, there was no proof...until supper. When the Sykes crew failed to show up at supper the men had their proof. Bill Sykes and his crew were gone for good. And guilty.

But they weren't gone, yet.

They must have needed some going away money. They hid out 'til Saturday. Then robbed the camp.

They did this by robbing the paymaster.

Senior, observant pig that he was, knew the paymaster to be a man of habit. Leathers was his name. He would drive in Thursday evening with the wages for the past week in his buckboard. He spent Friday conferring with the wood's boss and jobber on production and Saturday readying each hick's pay. Saturday morning he would eat an early breakfast. Alone. Then he'd go to his office, unlock the front door. This was when the crew cut the telegraph wires and rode quiet into camp. While the hicks were eating, Bill tortured the safe combination out of the paymaster and Missourah cut his throat. They emptied the safe and started riding quietly out. Bama and Junior were standing guard when the bloody paymaster stumbled outside. Bama shot him. The shot alerted the hicks who raced to the office. The robbers raced out of camp. A working-girl heard Bill chastise Bama: "Dammit! I didn't want any noise. Now they'll raise a posse!"

The camp did but the gang disappeared into the Big Woods.

They escaped west to the Pinelands. They could have prospered there with the logging skills and money they had, in time. But a murderous gang like Syke's does not take time. It's too easy to take from others.

Mr. Leathers lived. He couldn't yell anymore, talked raspy after Missourah cut into his voice box. Carried a grudge and a bullet and vowed his own evens.

He got 'em too. Later.

The gang cut a swath through the Pinelands. Then escaped south to Missouri. Holed up with kin there. Missouri was split between abolitionists and slaveowners. Being racists and haters, good with guns, blades and horses, they found sanctuary with the slaveowner's crowd. Eventually they joined Quantrell and his pack of "Reb Raiders." Got to kill and rape and pillage in the name of Southern Rights and Chivalry.

Back east they had prices on their heads. As raiders they enjoyed the protection of numbers. Even wore pieces of gray.

A good thing couldn't last. Senior chafed at taking "Bloody Bill's" orders. There wasn't room for two Bills. So the eight split off and split again and again. They took their uniform pieces and feudist attitudes with them.

Missourah saw one man die, not two.

He should have made sure of Bill's twofer. He didn't, which meant someday there would be evens.

We would meet again.

## Chapter 20

# Lovin' Peggy Sue

I woke up two days later, a true orphan. Dad was dead!

I looked around. I lay on a single mattress supported by two pallets. My bare feet stuck beyond the bed. A tarp hung between me and the woodshed. A chipmunk skittered down a hole. My head was wrapped in a bloody bandage. An empty bucket sat at the head of my makeshift bed. I sat up, got woozy. My mouth was dry. My head pounded. Where was I?

Cookie came in from delivering lunches. With news. The Sykes Gang had robbed and shot the paymaster. Cut his throat and the telegraph. A rider had been sent for the Sheriff. A posse was out but...they were long gone, he thought. Another rider was bringing in Mr. Glover. He would conduct payroll this evening. The paymaster got sewn up at the barber's, would recuperate at Mrs.

Jobber's. Leathers would make it, he thought. They played hell, that gang.

I asked for water. Cookie left. I stood, got my bearings. I was at Cookie's. It was Saturday, August second, 1862.

Cookie returned with a dipper of cold water from his spring. Half I drank, half I sloshed around, spat in the bucket.

"Where's Dad?" I asked.

"Beside Seagreaves. Funeral, after church, Sunday."

"I'll be there."

We made our deal and he left. He was so matter-of-fact, Cookie! That's the way it was in the Big Woods. Life was for the living. Death was for the worms. He charged a dollar a day for bed and board. Molly and her daughter would take care of me for another dollar. Glover would pay any money the Company owed me or Dad. If I couldn't make it to settlement, Glover would bring it to the funeral tomorrow.

So, for two dollars a day I could eat, sleep and get better at Cookie's. And how did he say it? Molly and her daughter would "take care of me?"

Uh huh!

I was skeptical because Molly was already "taking care" of another man. Arnie had squired her to church while Cookie was at the Fair. I saw him stick the dollar down her blouse at the pig's ear, heard him warned. So...

...Cookie and Molly and a thing going.

...Arnie and Molly had a thing going.

And Molly was a working-girl who had things going with men who followed her from the pig's ear to the sporting house.

This was okay as long as Molly stayed a working-girl. Not okay when she became a missus. I say "when" since the sporting house was the hick's resource for wives. These wives became ladies after a couple of kids and staying true to their husbands. The false ladies were those who forgot where they came from. The true ladies, like Mrs. Jobber, never did.

Molly and Peggy Sue checked on me daily. I healed fast, still do. Peggy Sue came with her mom from another log camp. Her mom was twenty-eight. Peggy Sue fourteen. You can do the math.

*I looked over at the worry-warts. Their mouths hung open at my descriptions. I had kept this particular journal hidden, decided to bring it out this morning. When you're over a century old, what harm could be done?*

*Peggy Sue was a frisky, full-blown girl when she "nursed" me, a working-girl in training. She said the best thing for my injury was honey and such. Cookie's larder provided the honey. She provided the "such".*

"Augustus..."

"Grandpa..."

*The worry-warts knew where this story was going. I pointed to the ever-present pot on the kitchen counter. "This is where I learned the benefits of honey," I explained.*

"Yeah, right," said Brenda.

"Go on, Grandpa," said Wicked Girl:

Once I got stable, Peggy Sue and I took a picnic lunch to Dad's grave. My first visit had been Sunday, at the funeral. He had been buried in canvas but deeper than Seagreaves, Crew Five said. We gathered rock, piled it atop and around his grave. She wiped my tears, chatted about things at camp, did her best to address my moping, gave me honey.

There in the woods, we became lovers. While wiping my tears she kissed me. I liked it. Kissed her back. Started tugging at each others clothes. She noticed the scabs on my back. I noticed she wasn't wearing bloomers. At the end, all she was wearing was her bonnet, all I had on was my cap.

"*Augustus!*"

"Kinda fumbly as I recall." I looked at Hayley.

"Go on Grandpa," said Wicked Girl, smiling:

We went on picnics daily after that. Always took honey. A couple of times a day, we'd need honey.

That honey pot went down fast as Molly and Arnie were hitting it too.

After breakfast one morning I rode alone to the site where Dad was killed. Moe was there, smelly, gathering carrion and flies. I crawled under the wagon, removed our hidden stash, some books, Dad's Bible. I then went to his grave and buried his Bible with him. I remember thinking, that Book's two owners died violent deaths. The time had come to bury it...for good. I grew up at Chancellorsville, started reading a Bible again.

I got back in time for my picnic with Peggy Sue. I did a good job on that reburial. I put every stone back as it had been. She never knew I had been there that morn.

After breakfast the next morning I helped Cookie salt and smoke some fresh meat. An old Indian had delivered a wagonload and the two of us unpacked it. He was old and scrawny and really strong. While carrying those halves I noted they were all young - deer fawns and bear cubs. "Good eatin'!" he replied. "I'll bring their mom's next month. They're workin' the farm fields now. These youngsters were fat and dumb." Cookie paid him twenty-five dollars in coin. I was impressed.

As he was getting paid Peggy Sue came around. He noticed her and whispered, "Nice filly there, Son. Ain't wearin' any bloomers, ya know."

"How can you tell?" I asked. I guessed but couldn't **tell**. How could he?

He cackled. "I've had workin'-gals, wives and daughters in my time," he said. "I can tell."

The old hunter drove off in his swaying wagon pulled by one swaybacked mule. "Daisy" wore a straw slouch hat with ear holes it it. That hat looked new. The wizened Indian and Daisy did not. Cookie called after: "Are you gonna make it home with that old mule, Joe?"

His name was Joe. Injun Joe.

"She'll get us home, I reckon. May have to take her to Dead Horse after that."

Dead Horse Hollow was where they "dispatched" animals like Daisy who had seen better days.

He'd shoot her between the eyes. Hope he remembers to remove that hat. I thought this. Did not say it.

I also did not say anything to Peggy Sue about her bloomers, or lack thereof. There are some things you just don't tell a working-girl-in training.

One week after "the incident," I breakfasted with the hicks but left early. Arnie Sorenson had borrowed ten the day before. He hadn't said anything about missing breakfast altogether. Why would any hick miss breakfast?

I caught them leaving camp. Arnie had "rented" a horse and buckboard. It looked like Mr. Leather's to me. He, Molly and Peggy Sue were headed to another camp further west. Bags all packed. All three excited about their new adventure. I was sad to see Peggy Sue go, sadder to see her so excited about going. Remembering I owed them seven dollars, I handed Peggy Sue a ten dollar gold piece. "Keep the change," I said.

They left in a clatter. Peggy Sue was biting the gold piece and holding on to her bonnet. It was blowing from the northwest, fixing to rain. Curious, without being obvious, I looked to see if she was wearin' bloomers. I still couldn't tell. How could **he** tell?

I decided it was time for me to go too. I packed up my personals, kept Dad's Colt and Bowie, made the rest all fit in a big backpack. Cookie came in. I told him about Arnie, Molly and Peggy Sue.

He shrugged. Crew Five is gonna miss him. Paddy and the house are gonna miss her. He never mentioned my missing Peggy Sue. "You know," he said, "I never had any success with women." He spat in the bucket. Seemed relieved. He knew something was going on because of lowering levels in the honey jar. By the way, I owed him seven dollars. I gave him ten, told him to keep the change. He kept it too. He was so matter-of-fact, Cookie.

Everything we had was mine, now. I sold Mr. Jobber Black Dan, Paddy my shotgun, Smitty my extra tools, the storekeep my rifle and pearl-handled pistols. I looked in on Leathers and Mrs. Jobber agreed to store my books - until Leathers recovered and Sorenson sent back the buckboard. I visited Dad's grave, piled on some more stones. I didn't say good-by to the hicks. They were out working. On the way I heard the cadence of the woods: Undercut - Topcut - Backcut - Down! Saw the top of the pine quiver, heard the hinge crack, felt the tree land.

The others went west.

I went east.

I was headed to Wellsborough. To sign up as a soldier for a "big" bonus.

The poster said The Pennsylvania Bucktails needed First Class Men.

The calendar said it was August seventh, 1862.

That girl was blonde, buxom. Reminded me of Peggy Sue.

I was seventeen.

It never did rain that day.

*I finished reading. Brenda and Hayley entered the room, sat at the kitchen table, turned to me. Hayley began it:*

"So, Grandpa, did you ever see Peggy Sue again?"

"Once, I think."

"Oh?" *Both girls spoke at once. This was also new to them.*

"I was in a veterans parade in Wellsborough. Fall 1870. I'd been awarded The Medal that summer, wore it around my neck. Saw a young blonde woman, bonneted, follow me in the crowd. Had a boy in tow. Then she saw Mandi waiting, and left."

"Was she wearing bloomers, Grandpa?" *Hayley grinned wickedly.*

"Hayley!" Brenda said.

I mused on. Ignored Hayley. "Peggy Sue taught me how a girl moves, smells, tugs at her hair..."

"Loves honey?" Hayley finished my sentence. Grinning wickedly.

"Hayley," You stop! Brenda was scolding this time.

"It's all there, Mom." She pointed to the journal that rested on my lap. "You were just using your senses weren't you, Grandpa?" Again that wicked smile.

"Hayley!" her exasperated mom said. "You watch your sauce! Do I have to use a spoon on your bottom?"

But Hayley was not intimidated. Brenda had lost a lot of punch when she cheated on Ralph.

"Won't hurt, Mom. I **am** wearing bloomers."

I couldn't help it. I looked. I still couldn't tell.

How could Injun Joe tell?

## Chapter 21

# 98 First Class Men

Dad was gone. Peggy Sue was gone. The Sykes Gang was gone. All I loved or hated were gone! You never get over a loss. Or a hate. Whoever said time heals all wounds tried really hard to forgive and forget. Or lies. Time scabs and scars wounds. It does **not** heal them.

That's the way it works for me, anyway.

I was healed...physically. I could have stayed at the camp until I was drafted. Or paid a replacement. Or hid out in the Big Woods. Or headed west. I had choices. All seemed practical. None seemed noble. Like I said - I could have stayed as a hick or went on as a tinkerer. I enlisted instead.

There was this poster at the store:

**Be A Bucktail**
**1st Class Men Required**
**$165 Bonus**
**Wellsborough Recruiting Marquee**
**Sat., August 9, 1862**
**R. C. Caufield, Lieutenant**

Dad had been a soldier. Why not me?

I was a "First Class Man," wasn't I?

The pay of $13 a month was shitty. As was the bonus...for three years. Some wag, probably Mr. Jobber, had penned in that detail. As if the Government was **not** telling us all. They'd tell us everything, right?

Right.

The wag's point was clear. Why risk getting killed for $13 a month when you could make that in a week here? The difference was in **how** you got killed.

Dad made a lot more than $13 a week...here... and he was dead. Dead! Killed in the Big Woods. I was green and seventeen. I didn't see the difference then.

When I was eighteen I did.

The pay was no big deal. I had money saved and invested. Well, Dad did. I inherited that money. Best of all, I inherited Dad's canniness with money. I also thought Dad would honor my decision. "I don't like it. But you got it to do," is what he'd say. It's what I said to his descendants. Their mother's didn't approve. Didn't talk to me for awhile afterwards. Accused me of talking them into it. I didn't. They made the same decision I made in 1862.

I answered my country's call. So did they. You know, I never heard a dying boy cry out for his dad. Ever. Those that could, cried out for their mom. I'll have to think about the implications of that.

I admit to being affected by the propaganda of the day. I had read **Uncle Tom's Cabin**. The chance to kill a bunch of racist Simon Legree's was impossible to resist. For me Legree and Sykes looked exactly alike. Oh, the glory of killing that Infidel, that Johnny Reb! I was going on a crusade! I was mad at God but I prayed, actually prayed, for some fighting when I got there.

God answered that prayer. He really did. Even with me still mad at Him. He has a sense of humor, God.

The Civil War challenged the "great experiment" called the "United" States. How could we be united while killing each other? There were at least three issues dividing the North and South. They were: 1) Anti-slavery versus pro-slavery factions; 2) Federal Rights versus States Rights; and, 3) Papists vs. Protestants. This latter issue was not nearly as consequential as the former two.

From 1860-1865 more than half a million American boys died. And we're still finding bodies, still counting! Huckleberry's been dead 82 years. He represents a type on either side - all killed were breeders. That damn war cost America a generation of young men. Created an imbalance in families. More women than men gave rise to widows, spinsters, prostitutes and polygamy.

I never had any trouble with polygamy.

*Grandpa!*

*Yep. They're still listening.*

The Brass mustered me out because of wounds at Gettysburg. My Regiment, the 149th, all shot to hell or heaven depending on your persuasion. My Company, A, started out with 98 First Class men, only had three still standing, four if you count Stickwalker. Of the four, only one wasn't dripping blood but he was walking wounded.

I went home, healed up physically, started my new life.

That war dragged on for two more years. By 1865, the Reb leaders knew they couldn't win. How much fighting can go on without ammo, food or shoes?

Those Johnnies were scrappers. I'll give them that.

Kinda dumb though, looking back. Their young men dying for $13 a month that could not be paid. Our young men dying for $13 that could. Still, as the wag indicated on the poster, was $13 a month worth it?

I spent two days walking to Wellsborough.

I left camp and went east to Knoxville where I met with Banker Glover. I found him training our paymaster Leathers. He was coming in half a day after being wounded at the robbery. Wore a sling and his voice was raspy but he was a tough nut, that Stan. Arnie must have returned the buckboard for him to beat me here.

Mr. Glover invited me into his office. Our box was on his desk. "Sorry about Angus," he said. "I told Fergus, after I heard."

I nodded. He knew I didn't have any truck with Fergus and Flo.

"I'm signing up, Mr. Glover."

He didn't offer any opinion. Knew if I had wanted it I would have asked.

He opened the box. Rifled through some papers. "Your Dad's will is here," he said. "And a paid-up life insurance policy for $500. Everything goes to you."

I nodded again. I knew.

We reviewed the stuff in our, well, my box. A bank book showed a balance of $640. There was another $200 in cash. We found receipts where Dad had invested with three timber companies: King's Arrow, Collins Pine, and Wright Logging. His King's Arrow interest was in uncut timber, Collins Pine was paying a $60 dividend every quarter, Wright Logging was defunct because of a typhoid epidemic. I signed paperwork transferring the McB brand to me, processed the life insurance claim with orders telling them to deposit that money with Mr. Glover. I had $400 on me from the sales at camp plus what we were owed. I put $100 in my money belt and $40 in my pockets. That left $1600 at the bank.

Not bad for a country boy. I thought.

I made out a new will giving everything to Ike McFee, Buttonwood, PA.

Mr. Glover asked, "To be clear, if you are killed, I am to pay McFee, correct? Not your next of kin?"

I knew Dad had supported Fergus and the farm. I had no intention of maintaining that support and told him so. Kinda hardass of me, I know. But I was seventeen and bitter, still smarting at Flo's harsh treatment. After Flo died, Mandi helped me change my mind.

Banker Glover sighed. "I will contact you if anything happens with the farm." He disapproved of my attitude but didn't say anything. Didn't have to.

As I was leaving I said goodbye to Leathers and wished him well. I spent the night, and $5 at the Wellsborough Hotel. Signed up the next day.

Officially we were Company A of the 149th Pennsylvania Volunteer Regiment, a sharpshooting outfit.

The first thing I noticed was that a "First Class Man" was anyone willing to sign up. No one was rejected. There were farm boys, town boys, fat boys, skinny boys, boys mostly. All could shoot. There were various degrees of proficiency but we did know how to load and pull the trigger. Compared with what I saw at Camp Curtin the Union got the pick of the litter with us Bucktails.

## The Legend of Augustus McBoone

The recruiter was a slim man, matter-of-fact like Cookie. His sign read R. C. Caufield, Lieutenant. The same as the poster. He had just witnessed an X. Seeing my size and beard and horny hands he shoved a paper at me. "I'll witness your X too," he said.

I read it first. He scowled. Saw I had a choice of a one, two, or three-year enlistment. I chose the one. Figured I could always re-up later. He handed me $55 in Union scrip which I stuffed in my pants pocket. I now had a total of $190 on me and resolved to put that fifty-dollar bill in my money belt later.

He also handed me a company cap, the biggest one he had. It fit. The cap was called a kepi. Had a tin insignia, a letter sewn above the brim. Company A.

I was leaving the recruiter when a voice hailed me. He had a booming voice, like Missourah's. "Is your dad here, Augustus?"

Father-son signups were common during the Civil War. I felt the pang of memory. Walked toward the voice. Walter Wright had been a jobber. Before that he and Dad had served together in the Mexican War. He had re-upped, now wore a blue jacket with shoulder bars. "You **know** the Major?" asked the recruiter.

I nodded. Didn't say he owed me money. I went to his desk, sat, took my kepi off.

Major Wright continued, "I don't see Angus. We served together in Mexico. We could sure use your dad."

"Dad's dead," I replied. "Killed by Bill Sykes ten days ago." I told him about the ambush.

He swore. Major Wright could be a salty dog. He hadn't heard. **Now** he knew why I was there. I knew why he was there too. He had lost his family and fortune to a typhoid epidemic. I didn't mention it. Dad had said "let it go," and I did.

"He's a mean one, that Bill. His crew too. Good loggers but I wouldn't have them. Too contrary. Can't abide renegades like them. We all felt safer after King's Arrow hanged Bill's backstabbing brother."

"They killed Seagreaves too. Then robbed our paymaster and wounded him. Took off west after that."

"They're a gang of bigoted bastards. Went west you say? Look for them wearing the gray. You might get a chance to pop one. Hope you do."

"Evens," I agreed. Stood. Put my kepi back on.

## The Legend of Augustus McBoone

The Major gathered us new recruits. We recited an oath to uphold the Constitution. He taught us to salute. Told us we'd be marching out that very day.

We were then directed to a third soldier in buckskin, our scout. He was older, in his thirties. He wore no trappings of rank. He did wear a bone-handed Bowie. He was lean, hairy, savage. I couldn't tell if his brown skin came from the sun or a parent or both. He had yellow, predator eyes and, next to me, the tallest man in the room. He reached into a burlap sack and withdrew a long black deer tail. "Have yer mom or sis or sweetheart sew that on yer cap," he said. He showed me where. He had a raspy voice, coarse and low like the paymaster's would become. He looked at me intently, like he knew me from before.

"My mom is dead. Never had a sis. My sweetheart left with her mom and her mom's new man."

That gave the savage the right idea about Peggy Sue.

"Never had a sweetheart," he said. "Too fickle. Have three wives, though. Won't put up with any runnin' off."

He meant it too.

A squawman then. A breed, the mixed-race product of a white parent and a red one. His thick rust-colored hair grew to his shoulders, stuck above his collar and out the lacings of his shirt. He pointed to my tail. "That was a big mountain buck. I'm wearin' his hide. Sold his meat to Wright's log camp."

A market hunter too. Like that lean old geezer that saw Peggy Sue wasn't wearing bloomers.

I took my tail to the back porch. Sat down, pulled a needle and sinew out of my pack and sewed it on.

Kinda skunky, I remember thinking.

I did a good job. That tail is still there, bullet-shaved, but still firmly attached to my blue kepi.

It was our badge, that tail.

Part of the Pennsylvania Bucktails we were. Company A, 98 First Class Men out of Wellsborough.

## Chapter 22

# HEADING OUT

Our destination was Camp Curtin, a training center northeast of Harrisburg. We'd walk east from Wellsborough to Mansfield then on to Troy. From there we'd ride a train south to Harrisburg. Then we'd walk again to Curtin. In a roundabout way a distance of 200 miles. We'd be at Camp in time for Sunday mess.

We walked two abreast, sometimes three. The officers used the term "march." But we hadn't been taught to march yet. Company A started out with 103 men - 4 officers, 1 sergeant and us 98 "First Class" men. Besides taking the oath and being taught how to salute, I learned the privileges of rank in the army. This meant the officers rode, the rest walked. The officers wore bars on their shoulders, the rest wore chevrons on their sleeves. That is, when we got uniforms with sleeves. The officers **gave** orders, the sergeant **enforced** them, us 98 **obeyed** them. The officers rode saddle horses, good stock. Colonel Shannon and Major

Wright rode at the column's front. Captain Stone and Lieutenant Caufield rode at the rear.

I never got to know Colonel Shannon. Glad I didn't. He seemed above the crowd. A loner, kinda aloof, he remained that way till Chancellorsville. He bragged once that there wasn't a Rebel bullet made to kill him. He got blown out of his saddle there and Wright became our colonel.

Captain Stone was the opposite. A gregarious, popular fellow, easygoing and approachable. According to Sergeant Benjamin he came from a politically connected family. I never realized **how** connected until years later.

Sergeant Benjamin was the workhorse of Company A. Big and strong, rough and capable, he liked being "Sarge." He had worked as a woods boss for Major Wright, had nursed him through the typhoid. They remained close all their lives, those two. Sarge set the walker's pace. Carried the Bucktail banner.

Behind him walked two newly promoted corporals. Asskissers both, they had volunteered to carry the Pennsylvania and United States flags. By the time we reached Troy the flags had gotten heavy and they had gotten demoted.

Behind them walked us remaining "First Class" men. Being the tallest I shared the last rank with the scout. It had rained in the night. There wasn't any dust. We talked. I learned he had done this before.

We left Wellsborough kinda noisy. Folks coming to town got out of our way. The walkers stomped, the horse tack jangled, a tenor started singing and the rest joined in: "Hoorah! Hooray! We're going on our way! Hoorah! Hooray! As we are marching to Georgia!"

What a sight! A bunch of cocky Pennsylvania boys strung out in columns of two, in common clothes and wearing skunky caps.

The scout and I were forced to amble, give the pair in front more distance. We were long-striding outdoorsmen, held back even while carrying the heaviest packs. "We'd get there a helluva lot faster if they let us lead. Oh well. It's the Army," he grumbled. We introduced ourselves, shook hands. "You got big hands, boy," he said. "You're not done growin'. I'm Saul Poorbaugh, from Kinzua original. Last eleven years in Buttonwood."

"I've been near there, to Fallbrook," I answered. "Dad logged in Buttonwood in the 1850s. For King's Arrow. I'm Augustus McBoone."

He smiled for the first time. Had large, yellow, strong teeth, all his teeth, predator's teeth. "Figured you were Angus' boy. Served under him in Mexico. Hunted for King's Arrow too. Heard ya say Angus was ambushed by Sykes."

I nodded. Swallowed hard.

Saul continued. Death was also commonplace with this man. "You be careful around Sykes. Sure you want evens but..." His voice trailed off.

Obviously he did not think I was ready to take on Senior. I knew I wasn't. Face to face. I'd shoot the bastard in the back, if he ever gave me the chance. "He took off with his gang," I said. "Went west."

"He's fast with that blade. Like my twin Jesse - Prefers a sure thing though."

Sykes had been the subject of campfire talk.

"His gang knifed Seagreaves the night before," I added.

"Served with him too. A good man but a fun-lover. Hotheaded. Liked your dad better. Everybody liked your dad. His killin' says Sykes is keepin' that feud goin." His eyes narrowed. "Why'd you sign up, Augustus?"

"Get away. How about you?"

"Money. Bounty for Reb scalps and ears. Walt made an offer I couldn't refuse." His eyes twinkled. This hunter enjoyed hunting men.

"You could teach us how to march then?"

"I could but..." his voice trailed off again. "Those asskissing corporals will get us there bye and bye."

I pointed to his long rifle. Thing probably weighed fourteen pounds. "That's quite a gun," I said.

"A Hawken 70," he said proudly. "Handmade. I bought two. Jesse kept the carbine. I took the rifle."

"How far does it shoot?"

"As far as I can see. And that's far."

He had eagle eyes, Saul Poorbaugh. Only one man could see better.

So...a mile? Two miles? (Two was a real stretch).

"That buck tail you're wearin?"

"Yeah." I felt the buck tail.

"Mountaintop to mountaintop, 2,750 yards."

"Jeez!"

"Like I said, if I can see him, I can nail him."

He wasn't bragging either.

Saul Poorbaugh was a killer who carried the tools of his trade. When he wasn't wolfin' or cattin' (bounty hunter terms), he was pinchin' (trapping). For trapping he used short weapons, his bone-handled Bowie and wood-gripped 44. He carried two other revolvers in his "possible" bag, his pack. There were also wood-handled "toothpicks" poking out the top of each boot. And one pocket bulged with his clasp knife, his "Sunday-go-to-meetin'" switchblade.

He made good money, killing. Reminded me of a tall, young and nasty Injun Joe.

We "halted" for water at the Tioga River west of Mansfield. I noticed Saul's growing impatience with the cockiness of a few recruits. The officers dismounted. I led Captain Stone's and Lieutenant Caufield's horses to the river, followed by another private ordered to do the same with Colonel Shannon's and Major Wright's mounts. All four horses were geldings. The boys gathered, shared canteens. The cockiest bragged, the smartest listened. I listened.

From the river the tower of the new Normal School dominated Mansfield. The "experienced" recruits were comparing the cloistered girls at the school with the available friskies at Curtin. Their leader was a flabby town boy with freckles and an ever-present flush. I called him Pink-Cheeks. A know-it-all, he had the temerity to question Captain

Stone. "When do we get laid? Here or Curtin?" He crossed his arms, expecting an answer.

Captain Stone obliged. He picked his battles. This wasn't worth a big show of authority. Maybe a small one. "First of all," he said, "We're **not** stopping in Mansfield. We have a train to catch. You may have a sweetheart at the Normal, like me, but they are cloistered. Second, it's an eight-mile quick-step to Troy, a one-hundred-seventy-five mile overnighter to Harrisburg, and another eleven-mile quick-stepper to Curtin. We are expected for supper. Then you'll find your bunks, arise fresh as daisy's Monday morning. The Army will provide food, clothing and shelter - **but no women.**"

The boys groaned. There was no time to get laid!

The Captain went on. "There are 30,000 soldiers at Curtin. A few officers are there with their wives. The rest make do with…working-girls."

At this the boys cheered. That bonus money was burning a hole in their pockets. They knew there'd be girls! They **were** gonna get laid!

Then Saul brought them down to river bottom so to speak. "I never saw more than one hundred women around any camp," he scoffed. "Do the cipher. It's three hundred to one! And you ain't gonna get those gals for two bucks. More like twenty. Unless you're married or got money you ain't gonna get laid."

Such a sullen crowd.

I had money but didn't want to spend twenty on a working-girl. Peggy Sue had only cost me ten for the week and I let her keep the change.

"Grandpa!"

"It's how soldiers talk, Hayley:"

At that news a couple of boys decided to return their bonus and go home. Sergeant Benjamin convinced them of the error of their ways. I think the officers preferred that Saul shut up but the cocksure attitude displayed by Pink-Cheeks and his followers pissed the scout off and he let them have it:

"Cap'n Stone mentioned clothing. Uniforms to match the caps. They're wool! Winter shit. Hot and scratchy. I'm keepin' my buckskins. Don't see any rank do ya? That's 'cause I don't like the idea of gettin' killed leadin' a noisome bunch of snotnoses."

He was challenging those boys. Telling them a harsh truth. He must have gotten the idea of snotnoses because of the sniffing of the two Sarge had beaten. But no one, I mean, **no one**, stepped forward and said, "Now see here!"

"I'm thirty-four years old. Here for the killin'. Don't give a shit about glory 'cause there ain't no glory in killin'." He paused, added, "Just money." He glared at the stricken assembly. Dared any to object to being called a snotnose. The two sniffers tried to stop. The tenor, Ambrose Kuhl, muttered, "Next to him we **all** are snotnoses."

Our column formed up again. On the way I saw Pink-Cheeks jostle Ambrose, who ignored the slight. One of these days he won't ignore that bully. I thought it. Didn't say it.

I got another lesson from Saul soon thereafter. "How old are you Augustus?" he asked.

"Seventeen."

"You got a quick mind. This is the Army. Here it's best if you keep yer mind open and yer mouth shut. Know who taught me that?"

"Who?"

"Your dad. In Mexico."

I did some quick mental math. Saul was twenty when he served with dad. Dad was six years older, wiser. Was he watching out for me like Dad had watched out for him?

Soon we were "marching" through Mansfield. Folks lined up to see us. Ambrose led us in song. Saul, who couldn't carry a tune in a bucket, whispered the veteran's take on each song. Kinda earthy, his assessment. After **Battle Hymn**, for example, Saul opined that no soldier ever sees the glory of the coming of the Lord, usually he doesn't see a damn thing coming! After **Yankee Doodle** Saul said Stickwalker told him all the Yanks were handy with the girls. I chuckled with him but remember thinking - that song was popular during the Revolution. How old **is** this guy, Stickwalker? When Saul left the ranks to help a lady on a buckboard and got handy with her, I was reminded of his carnal nature. When her husband objected and Saul's hand covered the hilt of his Bowie, I was reminded that he was a killer. Fortunately Lieutenant Caufield's horse got between Saul and the husband and Saul came back to the column. The buckboard sped away. Then the Town Band showed up.

You know, killers are valued but not liked in war. But I liked Saul. And, later, his twin Jesse.

*"Grandpa!" This was mother and daughter in unison:*

*A while back Brenda was threatening to spank Hayley's bottom. Now they were united against... me. The idea of my consorting with the squawmen bothered them. They had reason to object, I guess. But the twins were long dead. They were transferring that animosity because of our recent conflict with Jesse's son, Samuel.*

*When Saul got back from the war he and his wife Songbird had Hannah. She grew and attracted Jesse, bearing him a son in his old age. Samuel was born in 1898. Samuel went to France with Squire Hayes. Got in trouble over a girl Hayley's age. He was a killer like Saul and Jesse, the Allies needed him, so Squire and the Brass buried it. Samuel returned with the nickname Spike. Folks shunned him because he was a breed and dangerous and different. Spike's family was wiped out by the same flu that took Sandra. He lived alone in those mountains and grew more different. Most folks fear different. Squire and I did not fear Spike - then. He knew I had a special relationship with his dad and uncle. He also knew about Stickwalker. I saw his tracks around my cabin and figured he was curious. Actually, he was watching - Hayley. One day he threw caution to the four winds and tried to rape Hayley. Had her pinned. Ripped off her blouse. She bit and screamed. I came and knocked him off her with my stick. Bloodied him good. He ran off, still limber for a man in his forties. I couldn't catch him. Now I keep my guns handy. I've warned Hayley's dad not to go after Spike. Ralph proved his mettle with Brenda's former lover but Poorbaugh is a different kettle of fish. This man is a born and trained killer - fast, canny, deadly. A cutthroat that knows when to fight and when to run. Michael would go but he's past eighty. Ira is past fifty. Josh, when he gets* home, is twenty-five. Even then, he will need help. We can kill Spike but at least one of my family would die. In my prime I could have taken Spike. Not now. The only men capable of besting Spike in the woods are McEwen or Stickwalker. God, I hate risking someone else! But I'd pay every cent I have to protect Hayley...and more.

I speak of the devil and she appears:

"Grandpa! You've been mumbling again."

"Where was I?" (I knew. Just wondering how much of my ramble she or Brenda heard).

You were heading out to Basics. Mansfield's Town Band showed up."

I looked. My finger was still there. I started reading again. They hadn't heard:

Our ranks swelled as our color guard was joined by Mansfield's brass band. We made room, glad for the accompaniment and show of support.

There were hooters too. Mockers. Also a few scofflaws whose "rich" parents paid the three hundred required for a replacement.

During a lull Pink-Cheeks recognized a heckler he had played ball with. "Darren," he yelled, "There's gonna be a draft. They send you where they want in a draft."

Darren was nonplussed. "Where in Hell that is Ollie, I'll see you there."

It was prescient, his comment. It was Hell they got sent to. It didn't matter to the senders if the boys were enlistees or draftees. They both were Bucktails. The two met and died - at Chancellorsville.

Their exchange got me to thinking. So Pink-Cheeks first name was Oliver! Was this Cause worth dying for? Was I caught up in its glory or the grief of losing Dad? It didn't matter, I guess. I was in the Army now.

As if on cue, Major Wright halted us in front of a large colonial. Its clapboard painted white. Weathered, needed repainted. It was amazing how that man's voice would carry. "This house was a hideout for the Underground Railroad." he said. "Our Cause."

Saul harrumphed at that. The Major gave him the evil eye but turned back to the front of the column. He might have been doubting the wisdom of "hiring" Saul.

I asked Saul why the scorn.

"Sentiments go up with the smoke of battle," he said. "Keep your head down."

So far Saul had advised keeping my mind open, my mouth shut, my head down. I noted that Saul was not heeding his own advice on the second count.

He made a point of telling us where he stood. Our scout was not impressed with us "soldiers."

The band dropped off at the end of town. We continued east toward Troy. We "quick-stepped" it. Three hours and one tall mountain later we took another break beside a large cornfield west of town. Pink-Cheeks, one of the asskissers, sweating profusely, traded his standard and corporalship for a place back in line. His failure did not humble him enough to shut him up. "That corn is belt-high to a tall Injun," he said.

In response our only half-breed walked out into the field. It was belt-high. Higher actually.

Pink-cheeks was a know-it-all that didn't know it yet.

Saul said from the field, "You ain't seen a tall injun, Boy!"

Pink-Cheeks was confused. "You're 6 1/2 feet tall. That's not tall? What in Hell is a tall Injun?"

We found out later.

Saul knelt in a row. Came back with a handful of seedy black poop. "Sow," he said, "and her cubs. Sleepin' in the corn, eatin' berries."

I saw some weave in the cornstalks headed for a stonerow. "They're not sleepin'," I said. "They're runnin'."

I pointed to the field edge. Three black rumps scooted over the stone fence.

"You got sniper's eyes, Augustus," Saul said. "There'll be meat here, come fall." He then gathered us around and, indicating the stone fence, he said, "Bucktails! How far?"

Most thought 300 yards. Pink-Cheeks, used to being right, said 250.

I disagreed with them all. "I think it's closer to 400. There's a 100 yard dip in that field. It's hard to see."

"It's 377 yards," Saul said. He scoffed. "Some sharpshooters! Always, Always, Always, know how far. You'd a' kilt some heads of green corn today, shootin' that low. He smeared the bear scat on Pink-Cheek's forehead. The know-it-all trembled. "Smell it!" Saul said. "And remember! If you had been tradin' shots today you'd a' only got one off. Too low! And he'd a' got you" - he made a pistol out of his hand and pointed at Pink-Cheek's poopy forehead - "right there!" We looked. Saw a white spot in the middle of the dark smear. He repeated the lesson. "Know how far!"

This time Major Wright gave Saul a look of approval.

Pink-Cheeks was wiping the poop off. "How'd you know exactly? You didn't walk it off."

Saul just walked away.

I figured the Breed just knew. By experience. The same way Injun Joe knew Peggy Sue wasn't wearing bloomers. And, another lesson learned: Know the distance.

We gathered back to the columns, started toward Troy. That field ran into a smaller field which encompassed some farm buildings and a white frame house. Very neat, flowers bloomed along it. A big-eared man in coveralls was helping a lady with her baby into a wagon. He didn't seem happy about that effort. She seemed resolute.

We met later.

ALL ABOARD!

Major Wright was making sure his men were on the train. This was not a troop train. We were spread out among the other passengers. Seems the B & O refused to interrupt its normal Saturday night trip to Harrisburg.

Steam Engine 080 huffed and puffed healthily up hill and down dale to Harrisburg. Known as Old Warhorse because the Union depended on him for troop and material transport, we too, met again.

Major Wright, Pink-Cheeks, Saul and I shared a coach with the young mom and her two-year-old son. Her name was Mildred Jonas. She had been driven in by her brother-in-law. She was being met by her captain husband and staying with him at Camp Curtin.

"She might be horny." whispered Saul. "She'll find officers quarters is just a bigger tent on a wood floor. Hope she ain't a moaner."

Like I said - Saul Poorbaugh was a carnal man.

"How much longer is this conflict going to last?" she asked.

Pink-Cheek's answer was cocksure. He was out to impress the lady. I found myself really building a dislike for the guy. "No more'n a month after us Bucktails start shootin'," he bragged.

Not impressed, she looked at me quizzically.

"I honestly do not know, Ma'am."

Major Wright agreed saying, "It's been two years since Sumter. The Rebels have proven to be quite resilient."

Mrs. Jonas had not taken her eyes off me. I felt she was appraising me like Peggy Sue. "Hmmm," is all she said.

We disembarked the next morning in Harrisburg. Captain Jonas had a buggy waiting. She did her "We've missed you soo much!" routine. Pecked her husband on the cheek and climbed in with their son in the middle. The Captain seemed more embarrassed than glad. He was a smaller younger version of Big Ears. We Bucktails saluted as he drove by. He saluted back because he had to. His son had big ears like his dad.

Captain Jonas seemed stiff to me. Saul, who called things as he saw them might have said it best: "How in hell did that man **ever** make a baby?"

We shouldered our packs, gathered back in our column, started walking the eleven miles along Ridge Road to Curtin. The officers rode up and took their stations. The buggy rounded the next bend and was gone.

## Chapter 23

# J. E. P. Stickwalker

On the way **the Tall Injun** joined us.

He emerged from the treeline, strode beside Saul and me, just like he belonged. And he did. No one would **ever** argue.

I read of these men, originally thought giants a creation of fantasy. Dad taught me they lived, were very rare. A friendship with one was a lifelong treasure.

He was a full head taller than me. I kept stealing glances. How could he be so quiet? The rest of the column didn't even know. Lieutenant Caulfield spurred his mount forward to tell the Colonel and Major. Captain Stone, besides me, couldn't keep his eyes off him either.

His every aspect was...long: Feet, legs, arms, torso, face...all long. And he had the saddest face! What I thought at first were tattoos, were scars. Battle scars. Those huge yellow teeth only showed when he was grinning or gritting, the latter(while fighting) occurring more than the former. This Injun did not smile a lot. And when he lost teeth, from a blow or a shot, he'd shake it off and his teeth would grow back. Each hand had six long fingers. I assume he had twelve toes - He wore mocs with leggings. I never saw his feet. He was beardless with a mane of thick dark dull hair that draped his shoulders. Those shoulders were narrow, stooped. For all that height, he walked bent and still a head taller than me.

Like Saul he wore plain buckskins and a brown slouch hat. No buck tail. That hat was pulled low to mask shifting black eyes that could see farther than Saul. His nose was wide, nostrils flaring. Like a true predator he was always sniffing the breeze, always smelling.

He was, is, the quintessential warrior.

Like Saul, he came from a tribe. In his case, he was a purebred, the sole survivor of the Conestoga giants supposedly wiped out in 1762. Supposedly.

He looked me up and down. Then asked Saul: "He Angus and Mary's boy?

Saul nodded.

He knew Mom was dead. But when Saul told him that Dad was too, that sad face grew sadder. How bad news which panged me could make his face sadder was a mystery, a mystery made clearer when he remarked "Well, what goes around comes around, doesn't it?"

Again, Saul nodded.

"He handy like his Dad?"

"Handier," said Saul.

High praise coming from Saul.

"Hmmm," he answered, appraising me.

I knew then another of Dad's treasures was being transferred to me.

He talked to us, probably revealing more about himself than the rest of our time in the War, probably also because he hadn't talked to anyone in two years. So the words just kinda flowed. He had a low voice, very quiet. Saul and I were the only ones that heard. Of course Saul had probably heard this all before.

Recalling Saul's first lesson - I just listened.

He had fought with Dad and Saul in the Mexican War. Had gone on the Trail to kill Scots-Irish Texicans but then met Dad. Recalling a past "debt," he joined Dad. That was the first time he **ever** sided with the Americans. Before he had fought with the Redcoats. He was too young for the French and Indian War, would have joined the Brits in any event.

I noticed he said fight, not serve.

In The Big Woods if you were old, you were older than your hat. At 112 he was older than my great-great-grandfather Devon's hat. For his tribe though, he was **not** old.

He was born in 1750 to a tiny tribe of giants called the Conestogas. They farmed along the Main Branch of the Susquehanna. Before, they had lived up north along the North Branch of the same river and were called the Susquehannocks. There weren't many. Only a few tall warriors were required to defend their village. They didn't need guns or horses(they thought). Members of the Iroquois Confederacy, they came when called. Also thought the Confederacy needed them more than they needed it. They became more agrarian and peace-loving after moving close to the Dutch Mission.

I thought: Did he say "agrarian?"

He did. Used other big words that convinced me he was an educated man. In fact, he was multi-lingual, had a beautiful writing hand, could cipher as well as the Poorbaugh's.

He walked daily to the Dutch Mission. They weren't real Dutch. They were a sect of Pennsylvania Germans called Moravians. Locals called them Dutch because of their heavy accent. He never converted completely to their ways but they were tolerant and his tribe was too. (Tolerance was a rarity on the Frontier). His teacher was Mary Haverness Hart and he loved her. Mary became his second mom. She gave him his "English" name, naming him after three Biblical warriors and converting his Indian name.

He looked down and extended his huge right hand. We shook. Until then no man had a bigger hand than me. "My name is Stickwalker," he said. "Joshua Esau Peter Stickwalker."

A long name for a long man.

I named three of my sons after this warrior.

We "marched" on and Stickwalker kept on. Pardon me for paraphrasing:

The French and Indians lost their war against the English-speaking whites. This allowed a group of Scots-Irish to move near. They lusted for the Conestoga's rich bottomland. They were scrappers, these whites, rebellious in nature, hated to pay, would rather "take."

Fergus' stories in the barn came to mind.

## The Legend of Augustus McBoone

In 1762 a mounted company of "Rangers" attacked their village. Calling themselves the Paxton Boys, the likkered-up whites massacred the Conestogas, killing all but one - Stickwalker. The desperate boy, at 12 more than seven feet tall and trained as a warrior, charged the whites. He knocked two off their horses, brained them with his stick. He ran for the woods. A group of mounted whites gave chase. He eluded them, made it to the Mission School, dove under its front porch.

The Paxton Boys rode up. Mary Hart, the plucky headmistress of the school, came out.

She stamped her foot. Oh, she was mad! "You boys get out," she said. She pointed back the way they came. Mary spoke with a thick "Dutchy" accent. But it was English and the "Boys", who spoke with an Irish brogue themselves, understood her.

The Rangers milled around, confused. Likkered up they were but not too drunk to know that while white on red violence was accepted in Frontier America, white on white was not. Whites the Moravian were, of the True Faith though different from the Presbyterians.

I again thought of Fergus and Connie in the barn.

Their leader pointed his pistol at Mary. A follower rode up, their **real** leader, if you know what I mean. "Put it down, Lawrence," he said. "She's white."

"She's a damned Anabaptist," growled Lawrence. He kept the pistol pointed. His horse was getting jittery.

"Doesn't matter. She's Protestant and white. We gotta go."

"Gawddammit!" Their leader swore. He wheeled his horse. Stickwalker prayed Mary would not upbraid Lawrence for swearing. She wisely did not.

*"I think Mom would a'," said Hayley.*

*Brenda sputtered.*

*I think Mary was wise. (Note: The girls were still listening). Back to Stickwalker's story:*

The 'follower' tipped his hat. "Devon," the leader called, "Come on! We got a couple of bodies to pick up." Devon cantered away to join the group.

Mary stamped her foot again. "You can come out, Joshua."

When Stickwalker returned he found his parents, his sister, his relatives, his tribesmen - all dead. The Moravian men came and helped him drag all the bodies to a big pile. They argued for burying each one.

"Not the Conestoga way," said Stickwalker. The men left. He piled dried polewood on the bodies.

Made a huge teepee. Then set the pile on fire. He tended that pyre for two days. Then scattered the ashes to the Four Brother Winds.

Thus ended the Conestoga of old.

Thus began J. E. P. Stickwalker's vendetta against the Scots-Irish.

He looked down-mountain to the wide river. "Today I pay the taxes on all Conestoga land, and more," he said.

Fergus didn't tell this part I thought. Dad had told some. Stickwalker filled in the blanks. Most, anyway.

For the next eight decades he hunted the Scots-Irish. His reputation grew. The price on his head grew too. He roamed the Appalachians, befriended all the tribes, learned their language and the language of their enemies. During the Revolution he found the Hessian mercenaries to be racists, too, but not guilty of murdering his family. So he joined the Brits. During the Seminole War he fought with savage Indians and runaway blacks against the Americans. Andy Jackson, a Scots-Irish son of a bitch, doubled his bounty to $1,000. By then he knew German, French and Spanish. And, every Indian language east of the Mississippi. Still the Scots-Irish proliferated. By the tens of thousands they came. He couldn't kill them all! With no land left in the east they went west. Stickwalker followed. On the Trail of Tears, he followed.

Meanwhile, woe to any who dared threaten Mary Hart or her descendants.

This meant a lot to me and mine! I filled in our history from there. Having met the "Tall Injun" I could. He listened close, Stickwalker.

You see, the McBoone's are also descendants of Mary Hart. The name is Scots-Irish and Fergus told how far back we go. But that is only half the line. The other half, the Dutchy half, is through my mom. She was a great-granddaughter of Mary Hart. That makes me a white halfbreed, one-half Scots-Irish, one-half Pennsylvania German.

"So what am I, Grandpa?"

"We're all mutts, Hayley. All grades. There are no purebreds in America."

"We're like B 9, Bob 4 and Dick 5?"

"Yep. Stronger for it too."

*I read on: This part Dad told me:*

In the 1700s the whites did not mix. Or weren't supposed to. Even the Protestants barely tolerated each other. A strict taboo existed between the Scots-Irish Presbyterians and the German Moravians. A

## The Legend of Augustus McBoone

half-century passed before this taboo was tested - with desire. Elizabeth Hart Lehman, a Moravian girl, fell in love with Robert James Heisey, a Brethren. Since they were both Anabaptists this wasn't so bad. They got married in the Brethren church, moved north to Selingrove, built a farm, had children, did well. Their middle daughter, Mary, pushed the taboo further. She fell in love with Duncan McBoone, a backslid Presbyterian but good tinkerer. They ran off to the Williams Port area, had children, built a farm, got married in the Lutheran church. In that order.

"How come it's always the women who break the taboo, Grandpa?"

"Hayley!" said Brenda, still bothered that her daughter thought her tightassed about swearing.(She was).

I answered her honest. "I think pioneer women weren't afraid to go after what they wanted. Like Mandi. Some men were timid that way. I was."

This time Hayley sputtered. "You Grandpa? Timid? Ha!" I went on:

Duncan and Mary had three children, two boys and a newborn girl. A fire engulfed their cabin. Mary died clutching her newborn. Duncan dropped the two boys from the loft then Duncan dropped. Fergus(six) and Angus(three) became orphans and were raised by their grandparents in Selinsgrove. They kept the name McBoone.

Selinsgrove was not far from Paxton Township, Dauphin County. The Scots-Irish had settled there too. Fergus and Angus, being white half-breeds, never fit in with the Scots-Irish "purebreds." One day they were ganged-up on their way home from the store. Fergus did his best but it was eight to two with Angus then being the smallest of them all. Then the "Tall Injun" showed up. The giant, the wanted killer of the Scots-Irish, had a chilling effect on the eight and they ran off. The giant tended to the boy's hurts, walked them home, disappeared into the swamp. This was Angus' first encounter with the "Tall Injun." Years later both grandparents died. With their share of the inheritance the married brothers bought 200 acres from the Strawbridge Estate east of Knoxville. Fergus and Flo were flawed but stayers. Angus and Mary weren't as flawed but Mary died having me and Angus hit the bottle then the road. "Dad met up with you two in Texas. You know better than me what you did together there...Dad did say you three were awful good at killing Mexicans. Zach Taylor let you keep your booty and lifted the price on Stickwalker's head." I looked at Stickwalker. "That about right?"

"So far," he said. He rarely smiled but the corners of his mouth turned up where they had been down.

We "marched" on, quiet a while. I do remember thinking if a man's prime is determined by his ability to kill then Saul and Stickwalker were in the midst of theirs. Mine hadn't begun - yet.

*Hayley had a question. I noticed her mom still quietly seething about her daughter's observation that she could be a hypocritical church lady about swearing. Brenda could be an opinionated hypocrite! But she was trying. She and Ralph had patched things up. Were back in the bedroom - with each other. She was working on being a better mom, was always the greatest secretary. Were we being too hard on her? I have a hard time forgiving but noticed my heart softening like Stickwalker's smile. Back to Hayley's question:* "How come so many pioneer women were named Mary?"

"It was common practice to name a child after an important person in your past. Like Mary Hart."

"None of your girls are named Mary, Grandpa."

"None yet." I smiled.

"Augustus!"

Back to my reading. It's safer:

Saul broke the silence. "How'd you know I was comin'?"

"I've watched from the woods," Stickwalker said. "I sent you a letter two years ago."

"Songbird read it to me. She wrote back after I told Walt I was comin'. Sent it to the Mission."

"Probably still there. I haven't checked since... spring."

Time did not fly in 1862. Not like now - 1945.

"So, why are you here?" I asked Stickwalker.

Stickwalker looked at me like I deserved a dunce cap. "Why to kill Scots-Irish!" he said. "The South is where those bastards are. Those that see themselves as **racially pure**. White trash is what they are."

He spat. He had a real hatred for those people.

"White trash?" I asked.

"Term coined by the Cherokees in the 1820s," he said. "Before the Trail. Describes ignorant whites as poor, lazy, bare of feet, wives are slatterns."

"They didn't go on The Trail?"

Stickwalker shook his head. "They're the ones that moved in.They and their kin. I understand they haven't improved any. The most money they ever made is the $13 per month scrip from Jeff Davis. Least Lincoln can back up his scrip."

I knew about the scrip. Had some of the Union's in my pocket. Didn't know much about the Trail.

Saul chimed in, "Union offered me scrip at first. I stayed home. Then Wright and Caulfield came and offered coin for Reb scalps and ears." He added, "Songbird wrote that in the letter you ain't picked up."

"I don't care about any bounty," said Stickwalker. "It's those racist Scots-Irish white trash I want. Did you know there are Cherokee scouting for the Union?"

"From the South?" I asked.

He nodded. "Big, rugged men. You can't shoot at an accent anymore. You might be killing one of your own."

"Why?"

"Want their land back. I saw this in the Seminole War. Seminoles were open, like the Cherokee. Took in refugees, runaway slaves, the like. But, they like the swamps. Best place to hide - swamps. The whites, the trash, hated the swamps. Wanted the best - the farmland and towns. That damned Andy Jackson, now there's a racist Scots-Irish for you, sent the U.S. Army and they took it. Displaced the Cherokees. The Seminoles fought. Disappeared into the swamps. A few of the Cherokees went into the mountains. The fighters died. Most, though, went to the Reservation in Oklahoma . Those that lived. Called the Trail of Tears, that trek. 'Cause so many died along it. The Reservation, called the Nation now, is a shithole compared to what Jackson stole.

"But they're making it. Still taking in refugees too. Chocktaws, Chippewas, Blacks, me. Saw big puddles of oil there. They use it to roof-coat their shacks. I told them - never sell this land! There aren't enough whales in the world. But, you watch. Someday they'll have to fight for that shithole too."

I pondered his comment. Dad and I had seen oil patches in Potter County as well. Stickwalker joined my short list of far-thinking men.

Saul had a question. "We on the winnin' side this time? I think so, but what do you think?"

"The Union will win," he answered. "Not a question of **if** but **when**. The Union's got the money. The Rebs have got spunk, and better generals. Don't fight among themselves like the Union officers. So far."

Saul got excited at this confirmation. "You think we're in for the richest pickins' ever?"

"For you anyway. But you gotta stay alive. This scrap is more unpredictable than the Mexican War. I just want to be there when those Scots-Irish boys lose their land. See how they like it."

I whispered to Saul. "How many wars has Stickwalker been in?"

"Countin' this one, at least five. Scraps, battles, ambushes... maybe two hundred. He could carpet a big hall with his scalps...if he took 'em."

I believed him. Stickwalker walked softly and carried a big stick. He wore plain buck- skins, allowed nothing to reflect. A huge man, he **always** blended in. You never saw him unless he wanted you to. He could look like a tree trunk until he uncoiled, like today. Tens of thousands had passed by and never saw him there.

Take that long stick. Actually a war club. Think of two Babe Ruth ballbats, lengthwise. The tip, its barrel end was carved in totems and held holes for nails. The bottom half, twice the thickness of Ruth's bat handle, was grooved and knobbed - an atlatl it was, a spear thrower. The wood was hard, harder than ironwood and black with age and blood. It was tight-grained like sycamore, only stronger and heavier and would not shatter. He carried that stick like a wand, a third arm, an extension of his already long self. Saul and I were the only ones in camp capable of hefting that club.

Notice I said **heft**, not **wield**.

A quiver of a dozen fletched spear hybrids stuck above his shoulder. Their points were obsidian, sharper than steel. He wore a wide leather belt, carried a tomahawk as big as a single-bit and a sheathed Green River knife bigger than a Gladius. The handles were all the same - very hard, very black, very dull. There was no shine on Stickwalker, ever.

So, J. E. P. Stickwalker joined our band. I mean, he joined Saul and me. Never signed up. Never a Bucktail and always one. Probably killed more Rebs than all of us together. Came and went as he pleased. As I said earlier: Who would object? He and Saul became Company A's scouts. Were good at that. The best.

I became our armorer. I was the best at that too.

Stickwalker would not eat our food. Preferred to forage. Never stole. Didn't have to. Knew all the wild sources - roots, berries, mushrooms. His favorite meat was snake. Fried snake. Also bugs, big bugs - grasshoppers, beetles, locusts. All dipped in honey. Mmmm!

"Grandpa! Eww!"

*I loved hearing that. She may accuse me of grossing her out. But it's all true.*

## Chapter 24

# CAMP CURTIN

We stayed at Camp Curtin seventeen days. Long enough to get uniforms, rifles and trained. Sorta.

Assembling the rifles earned me a promotion. That's what the citation says anyway. I really think it was extending the ring on a fat lady's finger that brought that second stripe.

Another example of what goes around comes around I guess. I didn't realize it then but that lady wasn't done with me.

Camp was a tent city of thirty thousand soldiers. Bigger than the Bloomsburg Fair grounds and fenced high like a prison. You couldn't find a blade of grass anywhere. Several rubbed white oak pasture trees stood sentinel and provided shelter - for the stock, whose feed was delivered daily. A wide front gate divided us - one side funneled the men, the other the stock and supplies. The buildings were all barns which housed the stock. Soldiers grumbled the animals enjoyed the best accommodations - until they were butchered - then the complaining stopped.

Row after row of high teepee-like tents called Sibley's lined the soldier's section. Saul and I shared one. Stickwalker cut a hole in the fence and slept in the woods.

We "went" in latrines. An area the size of a ball park was cut in long narrow limed ditches. Getting caught peeing outside the latrine earned the punishment of digging and liming a ditch in the dark. When the wind shifted it made eating a real chore.

Two streams crossed camp. Filled with pollution and crawdads they were. Stickwalker would **not** eat those crawdads. Here we took our "warshin." If we had any. Most of us aired out our uniforms at night on a clothesline strung between tents. We slept in our short johns. I thought the bugs at log camp had beaten the soldiers here. Stickwalker wouldn't eat them either.

*"Eww! Grandpa!"*

I saw my first killing at camp. One private stuck his head outside his tent to get cool and fell asleep there. The camp bugler that woke us up cantered by and the horse stepped on the sleeping boy's head. Big horse. Small head. Popped like a cantaloupe, horseshoe imprint on one side of his skull. A detail buried him in the latrine. Scraped dirt and poop over him, read Psalm 23. Lieutenant Stone wrote his parents. How in hell do you tell folks their son stuck his head where it wasn't prudent? I observed the same to Saul who said it wouldn't be the first time imprudence cost a man his life. That proved prophetic.

We now had 97 First Class Men.

Our uniforms were wool and scratchy. Light blue pants and a dark blue jacket with one blue stripe already sewed on. I got two sets and orders to use the one set to make the other bigger. I used sinew. Split the back and lengthened the sleeves and legs. Like the buck's tail on the kepi that sinew has held for eighty- three years.

The Union didn't have any 18-inch shoes so I had to cobble my own. Consequently I did not share the same foot problems as the others. Stickwalker brought me some extra-thick leather from a buff hide stored at his cabin. "That's from a mountain buffalo," he said. "Got it while hunting with Injun Joe. He still up there, hiding from all his women, in Dodge Hollow?"

Saul nodded and I told about meeting Injun Joe at log camp and him not seeing any of Peggy Sue's bloomers.

Saul cackled. Got another crinkle from Stickwalker.

The word got out about my "handiness." I didn't have any sitting-around time, was busy fixing the whole while. This was especially true after we were issued the new Enfields. The breech-loaders were still packed in the box! I spent three days degreasing and assembling nine dozen rifles, another half-day sharpening their triangular pointed bayonets.

The fourth day we sighted our rifles in. Being a sharpshooting outfit we already knew how to shoot - we thought. We had to be taught **how** to shoot... in volley. The idea was not as much accuracy as speed. We had 58 caliber breech-loading single shots. We had to get off three shots per minute. I could do six, four accurately.

We learned a cadence: First Volley - Second Volley - Third Volley - Go! First and third volleymen were standers, second were kneelers. Sergeant Benjamin required three hundred shots a minute into the strawman.

He got them too. Straw literally flew out of the target which was only 50 yards away. The sharpshooters really hooted at that. But Saul insisted it be close. After I showed the Bucktails how to adjust the rear "buck" sight for one hundred yard increments they got less derisive.

In the Civil War most men fell from musket fire - either by sniper or volley. We had rapid-fire

Gatlings and cannons that fired solid balls, canisters or shot shells. You would be gloss on a rock if one of those cannon shells hit you. Mist. Still, what soldiers on both sides dreaded most was rifle fire.

We Bucktails thought we were sooo good. Took Saul to bring us down a peg or two. He scoffed at us. "That straw man out there is **not** a Reb. It's exposed and still. It's not yellin' or chargin', hidin' behind a tree or shootin' back. Right now the wind is blowin' at our back. What the hell happens if the smoke is in our face? Or the sun? We're gonna see pigstickers comin' at us through that smoke, outa the sun."

Lieutenant Caulfield tried to argue with Saul. He and Captain Jonas from the 4th Pennsylvania Cavalry had ridden up. "In five minutes there won't be any Rebs standing to stick us," he said.

"Bullshit!" responded Saul, not a whit deterred by rank. "Do the cipher! In five minutes we'd need fifteen shells. We got twelve. What we gonna fling at 'em that last minute? Boogers?"

The men chuckled. Lieutenant Caulfield allowed he'd have to think about it. The Captain frowned. Held his peace. This wasn't **his** outfit. He was the officer that reluctantly saluted us when we got off the train. Big Ear's brother. Mildred's husband.

## The Legend of Augustus McBoone

They rode off, the Lieutenant plainly perplexed. We did hear Captain Jonas say that the squawman needed whipped for insubordination.

Caulfield shook his head. "The squawman is telling us we need more shells. He's right. Whip him? Good God, Basil!"

My opinion of Lieutenant Caulfield increased after that. Can't say the same for Captain Jonas.

Saul had heard the peacock say he should be whipped. He didn't say anything but...Jonas was in his sights after that.

Lieutenant Caulfield requested our allotment of shells be increased to twenty-four.

We got eighteen.

Saul didn't like us bunching up to shoot either. "Volley shootin' is alright, if they're close. I think we should spread out some, get behind cover. Then volley shoot."

"Why?" asked Pink-Cheeks who peeked at Charlottesville when it was imprudent.

"Think on it, Snot Nose." Saul didn't like Pink-Cheeks but since the Bucktails were listening he thought they should be told. "When we're bunched up, we're easy targets. Volley or cannon fodder. If I was a Reb sergeant I'd tell my men to shoot low. Get kneelers and standers, that's why. Put us out of our misery later."

Saul's weapon of choice was his long gun. At least four pounds heavier and six inches longer than the Enfield it was made for mountain men to kill grizzlies. His Hawken could send a 70 caliber slug 2000 yards and still bore a hole in an oak railroad tie. It had a set trigger, that gun. That is, two triggers - one to "set" the gun to fire, the "hair" to touch her off. I filed that "hair" so it was touchy, mighty touchy. I made its bullets too. Etched McB in the base of the mold.

The last day of shooting Stickwalker approached Sergeant Benjamin. He'd been sitting, watching us practice, smoking that vile tobacco, no flies bothered Stickwalker. "Can I take a turn?" he asked.

Sergeant Benjamin shrugged, looked around for a rifle to borrow. Too late.

In seconds three projectiles struck the straw man: an axe in his head, the knife and spear side by side in the bull. The spear had impaled the target, supported it after it toppled back.

"Jesus!" swore the Sergeant, who had a salty tongue.

Stickwalker trotted toward us. He had righted the target, belted his axe, sheathed his knife. In one paw he held his stick, the other the spear. He handed me the hybrid. "Can you fix it?" he asked.

I examined its four-foot length. Straight. Hickory shafted. Eagle feather fletched. A broken six-inch point of black obsidian. "With steel," I said.

I went to the smith's. Sawed off the end of an extra bayonet. Sharpened it. Fastened it with sinew to the spear end. Painted the winding dull black to match the shaft. Stickwalker used it. Still has it. That buck sinew is strong.

Lieutenant Caulfield was at the smith's. His horse had thrown a shoe and didn't cotton to the replacement process. The gelding kicked at the blacksmith while the Lieutenant tried to soothe him. Stickwalker came, cupped his hands over the horse's eyes, spoke gentle to him, French I think. The horse calmed. I took a shoe, measured it, bent it one-handed, nailed it on. "You are a strong young man," said the Lieutenant.

"Not as strong as he," I answered, and pointed to a supply wagon. The smith had been struggling with replacing a wheel all day. Stickwalker simply picked up the end and held it while the smith replaced the wheel. Work finished, the human jack let the wagon down. He then found a shady spot in the barn and stretched out. The doors were open, the barn funneled in a pleasant breeze.

Stickwalker and I were making impressions that day. While I was showing my versatility and strength to Lieutenant Caulfield, Stickwalker was showing perceived laziness to Captain Jonas and two new recruits. My impression was good. Stickwalker's was bad.

How could Stickwalker **ever** make a bad impression you ask? Because some men are ignorant, racist sons of bitches, I answer. The new recruits, the Scagline brothers from Philadelphia, were all three.

At Curtin we ate twice a day, in shifts of 5,000 men. We got our chow while in a line then sat down. We had fifteen minutes. We were first. The trumpet blew for the evening gather. Stickwalker preceded us, sat crosslegged at the end of the table. He was as tall as the rest on their chairs and he sat on his rump. He looked like a dumb docile Injun sitting there, not eating, minding his own business, smoking that vile pipe while the flies bothered the rest of us. Captain Jonas and his cavalrymen were part of our brigade. They sat down at the same time. The Scagline Brothers had chosen a two-year enlistment as Union wagoners rather than a four-year prison term. This was their first and last supper. The two had seen Stickwalker lounging, always sitting, had not bothered to research him, had not seen him on the range. The Scagline's were determined to make a show. Racists to the core the two decided to have a "chat" with the Injun. The

## The Legend of Augustus McBoone

shoulder-strikers from a Philadelphia union were used to scaring "mere" men.

They didn't scare us mere men, least of all Stickwalker.

They sauntered over, Harry and Vernon Scagline, maybe 300 pounds each, big hairy unshaven men used to pushing people around. They hated Niggers, Kikes, Eyetalians, Micks and didn't know jack about Injuns, didn't care. The privates politely asked Sergeant Benjamin if they could visit with the red man, yonder. Sarge sized them up and shrugged. "Your funeral," he said. How prophetic that turned out to be!

"Trouble," muttered Saul as they approached. He didn't seem too concerned.

"I see them," answered Stickwalker. He placed both hands under the table. Hunched his shoulders so he'd look smaller.

Harry, the oldest, got to Stickwalker first.

Saul moved a little, lengthened his leg.

Big mistake, Vernon, I thought.

"You know how to march, Injun?" asked Harry.

"Yep."

"How to sleep?"

"Yep."

"How to shoot?"

"Yep."

"But...no gun?"

"Don't need a gun."

Harry leaned close to Stickwalker. Placed his right hand on the back of Stickwalker's neck intending to squeeze it. His left hand on the table. He smelled horsey. He started to whisper in Stickwalker's left ear and his eyes widened.

"It's comin' now," I thought.

Harry discovered he couldn't get his hand around the Injun's neck, he couldn't squeeze. This man was a helluva lot bigger than he thought. At the same time he saw the knife.

There was a flash, a flurry of movement and Stickwalker towered over Harry. Vernon stepped backward and tripped over Saul's outstretched leg. He sat, looked up...

At a glowering nine-foot tall giant.

"Harry!'

But Harry was looking down at his thumb. The four fingers of his left hand still held the table but his thumb was wriggling by itself, an inchworm inching along.

Then the point of Stickwalker's Green River scraped the underside of Harry's chin. A couple of whiskers fell. I had done a real good job of sharpening that knife that morn.

Then Harry's severed hand started gouting blood toward Saul. "You better get your brother to the surgeon," he said. "God, he's bleedin' all over!"

Stickwalker lowered his blade. Harry and Vernon rushed out. Harry was holding his stump and whimpering. His thumb, not aware it was dead yet, moved another inch.

I didn't know fingers moved like that.

Stickwalker picked the thumb up, bit on it like a pretzel, chewed and swallowed.

Half the thumb was left.

"Pass the salt," he said.

"*Eww! Grandpa!*"

*I loved hearing that.*

A glance passed between Saul and Stickwalker.

Uh-oh, I thought.

The two went on a scout after midnight.

Harry and Vernon were buried before noon. In a latrine. They had been found, after breakfast, in their beds, their throats slit. Stickwalker watched, smoking that pipe. The gravediggers backfilled over the bodies and left. No one read the 23rd. I doubt anyone sent a letter to Philadelphia either.

Seventeen days is not a long time to train a soldier. We got our uniforms and guns, learned to shoot in volley and to march in formation. To the Brass it was important that we get there and shoot. The rest we learned on the job.

The Brass also wanted us to know who they were, what colors they wore, who was Boss. The rank and file called the Brass the **Powers That Be**.

To distinguish function our army wore different colored insignias. The Infantry wore blue, the Cavalry yellow, Artillery wore red, Medical wore green. Within their colors were the Powers That Be. It was kind of a **pyramid**. The President was the Big Brass. Since he was **elected** he got to wear what he wanted, usually a black suit and a high hat. Every rank on down was **selected**. First was **General** of the Army. Under him were Generals of the **Army Corps**. A **Corps** was comprised of **Divisions** each of which was led by a **Major-General**. Each

Division was made up of **Brigades,** headed by a **Brigadier-General**. Each Brigade was made up of **Regiments** then led by a **Colonel**. The Regiments were alphabetized into **Companies** which were headed by a **Major** or **Captain**. Each company was split into **Platoons,** each led by a **Lieutenant**. Then came the workhorse of every army - the **Sergeants**. He wore three stripes, called a chevron, and led a **Squad**. (If he was Cavalry his squad was called a **Troop**). Under the Sergeants were **Corporals** who wore two stripes. Under them, and everybody in the whole wide world it seemed, were us **Privates**. We wore one stripe, did what we were told, went where we were told. We were mollified by calling us "First Class Men."

This was the ideal structure. By the time I got there the structure had morphed into ranks determined by politics, ambition, ability or luck. The latter two helped me for by July 1863, everybody in the whole wide world called me Lieutenant. Well, Saul and Stickwalker called me Gus.

Here's the beginning:

Before we left Curtin, Lieutenant Caulfield left me another stripe. I was now a Corporal. I was not, as Saul said, an ass-kisser. I earned my promotions. My first citation told of my handiness, how I'd assembled and sighted-in our rifles, how I was able to help the smith. It did not mention the fat lady's ring.

Colonel Llewellyn was a surgeon, a real-deal doctor who ran his roost so to speak. The roost did not include his household. His wife Polly ran that. I mean, name a doctor who has **time** for that. Polly had come to Curtin, had followed her husband in his various duty stations. That was a passel, they had been married thirty years, had seven sons. Each son was a Union soldier stationed somewhere, not there. Their years together had been good ones, especially for Polly. She had put on a few "extra" pounds. Maybe one hundred extra. To use the polite vernacular of the day she was "pleasingly plump." You had to be polite around those two. He was **the** Colonel. They were the most influential couple in camp. They earned it. He had turned down promotions to general - that would take him out of the operating room where he was needed most.

Polly's wedding band was pinching. She couldn't get it off. It hurt. So, the Brass called me. Stickwalker made a stinky slippery salve that cut the swelling. He told the recipe to me (it's base plant was leeks) and I removed the ring. It slipped off easy, just like Flo squirting out a baby.

*"Grandpa!"*

I measured her finger with sinew. She needed a band twice the size of the original. I took the ring to the smith's where I cut and melted it. I then cut and melted a $5 gold piece. Rolled them together.

I made it wider and thicker, stuck it on a poker to the place I wrapped the string, cooled and polished it. That ring shone as bright as the day she was first shagged.

"Augustus!"

"Grandpa!"

Yep. Both still listening:

Colonel Llewellyn put it on. Polly was thrilled. Gave me a big matronly hug, whispered she had seven sons but there was always room for another. I said "Aw shucks, wasn't nothin'," and left. Forgot all about that gold piece.

Millie Jonas told me later that she showed all the officer's wives.

"Just **where** did Mrs. Jonas tell you Grandpa?"

This was Wicked Girl who knew some of the story.

"Later, Hayley:"

I sewed that second stripe on with sinew. Saul said, "Good. It's blue and dull. Not shiny like the Cavalry's. Those boys are targets for snipers." I earned another title with that stripe. I was now Corporal Augustus McBoone, Company Armorer.

I got a $5 raise too. From $13 to $18 a month. It was sixty-six days before I broke even on my investment in Polly's ring.

What goes around comes around my dad said.

## Chapter 25

# MARCH TO D. C.

Rumors that Bobby Lee and 50,000 Rebs were marching on D.C. began the morning of our tenth day at Curtin. By night his force had grown to 500,000. This rumor was not started by the wives. It started with their husbands. I had learned at log camp that gossip was also relished and spread by men. It was human nature to tell tales but men liked to blame women.

Anyway, with Bobby Lee coming, the Powers That Be thought they required protection in D.C.

In a week dandelions started springing up in the parade ground. There weren't enough recruits left to stomp them down. I watched the grass spread. Soldiers were leaving faster than they could be replaced. When our turn came Old Warhorse was full so we had to walk.

Well, we peons walked. The officers rode.

## The Legend of Augustus McBoone

Our officers rationalized our Company needed practice. What it really meant - the Union was not relying entirely on balloon sightings to see if the country north of Washington was free of Rebs. The Powers That Be wanted Company A to find out.

We didn't find any Rebs. The balloonists were right. We did have some adventures I will recount here.

Before we left we had to get a company picture taken. That man Brady made us stand in formation, bayonets fixed, rifle butts on the ground. That's me and Saul in the back. Stickwalker said it was bad luck and wouldn't do it. So, no Civil War image exists of the giant. Only one of Saul. In fact, for most of the other boys, all dead now except me, that picture may be the only youthful image of them. Most, like Pink-Cheeks were dead in less than a year. Company A, wearing our bucktails, stood there. 102 of us including officers, in total, in our glory. I could name every one. A year later that photo could not have been taken. 75 were dead. Of the 27 living 24 were still hospitalized and 3 were mustered out. Two of the last three carried visible wounds. The one seemingly unwounded carried wounds that were invisible - the kind that **never** heal.

Marching was simple - for me. A few newbies had trouble but the walk to D.C. cured that. Right face, left face, forward and halt - that much we knew, by D.C. Other maneuvers, battle maneuvers, we learned after D.C. We kept the same formation as we had approaching Curtin. The one change was we marched four abreast instead of two this time. The roads were wider and other travelers got out of our way. Saul grumbled about us being bunched up. His point was made at Charlottesville. But that was the next May and cost one rank of boys too dead to spread out.

Stickwalker, Saul and I made up the rear. We were **always** being yelled at to close ranks. Saul, the main dawdler, "explained" us as too long-legged to maintain the eighteen inches required by the Army. I noticed the officers kept a good distance between their mounts and our host **after** hearing Saul complain.

You could be insubordinate and right in Company A. Not so with the 4th Pennsylvania Cavalry. Captain Jonas would have you whipped for not following the rules. He was more bureaucrat than soldier, that martinet, and it cost him. Saul called him a g-d peacock.

Since it took a week to get to D.C., behind us rolled two covered wagons - one with supplies to support Company A, the other to support, well, me. This particular wagon was driven by Ambrose Kuhl. He drove my armorer's wagon which contained a small forge and grindstone, gun and wagon parts, tools, and gunpowder and ammo designed to last until we made permanent camp. Since he had the best voice it also contained his guitar.

I still carried the heaviest haversack. I was a corporal and could have placed that on the wagon but my pack carried special tools, Dad's tools, and I was reluctant to relinquish control. I was seventeen, tall and strong. The extra weight no big deal.

We learned this new cadence on the road:

**Go left! Go right!**

**Go left, Go right, Go left, Go right!**

**You left your wife and 48 kids without any provisions!**

**Go left, Go right! (Repeat)**

Saul said, "Never knew a man with 48 kids. Did you Stickwalker?"

Stickwalker didn't either.

Saul continued. "There was a chief at Kinzua with a longhouse, six wives and thirty kids. Twenty-four daughters and six sons, he had. The kids got to fightin', the wives to bickerin'. Raised such a racket the chief took off. A week later his Council came lookin'. Family hadn't realized he was missin'!"

I couldn't help it. "He must have kept 'em well provisioned," I said.

"*Grandpa!*"

*Still listening:*

"That he did." said Saul

"Where'd he go?" I asked.

"Walked east in the Big Woods to the White Knoll area. Built a shanty head of Dodge Hollow. Became a hermit. You met him. Name of Injun Joe."

"Injun Joe! He'd been a chief? He told me Peggy Sue wasn't wearing bloomers. How'd he know?"

Saul laughed. "If you had thirty females after you all the time, you'd know."

"Do Injun women wear bloomers?" I asked this kinda quick, not thinking of the consequences. I wanted to know.

"*Why, Grandpa?*"

*This was Wicked Girl. I ignored her:*

Saul was insulted. His did, in the winter. He then changed the subject. "Stickwalker," he said. "Were all Joe's wives red? Weren't a couple white?"

Stickwalker nodded and grinned. A rare sight! Just the mention of Injun Joe was funny.

"Where is White Knoll?" I'd heard of it. Never been there.

"Way north of here," said Saul. "In the Big Woods. High country. Lots of trees, critters and snow. And now, Injun Joe. We been there, me and Jesse. You been there Stickwalker? Before Injun Joe?"

This time Stickwalker talked. "Long before Joe, who is old enough to be Saul's daddy. Between wars. Hunted up there with Cornplanter. He was a Seneca chief too. His dad was white, John O'Bail, an Irish fur trader." So O'Bail was Cornplanter's white name.

Saul who had a red dad and a white mom thought the tribes a lot more accepting of other skins. This was true answered Stickwalker, if they liked you. If they didn't they'd tan your skin and stick your head on a pole...

"Halt!" ordered Sarge. We took a water break by a stream crossed by a covered bridge. The wagons were each pulled by two draft horses. I grabbed two empty canvas buckets and took a path to the stream. Ambrose followed. While filling the buckets I examined the bridge. Ten ends of squared timber supports were exposed, nine branded with a King's Arrow, one McB. I showed the brands to Stickwalker, Saul and Ambrose. Heard the Big Injun mutter "What goes around comes around!"

Along the way Stickwalker noted we were only a few miles south of his warrants along the Susquehanna. We marched west to Carlisle then took a pike by the same name south to Gettysburg. Found a quiet pastoral town, maybe three times the size of Wellsborough. We didn't see any Rebs there in August 1862 but by July 1863 they were all over the place. We took Emmitsburg Road south from Gettysburg, could see Seminary Ridge to the west, Cemetery Ridge to the east, crossed the Mason Dixon Line nine miles later. We were now in Maryland. Still no Rebs.

It was typical summer weather, warm nights, hot days. Beautiful rolling farm country. Older men in coveralls, their bonneted wives and daughters, some boys, worked the fields and orchards. All busy piling hay, shocking corn, gathering produce or picking fruit to put by or sell. Along the main we saw the ravages of confiscation and war. We saw no young men.

At sundown one evening Saul and Stickwalker returned with a bushel of peaches they bought from a lady "manning" a produce stand along a side road. Buying meant that Stickwalker paid. Otherwise the bushel counted as a spoil of war.

We sat around the campfire, telling stories, singing songs, peach juice streaking dirty faces. Pink-Cheeks, pig that he was, finished first. He rolled the pit around in his mouth, sucking the last of the juice. Ambrose Kuhl sat nearby. He had just set aside his guitar, just finished his song. Ambrose was a skinny farm kid. Pink-Cheeks was loud and mean, Ambrose quiet and kind. Pink-Cheeks was used to getting his way, Ambrose stayed out of everyone's way. His pit cleaned, Pink-Cheeks approached Ambrose. He spit the seed square in Ambrose's face, it's sharp end stuck in his cheek. Pink-Cheek laughed, pointed at Ambrose like Junior Sykes had pointed at me. Pink-Cheeks did not see Ambrose's eyes slit. The ground erupted at Pink-Cheek's feet. Ambrose rose fast and mad and swinging. He caught his adversary square and knocked him down.

I was the Corporal, senior to those privates. Nearest to them too. Saul and Stickwalker never moved, content to see the show, correctly expecting Pink-Cheeks to get his due. I was expected to assert some authority, I know, but it took **forever** for me to get there and break up those two.

"Augustus! You allowed that fight to continue?"

"Yep. I was at the Turkey Ranch when Ralph thrashed Mort too."

Brenda shut up.

*Hayley didn't say a word.*

Ambrose had him down. He whaled as Pink-Cheeks wailed. I finally pulled Ambrose off. Pink-Cheek's nose streamed blood, his lips were smashed, there was a gash over one eye. Ambrose had the red mark on his cheek and the pit inside his hard fist. He struggled, pleaded with me to let him finish the job. I told him he had. Two buddies escorted Pink-Cheeks to his bedroll. I dragged the fuming Ambrose to his wagon where Stickwalker handed him the last peach. Ambrose's had been smashed in the fight. Ambrose thanked Stickwalker for his generosity.

"Worth it," he said.

I never saw Stickwalker eat a peach. He was kind and generous as was Ambrose.

Just don't piss either one off.

I was struck by the number of Copperheads tolerated by the Union. Still am. The literal snakes ended up in our cookpot. The figurative ones, the Reb sympathizers, should have. Actually, we didn't have a pot big enough to boil their little fingers, there were so many. In two instances I witnessed these turncoats biting their own tail.

We were in Reb territory. We hadn't seen any yet but we'd crossed into northern Virginia. Virginia was a member of the Confederacy, Bobby Lee's home state, he was bound to find out about our incursion. We were hoping he'd get mad and make a mistake. He might have gotten mad, but he made no mistake, which was why the war lasted four long years.

Well, he did make one. In July 1863. It cost the Confederacy the war.

One morning we kept the sun at our back. Wasn't D.C. south?

"We're bait" said Saul. "Cannon fodder. Don't worry. We've scouted far. There's no sign of recent Reb activity."

We still managed to raise dust and ruffles on the way. The dust came first. The ruffles later.

*"Did you know those Virginia girls sewed ruffles on their bloomers?"*

*"Grandpa!"*

*Still listening:*

We marched into that Copperhead countryside where we were "supposed" to act civilized, "expected" to be polite. It was the "Christian" thing to do. I'd heard **that** before.

*"Grandpa! You're being ornery and snide!"*

"You try telling that to a company of Bucktails, Hayley."

"You're the only one left. I'm telling you!"

Back to my story:

Most Copperheads dared not provoke the occupying Union army. The women usually just turned their backs. A couple of male tail-biters, however, got openly hostile.

The first of these shocked his corn along the road. His farm had **not** been overrun by the Rebs. He was an excellent farmer, coveralled, a massive hairy bull in his late prime. A girl in a yellow bonnet helped him. She turned her back to us. Still working, she swayed provocatively. To a man, we stared.

The burly farmer stepped between us and his female. Held a long scythe. I thought he was protecting his wife.

A rail fence also separated the field and the road, the couple and us soldiers. Captain Stone rode up, tipped his hat, asked if we could water our horses from his pond down the road.

The Captain **asked**. Very polite. Very controlled.

I can hear the answer today. That bearded sob told our Captain to get the hell off his land!

## The Legend of Augustus McBoone

"No!" said Hayley, recognizing the affront.

It was custom to allow a company of soldiers water, no matter what side.

Captain Stone said, "Yes, Sir!" Tipped his hat again and rode back to the rest of the column. He rode by me, his jaw set, his face firm.

The girl turned to face us then. She was young and pretty. And married. The low sun glinted off her wedding band. And off the ring in the farmer's left ear. It did not reflect off the scythe blade. That needed sharpened, I thought.

All that earringed Copperhead had to do was let us go. But he had a temper. He just could **not** let us pass. "His son was an officer with Bobby Lee and proud of it, he yelled! He had stayed behind to tend this big farm."

"And his son's wife," said Saul marching behind me.

"What do you mean?" I was naive, believed in chivalry and all that.

"Look at the girl," said Saul. "Bruises on her cheek and wrists. That son is dead. She's a widder, I'd wager."

Captain Stone had heard Saul. "Don't take that bet, Corporal." He had seen the bruises too.

Saul continued. "The missus is lookin' out that house winder, yonder."

I looked then. Saw another yellow bonnet. Saul had great eyes. "Huh!" I said, surprised. Ambrose Kuhl, driving the team behind us had heard. He too was surprised.

But not the Captain or Saul or Stickwalker. Older men. They knew.

"Forward, ho!" yelled the Captain. He stole some of Sergeant Benjamin's thunder, had to let off some steam. There was a hatch on the pond. Fish bumped the surface, made little circles.

We marched up a slight rise. 880 yards out Saul stopped my wagon. The farmstead seemed even prettier a half-mile away. "Damn your Rebel loving way," exclaimed Saul as he rested the long rifle across the wagon and aimed. He set the back trigger. Stickwalker got behind Saul, bent a little. No breeze. No ripples in the pond. Just dimples from the fish.

The Hawken boomed. Red dust flew from the chimney.

"Center, high," said Stickwalker.

## The Legend of Augustus McBoone

"Where I aimed," exclaimed Saul, starting his reload.

While the farmer and the yellow bonneted girl ran for the house, I joined in. I got two off with my Enfield, both direct hits.

The farmer brandished a rifle at the window. Saul splintered the sash beside him and the rifle disappeared inside.

Saul's next 70 caliber toppled the chimney.

The men cheered. The bugles bugled. The men sang "Yankee Doodle."

That evening we camped in a wooded copse three miles west of the valley. Saul and Stickwalker went on a scout, splitting up, Saul going east, Stickwalker west. Stickwalker got back hours before Saul. That morning Saul turned in a salt and pepper scalp with an attached left ear. Lieutenant Caulfield paid him three silver dollars. Told him to keep the ring. It was worth at least two dollars.

"I bedded both wimmen!" he bragged. They weren't weepin'. Jesse couldn'a done better."

"Who's Jesse?" asked the incredulous Pink-Cheeks.

"My twin," answered Saul. "He stayed behind with the wives. He's too hotheaded, mean. Not fit for war."

Captain Stone sent me and Ambrose back to bury the body and repair the chimney. It was the noble thing to do. Who else could fix the chimney before winter?

They were glad to see us, those two. Fixed us lunch. We did the work and caught up with the company. I even sharpened that scythe.

Saul was right. There was no weeping.

The second Copperhead incident occurred west of D.C., while we were still in Virginia. A big wagon, loaded with supplies for the Union Commissary, had gotten stuck in the ditch. The driver had passed us on our right, whipping his team, in a big hurry. We found out later why. The soft gravel had given way. The heavy-laden wagon rested there, sunk to its axle.

Travelers passed by, too busy to stop and help.

The driver sat on the plank seat, cursing and whipping his mules and the black man in front. "Damn your lazy ass Ratchet, pull that team!"

## The Legend of Augustus McBoone

Ratchet was the first real slave I had ever seen. Some folks think because they own you, you're dumb. Ratchet was not.

"You can't force 'em, Suh! The load's too heavy."

In answer the driver sent a long lash Ratchet's way. It opened a gash along the back of the slave's neck. Had to hurt.

"I can unload us, Suh! Won't take long."

That man kept cursing and whipping. Those two thick-hided mules seemed oblivious to the abuse. Used to it. The slave cringed at every crack.

Crack! Crack! Crack!

*"Go get him, Grandpa!"*

*Hayley knew this story.*

I saw red.

He thought I was helping. "Soldier, I was just..." was all he got out. I threw him bodily into the muck. His whip went flying.

A skinny small man. The mouthy kind that thinks they're bigger than they really are.

The cock of the walk where he came from.

Not here.

He scrambled back up. Muddy, mad, screaming profanities, threatening...me.

I ignored him. Turned to help Ratchet. Heard Saul say, "Really?"

The small man had retrieved his whip. Drew it back to lash at me. He thought he was really good with that whip.

The huge bore of Saul's Hawken was pointed at his belt buckle. It didn't waiver.

Stickwalker, who had hung back, came up then.

Imagine this scene: A small slaveowner facing three large men. One is in uniform, the other two are savages and one of these is a giant. The big men were all armed. He had a whip.

He had guts that little man. More ego than common sense. Saul set the trigger on the Hawken. We heard the audible click. The cocky slaveowner tossed his whip into the wagon.

Knowing Saul had the situation under control, Stickwalker and I turned toward the wagon. A streak of blood ran down the back of Ratchet's shirt. The mule team chewed grass he had fed them, hides too thick to feel any pain. Good teams respond to voice commands, not whips.

I handed the reins to the Negro, instructed him when to pull the team. Stickwalker and I got behind the wagon, lifted and pushed. Our teamwork paid off. The wagon bed slid off the hump holding it, the wheels got purchase, Ratchet pulled the team and wagon up to the road.

The Major rode back. In his deep voice wanted to know what all the commotion was.

The little man whined. "I was whippin' my propity when this sumbitch threw me off my wagon."

That right, Corporal?"

I nodded, opened my mouth to explain but Stickwalker broke in.

"He thought about whipping the Corporal too. But did not, upon reflection."

The Major sized things up quick. "You intended to whip one of **my** men?" His intent was clear. That whip could be used to whip him.

Ratchet spoke up, defending his master. "But he didn't, Suh! He was just mad, Suh!"

I'm thinking, every white man to Ratchet was Suh.

"What is in the sacks?" The Major asked the owner.

"Oats. Grain for Yankee stock!"

He spoke as if Yankees were just below slaves, in his estimation.

"You get paid yet?" asked the Major.

"Half. The balance upon delivery."

"We pay better than Jeff Davis, don't we?"

He nodded, sulking.

"Your farm close?"

"Back down the road a mile."

"So, if you hurry, you can deliver two loads a day?"

He nodded again. Although he did not expect to get paid for that second load. That was intended for a secret barn in the opposite direction. I learned a lot that day.

The Major then pulled a rank of four men from the column. "You men escort this wagon to its destination," he ordered, adding, "Both times. Then report to me."

The Major made certain **two** loads of grain got delivered to our commissary that day. That little

Copperhead didn't like it but now had four Yankee soldiers "guarding" his wagon all day. And, knew where his farm was. Where the hell was Bobby Lee when a man needed him?

He thought this, I think. He didn't **dare** say it.

The little man climbed aboard. Ratchet climbed alongside and clicked the team.

The four soldiers showed up as I was leaving Major Wright's tent. I thought he was gonna bust me.

"Augustus, you need to save that anger for the enemy."

"With respect, Sir," I answered. "He **is** the enemy. That second delivery was for Bobby Lee. Until you caught on and interceded."

"Our enemies are the Rebs, Augustus." He called me by name not rank. A good sign. "He has the right to whip his property. That colored man **is** his property."

"Doesn't Ratchet have any rights, Sir?"

He sighed. "That's what we're fighting for, son. That may change. It hasn't yet."

I knew the Major was advising me as a friend. But I was young and idealistic and bothered by the situation.

I was also bothered by an earlier conversation with Ratchet, before he climbed aboard the wagon. I had the money. I was thinking of buying him, having him serve the Company as "contraband," then setting him free.

"I can't allow that, Suh."

"Why not?"

"I can't leave. Got a wife and kids back there. What if I'm killed? Where would they go?"

I remember thinking: I sure got a lot to learn.

## Chapter 26

# RED REB

We guarded our section from September 1, 1862 to February 14, 1863. We didn't know jack about sentry duty. Learned by doing. "Jes' know what the hell yer shootin' at," said Saul, concerned about one of us shooting **him**. (He and Stickwalker snuck out at night).

They never got caught but Saul was making certain a mistake never created a victim.

The Reb's lost their second greatest general, and maybe the war, in this way. When he heard of the death of Stonewall Jackson, Saul said "Imagine him bein' shot by one of his own men, and him not deservin' it!" I noticed he emphasized the latter.

The presence of half of the Army of the Potomac deterred the Rebs from attacking the nation's Capital. It could have happened but Bobby Lee's intention to split Maryland from the Union got thwarted at Antietam sixteen days after our arrival.

## The Legend of Augustus McBoone

In the bloodiest battle yet, General McClellan's Union forces "bested" General Lee's Confederates. That's what Mac told our northern powers anyway. Who actually won is still being debated. In terms of casualties we lost 12,000 to the Rebs 13,000. Therefore, the Union won.

And, Washington and Maryland remained in the Union.

Our presence helped.

Saul said it best. "From Mason-Dixon to Virginny, 2/5ths of the folks are fer us, 2/5th agin' us. The 1/5th remainder don't give a shit!"

He couldn't read or write but he sure could cipher, that Saul.

Mac blew it at Antietam, though: By maintaining the irritating pattern of allowing Lee to retreat - to live and fight and kill another day. I wasn't at Antietam. Busy protecting the Powers That Be in Washington. I fought at Chancellorsville and Gettysburg. Like Antietam, the carnage was awful. And, when I say I fought, I mean **I fought!** I smelled Johnnie's breath - before I stuck him.

*"Grandpa! You're getting carried away!"*

*"Sorry Hayley." Back to my story:*

In each case the Union general in charge blinked - Hooker at Chancellorsville and Meade at Gettysburg - both let that slippery Bobby Lee and his surviving Rebs get away. Just like Mac.

I wish we had pressed our advantage. Put them away early. I've heard the reasons - exhaustion, wounds, weather. But those are more excuses then reasons. **We** had the reserves, they didn't. In the long run, it would have been a helluva lot easier on the South. We allowed the Great Conflict to drag on another two years after Gettysburg, a period that hardened the northern resolve. Led by no-nonsense Union hardasses like Grant, Sherman and Sheridan our troops laid waste to the south and west. We were determined to show the Barefoot Johnnies we were Bull of the Woods. We called our occupancy Reconstruction - a fancy name for Subjugation. The south called us Carpetbaggers.

Angus, who was stationed in the South, attested to more Union harm than good those post-war years.

*"Grandpa, why do 'they' call political stuff fancy names?"*

*"Dunno Hayley. 'They' are usually far away from the blood and guts spent to keep a place."*

I never fought for Grant. Like me, he had a soft side he didn't like to show. We both teared up when he pinned The Medal on me in 1870. It took us back, that ceremony. Why we teared up. I smelled whiskey on his breath. I didn't know he drank too much! It didn't show. Didn't matter to me. Whiskey-breath was normal back then.

I was taken back to that first day at Gettysburg, when the Bucktails slowed the Reb advance. But at what cost! Our outfit was so shot up that Colonel Llewellyn disbanded Company A and sent us three standers home. And, we were walking wounded. Our casualty rate was ninety-nine percent. Per the Colonel's records. Actually it was one hundred percent. The one poor soldier who appeared unscathed was hurt in the head. He who never drank before, drank himself to death sixteen years later. He, who had the sweetest voice, never sang again. Ever.

Back to guarding D.C. I warned you, I ramble.

*"That you do, Grandpa."*

Back then most of the city spread north and east of the Potomac river. The lowlands were swampy. There had to be a political reason for putting our Capital there. Seemed forced to me. I'm too practical I guess. Stickwalker foraged in the lowlands, loved it.

My squad guarded a perimeter of one thousand acres within the western quadrant of the "city." We slept in wedge tents set on a wooded hill. Our area was rural and contained our hill, a swamp, farm fields and a section of the river. High wooded bluffs faced us on the opposite side. We felt we were a real part of The Army of the Potomac after guarding it for five months.

"Good place for a shooter up there," noted Saul, indicating the high bluffs. "Me and Stickwalker better check that out some night." That night came too late for one sentry.

The other two corporals and I split Company A into three squads of twenty-eight privates each. Guarding was a twenty-four hour duty, seven days a week. I organized my pickets into four seven-man teams, each team worked the same number of days and nights. I took a turn at night, saved my armorer's work for the days. I've read reports of boredom at camp but I never was. There wasn't enough time to do all I had to do! Created work for myself I guess. The days flew by.

I did my best to be fair. I liked the men and they liked me. Respect might be a better word. Other men weren't fair. Captain Jonas and his cavalry unit for example. He went by-the-book even when the book was wrong. His company had a high desertion rate. Ours was zero.

D.C. bustled with government and military activity. The business of both was patronage. Corruption seemed expected - unless you were a soldier and were caught. Then "military justice" didn't seem different from "frontier justice" except executions were carried out by a firing squad instead of a rope. We heard Jonas had trouble getting volunteers for his squad so he shot his captured deserters himself.

D.C. to us country boys was **huge**. The Union Commissary, Field Hospital and Weapons Depot seemed as large as Camp Curtin. For those functions only. Once a week I sent a team to guard a section. The thing they complained most about was the rutty roads.

D.C. served as a haven for intrigue and violence. Bordered by slaveholder states to the south, abolitionists to the north, and wavering Maryland in the middle, an undercurrent of strife boiled in support of each cause. I hated the city. Saul loved it - at night. A soldier **never** ventured into the city alone. Gangs, gamblers and shanghaiers roamed the streets preying on sinners.

And Poorbaugh and Stickwalker earned bounty money preying on them. The really bad guys, not the poor sinners.

How can a sinner be poor? After the crooks got through with them, they were!

Our "scouts" patrolled nightly and reported to me. I delivered their scalps and paid bounties from Captain Stone's strongbox. In specie. I took exactly what was due. I never asked for pay but they voluntarily paid me ten percent for my "emissary" work. I suspected their "victims" were more criminals than Copperheads. If the Captain suspected the same he didn't say and the D.C. police didn't either. It was kinda like Injun Joe's ken of lady's bloomers. How'd they know?

Newspapers reported crime went down with us Bucktails there.

We picketed 165 days. Bobby Lee never showed. Aside from two riverfront incidents the guarding itself was uneventful.

The first incident occurred our fifth day there. A sniper got one of my pickets. Shot him clean through. In broad daylight. Red Reb was our name for this shooter. I never knew his real name. Never got close enough. He waved a red bandanna from his vantage point then disappeared. His vantage point was a high bluff 1500 yards away. Across the Potomac. 8/10ths of a mile.

He was patient, that shooter. He waited for days to establish his target's pattern, shot once. Private Bronson had a habit of standing still, looking around and making a smoke, while out in the open. Our downstream picket heard the impact, then the shot, saw Bronson fall. He ran for cover, shot at the smoke, yelled for help. From the woodsline

## The Legend of Augustus McBoone

we could see there was no help for Bronson. We also saw Reb wave his red bandanna before he disappeared.

"Cocky sumbitch," said Saul kneeling close to me. "Pretty good shot though."

I'm thinking, only pretty good! He's dead, ain't he?

Saul and Stickwalker jogged upstream, found their stolen rowboat, snuck over. Found his vantage point, not the shooter.

"He shoots a buffalo gun," reported Saul. "Sharps I think. Gets there early. Waits and smokes. Probably an officer, has **real** tobacco, shoots prone. Has a spotter. Bet one of 'em has a scope of some sort."

We waited until after dark to retrieve the body. Saul, examining the chest wound, was critical. "He didn't allow enough windage. Should aim six inches right to get all the heart."

I'm thinking, a half a foot in almost a mile!

Saul continued. "The breeze must a' happened just as he shot." He turned to Stickwalker. "Was there any wind today?"

Stickwalker didn't recall any but did note he was shooting across the water and downhill.

Saul remained unconvinced. "Could be a pattern. Like Reb artillerymen always shootin' high - I think it's a pattern."

Our river pickets stayed alert and in the woods after that. I forbade any smoking on duty. Anywhere. Our scouts could see a flare, smell the smoke, use either to trail and scalp an enemy or shoot at a distance day or night and still get away. Why couldn't they? I told the men unless you want to meet God early, do your business behind a wide tree, and keep the tree between you and the river.

Captain Stone wrote Bronson's parents. He wrote great letters, the Captain. Their son had been killed by a Reb sniper. He did not suffer. He was a good soldier. Company A was sorry to lose him.

He told the truth. No graphic details. "It's a valuable lesson," he said to me. "But costly. Damned costly." He only swore when he meant it, the Captain.

We buried Bronson at night in a hilltop grave overlooking the river. I made a cross. Major Wright spoke the 23rd. From memory.

He'd get more practice, reciting that.

The Brass put a $200 bounty on Red Reb. But we didn't get him, in D.C. We hoped he'd bought it at Antietam but he returned to plague us several times after that. He victimized us at Chancellorsville and Gettysburg. We knew it was him. He always waved that red flag. And shot left every time.

I discovered that winter was a lot milder in D.C. than in the Pennsylvania Northlands. Still, the farm boys complained about the wet and the town boys about the slop. I concluded it was also human nature to complain. While loggers and soldiers both complained about the weather only soldiers complained about their food - with good reason. The ham was slimy, the beans buggy, the hardtack hard. I had acquired a taste for Stickwalker's forage so for me and Saul the army food was... tolerable. Stickwalker's favorite was live snake boiled in corn oil, beetles in honey a close second. Of course forage was seasonal but not so much in D.C. He kept the snakes and beetles under a pile of boards according to Saul. A bee tree in the swamp held the honey.

I grew taller, thicker and stronger at D.C. Let my belt out two notches. Saul remarked my growth was due to my aging from seventeen to eighteen. But I give all the growth credit to Stickwalker, none to aging or the Union.

During my time at D.C. I "celebrated" my eighteenth birthday, suffered through numerous mail calls until a Christmas Surprise, witnessed the Emancipation Proclamation and started a maintenance relationship with Old Warhorse that lasted sixty years.

Those events are ahead in my story.

Aside from glimpses of Red Reb, Bobby Lee's "graycoats" never showed. All those hours, all those miles walking picket, all based on rumors. I don't doubt that there were thousands of Rebs in D.C. that winter but none wore a uniform and very few caused us Bucktails any trouble.

Like I said trouble (crime) went down while we were there.

## Chapter 27

# HALLOWEEN

I spent the night of my eighteenth birthday with Saul in the belltower of a Methodist Church. I had seen the tower on my rounds, grew curious about its vantage point. In case of an invasion a Bucktail sharpshooter could do a lot of long-range damage from up there.

I resolved to take a better look so I took in the service the Sunday before my birthday. This meant I had to clean up. I filled a horse trough with river water, used sand for soap, used the same water for my pants and shirt and extra set of drawers, hung the clothes on a rope to dry. I decided not to shave. Trimmed my beard instead. By then my mustache and beard was dark, full and soft and in fashion. Made me look ten years older than my almost eighteen years. I brushed my jacket and kepi, polished my boots and belt, left my weapons except a clasp knife and a toothpick at camp.

Several of the wealthier Union soldiers, even those with wives in camp, employed freed Negroes called "contraband" for menial tasks. I could afford one but thought a "boy" would get in my way. I did find racial prejudice on both sides of the Mason-Dixon. I should have expected that, I guess. Was surprised at its prevalence in D.C. What were we fighting for?

Anyway, I went bright and shiny to church and found myself the only one there in uniform. After a while I realized I was also the only one there that wore the blue. Had the men not been in black broadcloth they would have worn the gray. Even after hanging my cap on my belt I still stuck out. I wasn't the heaviest there but was the tallest and broadest-shouldered. It was kinda fun looking across at the dusty tops of stovepipe hats until the men removed them. Then they exhibited standard pates of the day. I was reminded of log camp. Again I stuck out: I had a full head of wavy dark hair, a dark beard, and not a trace of gray.

I followed a young woman with a nice sway into the sanctuary, sat behind her. Blonde curls sprang out from her bonnet. She wore long gloves, was probably properly bloomered (I still couldn't tell). She was pretty and demure and when she removed her gloves to open her Bible, I **knew** she was bloomered. She was married and had to be bloomered - for church anyway.

I had seen the tower access on the way in, then sat behind the girl in the middle of the pew. Soon I was hemmed in. So I followed the service, stood when they stood, sang when they sang, listened to the sermon.

I listened too. I was wary but heard it all. They had a guest pastor that morn, a high-powered young preacher named D. M. Brands. The girl sang with a soft drawl, seemed rapt in his speaking and the men around her were very protective. I guessed she was a recent Confederate widow.

I was half-right. She wasn't a widow.

Reverend Brands preached from Psalms. Everyone opened their Bibles except me. I didn't have one. Had buried ours with Dad. I did resolve to get one after hearing Reverend Brands. He offered to sign their Bibles after service.

I did **not** know Psalms was the most important book of the Old Testament. I thought Exodus was. That's where the Ten Commandments are anyway. He backed his comment by explaining how Irish monks grabbed Psalms whenever their monastery was threatened by pagans. The abbot ordered them to take those particular scrolls and skedaddle. Hide and protect the Psalms - all we believe is in there! I also resolved to pay closer attention to Psalms when I got my Bible.

Then he switched from history to salvation. (Southern preachers talk about this a lot). Caused a stir when he said **you alone** determine your salvation. It's **not** based on the color of your skin or uniform. I swear to God he looked right at me when he said that. Then all eyes turned from me to a white matron who obviously was used to having her way and say. "So my darkie can be saved too? He can go to the same heaven I go to?" The Reverend nodded and smiled. "Well, I never!" said the matron whose image of heaven only had white folk in it. During the commotion the Reverend winked at Mrs. Bonnet.

I caught that wink. Thought it was kinda cheeky toward a married lady, even a widow. The congregation succeeded in shushing the matron and Reverend Brands finished his message. I wondered if they would **ever** invite him back. Although very engaging and knowledgeable he talked "equal" talk and his opinions would get him in trouble in the Old South. And that matron was definitely Old South. Her name was Clara. She was an opinionated old brick but those opinions were shared by all there. I was in a nest of Copperheads and boiling oil was not gonna help me out one bit. I was on my own. My only salvation there - youth, my size and the toothpick in my boot. I shifted my feet so I could grab it but soon discovered I didn't need to. This was church. Sanctuary. They would treat the Yank with respect. On Sunday.

After service the young lady, approached the preacher and bussed his cheek. Mrs. Bonnet was Mrs. Brands! It turns out, he was a Reb chaplain, visiting from Charleston.

Outside I passed two men smoking beside an expensive buggy. They smoked **real** tobacco. One of them approached me. "Corporal, where are you stationed?" He asked this in a friendly way. I noticed he had sharp eyes and held his cigarette between the thumb and forefinger of his left hand. I shook his right. I pointed to our hill, told him my name, said I was with Company A of the 149th Pennsylvania Volunteers. "We're part of the pickets guarding D.C." I said. "We haven't seen any action yet."

He drawled. "So, you haven't killed any Rebs?"

"Hope I don't have to, sir."

"Me too," he said and walked back to his waiting friend.

I walked toward our hill, wondering. Was he hoping I didn't have to kill anyone or he didn't have to? I didn't ask his name. He didn't offer. He wore the gray, I the blue. We would meet again.

Saul and I snuck into that belltower on Halloween. I say "snuck" because that's the aspect we assumed. Didn't have to. The front door was unlocked, no one inside. This Copperhead church was ignored, only busy on Sunday. We climbed the narrow staircase to the tower, opened its trapdoor, walked around the big bell, set our rifles on the rail, peered out into the night.

I was right. A sharpshooter could do damage from there. We talked about our sniper's getaway: Down the stairs too slow, down the bell rope too noisy, down an unexposed side, just right. Would need a long coil of knotted rope so the marksman could slither safely down. Is there any kind of safety in war?

Saul then produced a flask. Offered me first sip. Wished me a happy birthday.

It was good. Not the same as Fergus' but there's a difference between bourbon and scotch. I didn't ask Saul where he got it. Some well-to-do Copperhead that didn't need it anymore probably.

The night was clear and cool. A salty breeze blew in from the south. A full harvest moon rose. The V of a flock of honkers crossed it. As the city lights dimmed the stars grew brighter. Not as bright as Steam Valley's but okay. Saul pointed to the Hunter and the Seven Sisters sparkling out of sequence in the night sky. He told of the Great Lusting Bear and Jesse's desire to snag one of those sisters. He told of Job and Blacksnake and the twins howling at the moon.

I told of Pastor Brands description of Irish monks hiding from pagans.

Saul chuckled. "Like me and Jesse?"

I didn't think so...exactly. My take on pagans of old was they worshipped a bunch of Gods while the Christians worshipped the one true God. Then argue about whose was the truest.

"If there is only one God how can there be three?"

The cipher-man saw three not one. "Where did you hear about the Trinity?"

"Songbird. I didn't argue but it don't make sense. How can three be one?"

I said, "I believe in one supreme God. The other two, His son Jesus and the Holy Spirit, do His bidding. They are powerful, though. Stronger than angels. When the top angel rebelled, Jesus bootkicked Satan and his minions to the earth."

"How many are a minion?"

"I don't know. More than we can count."

"Jeez!" Saul really meant to swear. In so doing, he gave credit where it was due. Then he added: "Our mom made us attend the mission church in Kinzua. She was white. Our dad made us follow the stars. He was Injun. Cornplanter, he was mixed like us, had a brother who blended it all together. Stickwalker knew Cornplanter."

Stickwalker was the authority on everything.

"Dad said to keep some slack, you never really know until you're dead."

"Wise man, your dad."

I continued. "Pastor Brands emphasized a personal relationship with God. Said our salvation is not determined by skin or uniform color. Made an old woman mad."

"You make your own way, Gus. When you die you hope He'll let you rest. Otherwise you can become a haunt like Blacksnake. He rides the Four Brother Winds and will 'til Bear Mountain is rid of all the big cats. That's a tall order, even for us Poorbaugh's. Only God knows when all the cats are gone."

"Can't howl at the moon here," Saul said. "Too many ears. Ya know, Jesse and me only did that to tick Songbird off. She'd get preachy and we'd get more pagan just to spite her. He's a pistol, that Jesse. Mean. But still a pistol."

We were quiet after that. Contemplated our world views. Saul and Stickwalker had been mission-trained. Their world was a blend of cultures. I had been dad-trained. I learned from his Bible, as Dad interpreted it. We agreed on two things, two essentials that kept us together. First, there is one Boss God. Second, for all the rest give slack.

I posted myself near the riverfront on the nights the two went "scouting." I didn't want them shot by mistake. Saul assured me they were careful. This was true for I never heard them leave or return without them warning me first. Still, I fretted. You never knew. All it took was the snap of a twig and the cock of a hammer.

They usually brought in a scalp or two. I'd pay the bounty in specie out of the Company strongbox, dry the scalp on my wagon, stuff it in a footlocker after drying. Some days my wagon smelled.

Copperhead scalps were worth $5 each. A Reb soldier brought $10 but required a uniform patch. Otherwise it was $5. A Reb officer brought $15 but required a shoulder insignia. A Reb general brought $50 but was deemed too difficult because he was always surrounded by guards. Consequently, the foot locker grew a cushion of scalps. It was too dangerous to mess with patches. $5 was better than nothing and didn't require any identification.

I made money too. Got paid ten percent. I never asked why. Just covered for them and paid them for doing their thing, I guess.

## The Legend of Augustus McBoone

When it snowed they were easy to track. How could you hide Stickwalker's stride and 24-inch mocs? Fortunately, snow didn't stay long in D.C. Those times they took the rowboat they had confiscated and hid in the tall reeds then stole into the harbor - those times they'd wipe their tracks with a wide broom I made. Those times I was nervous.

Women were available too. Saul disliked paying so the women Saul dabbled with were married. Army officers and government officials were always off to "important" meetings followed by late-night drinking. Saul had been calling on a clerk's wife, Mrs. Hanratty. She was a moaner, Mrs. Hanratty! Had to clamp his hand over her mouth. Adventurous too. "Her man didn't know what he was missin'!" Liked it doggie, with Saul wearing her pillbox.

I thought carrying on with a married woman was dangerous and said so. The image of the naked Saul wearing her pillbox was kinda pagan. Stickwalker, grinning, confirmed the story - he was protecting and watching. I wondered if Mrs. Hanratty knew she was being watched. Saul shrugged. "What about your conscience?" I asked.

He scoffed. "There's no such thing as conscience in whorin' and war." he said.

*"What's doggie, Mom?"*

"Later, Hayley..Augustus! You stop!"

"Now, Mom!" She could be bossy, Hayley.

Brenda sighed. "It's how your dad and I do it sometimes. We call it backdoor."

"Oh."

Both gals were blushing. I wasn't. I was happy they were still listening.

## Chapter 28

# CHRISTMAS MAIL

Of all guarding our thousand acres, only three never got any mail - Saul, Stickwalker and me. This distressed me. The other two were older and didn't expect any. I was reminded of my orphan status at mail call. I thought Peggy Sue would write. Maybe she didn't know where I was or didn't know how. I knew how but didn't know where she was. Maybe she just didn't care. Like her mom she went from man to man, a true "working-girl." I had people, Fergus and Flo, cousins like Connie, but none that **really** cared. I told myself this anyway, whispering into the haversack which doubled as my pillow.

We would talk, Stickwalker and I. Mostly about Dad. In English. When we discussed ourselves he talked in spurts. His last relationship was on the Trail of Tears twenty-eight years before. He "took up" with a tall Cherokee woman, saw her and her "younguns" safe to the Nation, built them a cabin. He went hunting one morning, returned to find a "buck" there. The kids acted like he was their daddy. These things happened on the Trail. She was willing to share, but their bed, built big, still only held two. He left. He acted kinda hasty, upon reflection. Everybody liked him, including the buck! She's either dead or dried up by now. He wasn't. Still had his moisture at 112. Moses still had his at 120. Could see far too! He shoulda looked in on the family after the Mexican war. But he didn't. They all went their own way after the war: Dad and Seagreaves to the Gold Fields, Saul home to Kinzua, he to Alaska. On the way he saw huge red trees, rain-forest, brown bears bigger than the blacks at White Knoll. He found gold, panned it, crossed Canada, bought the mission and warrants surrounding it, pays taxes to Dauphin County, Pennsylvania. Built another cabin in the middle of the swamp. Did I know swamps were cheap? And no one goes there? Ever?

At Christmas we **all** got mail. Saul and Stickwalker each got one letter. I got two. Surprise! Surprise!

Stickwalker's was a packet forwarded from the mission. Inside was the letter from Saul, a note from the Moravians wishing him well and the bill for that year's taxes. He pored over that short note, returned it with Union scrip for the taxes. Seems the honest missionaries always paid his taxes.

Saul got a letter from Jesse. Written by Songbird and read by Stickwalker, it went like this:

"Dear Saul. Our wives and daughters are fine. They miss you, Songbird especially. I don't (ha!). Huntin' and trappin' great. Got a cat last month. Am sendin' you part of yer share of bounty. Should spend the rest (ha!) but won't. Blacksnake still wales. So, more cats. No wolves. Keep yer head down."

Two ten dollar gold pieces were wrapped inside.

"He's a pistol, that Jesse." Saul said this while pocketing the coins.

The two I got were from Ike and Lady Louisa and Mr. and Mrs. Glover. Both were headed with "Dear Augustus."

Ike and The Lady's said: "We heard from the War Department regarding the disposition of your belongings, if necessary. We pray it is not! We sent the letter on to Mr. Glover. His return had a copy of your will. Very sorry to hear about Angus. He was a good man, your dad. Stop in when you get back. Enclosed please find some Christmas from us. P. S. Keep your head down."

Mr. and Mrs. Glover's said: "We sent Mr. McFee and Miss Longsdorf a copy of your will. We also placed the War Department letter in your box. Expect a visit when you return. Keep your head down. P. S. Edna darned you a pair of socks. Edwin stuffed some Christmas in each."

## The Legend of Augustus McBoone

Inside each sock was a five dollar gold piece. The Glover letter, very formal, told me the missus had more to do with the daily routine than I expected. I didn't know her first name until then. And I had stayed at their house!

The McFee/Longsdorf missive: More informal also contained ten dollars. In a federal note. I was struck by their similarities. They all got to D.C. with the money intact and they all urged the recipient to keep his head down.

Ten dollars was a big gift in 1862. I sent each double and assured them I was well and would stop in upon my return. I did say their gift was the only gift I had ever received outside of Saul, Stickwalker and Dad. Saul's gift too carnal to tell about.

Stickwalker wrote Saul's response. Saul sent fifty dollars and asked Jesse to buy Christmas for the family. Use his share of the cat money when he grew short. And please do not send him any more money! Bounty work is fine here and I promise to keep my head down. Stickwalker is here and Augustus. There was another side to that letter. I did not know about it for eighteen years. I stuck the fifty-dollar greenback in Saul's letter home. After he died Songbird dug that letter out. The back side said "No action yet but it's comin'. If I don't make it look after Gus for me. He's a good youngster, handy like his Dad. Stickwalker and I both fear he won't keep his head down."

That letter is pasted in my Civil War journal. It's written in Stickwalker's formal and flowing hand. In English. It's nice to know, even now, how much they cared. We had each others back, back then. But it was never stated, just done.

It was also nice to know that Ike, Lady Louisa and the Glover's cared. I made them a promise that I'd get back so I kept my head down. Tried to anyway.

I was sure glad I posted their returns the next day as I got real busy later. We corporals were ordered to double the guard over Christmas. This meant double the work and the men grumbled. A couple threatened to join the two hundred deserters that plagued the Union daily. My threat to send Stickwalker after any who left their post was met with compliance. Those who complained wisely decided to stay.

What the Powers That Be ordered was textbook defense. Ever since Washington's Crossing surprised wassailing Hessians in 1776, occupying forces near rivers were extra cautious at Christmas. Stickwalker had been there. A young fighter, hidden in the woods. He heard the oars and rushed to warn the celebrating soldiers. Warned them in German but they were too drunk to listen to a redskin, even a big smart one. He slunk off. Their commander got killed. The g-d Americans won that battle.

I took my double turns and disappointed Saul. He had promised to take me to a "clean" (no bugs) brothel and get me laid for Christmas. He thought it had been too long since Peggy Sue. While I guarded he scouted. Took his anger out on a couple of wassailing Copperheads. "Nobody's ever gonna miss those two," he said after pocketing his ten dollars.

They weren't Copperhead as much as criminals. And Saul was right. Nobody did miss them. Ever.

No Reb troops crossed the Potomac either at Christmas. In this the Powers That Be were wrong. Again.

My journal indicates we doubled the guard until January third. I recall clammy weather. We wore slickers on duty, stayed inside our tents otherwise. I didn't get much sleep. Didn't need any. I was young and full of sap and vinegar. Able to guard at night and armor during the day. I etched more rifling to the seventy-caliber bullet mold, inscribed "McB" to the base of each bullet cast. I also sharpened Saul's Bowie and Stickwalker's Green River. Per Saul both blades had "dulled with use."

*"What kind of sap were you full of Grandpa?"*

*"Hayley!"*

"Mom! McB makes vinegar here. And syrup from maple sap. He writes about moisture and sap in these journals. But that's not the same, is it Grandpa?"

*I pulled a Fergus on Wicked Girl and ignored her. Comforting to know they were still listening:*

Church bells rang in the New Year. Morning, it was, 1863. I could hear them clanging in the distance. I groaned. Rolled back over.

Pink-Cheeks shook me awake. The morning picket's first job was to do that. He reeked. The stench from last night's revelry followed him. I opened my own bloodshot eyes. Just another Tuesday. "Aren't you on duty?"

"Due there in an hour. Exchanged with Ambrose."

"You two kiss and make up?"

"We didn't kiss. Shook hands after I apologized for the peach pit thing."

"You should tell me when you trade duties."

"I tried. You weren't here."

"Oh," I said and stood. Noticed that Pink-Cheeks had lost the baby fat since Curtin. He weaved off to relieve Ambrose. Saul came up. None the worse for wear. He had an amazing capacity for Bacchus, that Saul.

He and Stickwalker had taken me out for New Year's Eve. Discovered I liked whiskey as much as Dad and Fergus. Next morning my head pounded, my mouth tasted like cotton, my stomach churned. Stickwalker brewed a vile oily tea. It helped. Resolved **not** to do that again.

I had taken my turn that night. No activity except wind lapping the waves, whistling through the trees. The two invited me along for a "scout." I climbed in the rowboat, took my turn rowing on the way to town. I guess the current pushed us on the way back. I didn't remember that part. "We do any good on our scout?" I asked while sipping another cup of tea. The haze was lifting, the world starting to clear. It wasn't the weather. That was still clammy.

"Naw," chuckled Saul. He dipped hardtack into a metal cup of black stuff we called coffee. "We took you to a clean place (where the working-girls did not have clap). Somewhere between '62 and '63 you passed out. Stickwalker carried you to the boat."

I didn't remember. He continued.

"You got a poke comin'. I negotiated fer ya."

"How's that?"

"I gave the boss-gal five bucks. Then you passed out and she wouldn't give the money back. You're to get it in trade later."

"She'll remember?"

"She will. Or end up a Copperhead."

"But she's a lady!"

Saul scoffed. "She's no lady."

"Well, she's not a Copperhead!"

"She ain't a Yank, either. She's a high-class whore who runs a boarding house. Long as yer money's good she's got a room and a gal fer ya."

I changed the subject. "How'd you get me here?"

"The boat and Stickwalker."

"None of the pickets saw?"

"We weren't hailed. Snuck right by Ambrose. He might a' looked the other way. It was dark and foggy, remember?"

I shook my head. Finished that tea. Felt better.

At sundown that evening, while I was on duty, the church bells pealed again. Not the closest, I recall. It wasn't Sunday or the New Year. What was happening in town?

Saul and Stickwalker went to find out. Came back and I warned my bored replacement. "Keep awake, dammit! You want to get home don't you?" I didn't have many rules. Staying awake was the firmest one. We walked back to my tent. Sat on three stumps I had sawed while building the officer's quarters.

"Big doin's in town," said Saul. "More excitement than New Year's. Lincoln signed the Emancipation. Freed blacks and abos are whoopin' and hollerin'. A black whore is gonna cost the same as a dirty white now." The carnal Saul always counted the cost. The racist Saul figured every black working-girl was crabby.

Ambrose heard and sat on another stump near us. "He can do that?" he asked. "Take someone else's property?" Ambrose had been mulling this over since the incident with Ratchet in late August. I had noticed him calling the armorer's wagon "his." He had acquired some possessions in D.C. He didn't have a lot, Ambrose. Sent most of his money home. The nice things he saw made him realize he was poor. He never saw a black in authority. Most he saw were contraband or slaves. Pretty squalid. The accepted view, even in the North, was they were beneath whites. They were Darkies. He couldn't afford to hire one but he learned to call them Darkies. These were part of the negatives of D.C.

Stickwalker grunted the answer about taking: "Andy Jackson did in the 1830's. He and his g-d Scots-Irish trash! Took Cherokee land. Sent soldiers to the Ross Plantation in Tennessee. Confiscated his land, buildings and slaves. Ross was 1/8th Cherokee, 7/8th white. But, he'd been elected the Cherokee Chief. A squawman, they said. Wife's name was Qatie. She died on the Trail. My woman and I buried her. Place Jackson took is called Nashville now. Helluva thing. Taking someone else's stuff."

"What happens next?" asked Andy.

"Whole lot of nothin'," said Saul. "The North'll celebrate then go back to abusin' the poor black bastards. The South'll ignore it and keep doin' what they're doin'. Blacks may find they eat better as slaves. Either way, we'll fight it out come spring."

I thought it might turn out to be a whole lot of something, myself. Turns out we were both right. In the near term, Saul was correct. In the far, I was. The twentieth century saw change. The nineteenth did not. Saul was dead by then.

"Oh," said Ambrose and that was that. A near term solution. He grabbed his Enfield and went on picket duty. Walked past the place Stickwalker carried me the night before. He hadn't looked the other way. Unless there was a full moon and snow on the ground you couldn't see past fifty yards in the D.C. dark.

## The Legend of Augustus McBoone

We were eighty.

On January second, we got a visit from a Power That Be. He was rich and local, head of the Hospital Commission. His wife helped. Made bandages. Not like Polly Llewellyn who waded right in. She kept her distance but did her part. She thought. They were part of the conflicted community who had friends on both sides. In their case more North than South. So, instead of wearing a uniform he paid a replacement and volunteered. Like Polly she had sons, at least one was not conflicted. He ran away. Joined the Union. Trained to be a bugler. Wrote his mom every day. After Christmas the letters stopped.

She knew something was wrong! Teddy was fourteen. Very idealistic. She expected a triumphant letter after the slaves were freed. It hasn't come. Yet. Oh, the optimism of a mom!

Teddy was not a Bucktail. His outfit guarded an area south of ours. He was a drummer, learning to be a bugler. Practiced daily, he did.

"Took the same route?" I asked. "Same time?"

His chastened Captain nodded. His orders had been to keep the boy out of danger. No safer place than the Drum and Bugle Corps was there? He hadn't been needed so the bored boy practiced. Wrote letters home. Fell through the cracks.

These things happen in war.

I directed a search party. Sent Saul across the Potomac to root out Red Reb - if he was there. I joined the party that Stickwalker led. We kept to the treeline. Stickwalker's nostrils flared.

A half-mile south of where Bronson was hit he picked up the smell. Then the crows flew off, squawking. They had pecked out his eyes, opened his body wound. He sat there supported by his drum and a high clump of grass. His bugle lay in the grass. The big bullet struck a decorative plate on his shoulder belt, passed through his heart, exited out his rib cage.

"Dead before he sat down," said Stickwalker. He removed the belt and drum, handed them to me, carried the boy's smelly body back to camp. Even bloated, the boy was small - fourteen goin' on four. His lineage ran small. His mom was shorter than his dad who had the thinnest pencil-neck I ever saw.

Saul came and examined the body. Red Reb had made the shot. The signs were all up there. He had patterned the boy, heard him coming, waited 'til the lad started an about-face and nailed him. "That sumbitch pulls left, I tell you."

My sentry had heard the shot but no impact. I had counted my men and sent a message to Company

## The Legend of Augustus McBoone

B who had the same report. No missing men which meant a distant shot. Could be a hunter, an accident, anything. That sentry handed me Teddy's bugle. I gave that and his drum to the dad. They wouldn't let the boy carry any weapons.

We buried Teddy across the Potomac on Bobby Lee's land at Arlington. The families knew each other and Mrs. Lee gave permission. I shined up and drove their buggy to the funeral, the parents sobbing in back. Their minister conducted the ceremony. His Captain came. The Drum and Bugle Corps performed. Our Major Wright, he with the strong voice and who had lost his entire family, recited the Twenty-Third.

Our Colonel Shannon couldn't be bothered.

Saul and Stickwalker lurked nearby. They made sure Red Reb could not make another long shot. He might have been one of the top-hatted mourners, but I didn't see anyone I knew.

Saul said, "He was just a kid. Blowin' a bugle!"

Stickwalker was more philosophical. "These things happen in war," he said. In English.

## Chapter 29

# FIXING OLD WARHORSE

I just finished mending harness for "Buster" when Captain Stone came by. Buster was the name Ambrose had given one of the Army's draft horses that pulled the armorer's wagon. Buster was a gelding, with us since Curtin. He and Ambrose had cultivated a friendship. For me, he was a draft animal. He did what I told him to do. "They need you in the train yard, Corporal," Captain Stone said. "Sergeant Benjamin will command your squad until you return."

I did what they told me to do too. Mostly. Was I a human draft animal? I wondered this. Did not say it. There was work in the train yard. I loaded my tools into the wagon, hitched Buster to it, followed the Captain into the city.

I changed horses that day. Went from grain-fed to steam. My sixty-year maintenance relationship with B & O number 0-80-0, Old Warhorse, began.

## The Legend of Augustus McBoone

The "old" boy had seemingly puffed his last. Couldn't hear him coming anymore. Just stood outside, black and cold and raindroppy. He couldn't fall over, but he sure looked like he wanted to. Like a huge tired elephant he had quit pulling. Even his clapper was rusted and listless.

There were other mechanics but it soon became apparent I was the only one capable of fixing him. Or strong enough. Or that cared. The others wanted to strip him for parts, to scrap him. I grabbed my hand sledge and grease gun. The locomotive had seized up, needed TLC. Tender-loving-care. That meant banging the hell out of him.

Captain gave me another stripe. Made me a sergeant. That way I could order the other mechanics without taking any lip. I soon earned their respect though. I was the tallest, strongest, and cleverest. They never knew I was the youngest.

This is what happened to Old Warhorse:

They used him up. The Union had too many resources - men, materiel, money. The Big Three. They needed to employ the fourth one - maintenance. When a rifle didn't work, they threw it away. Old Warhorse was too big and expensive for that. So, for an extra stripe and another five dollars a month, they got me.

The locomotive responded well to my rough treatment. Kinda like a woman - you gotta teach 'em who's Boss.

"*Augustus.....*"

"*Grandpa!*"

*Yep. Still listening. Both of 'em, too:*

Warhorse and I were the same age, not even close to our prime. But he hadn't seen an oil can or a grease gun since the beginning of the war.

I loosened his wheels, hitched him to a ten - ox team and pulled him into the B & O repair barn. I welded his leaking boiler, greased the seized parts, oiled the squeaking ones. He slurped oil like a thirsty soldier, downing drums of it. I ground away rust and repainted him. That took drums too. I replaced his fire box, used hard coal instead of wood, made steam. The blast from his whistle was my first successful test. The ding from his reclappered bell my second. Now you could hear him coming!

It was great work for me. The cavernous repair shop was heated by a huge wood stove. For the first time in weeks I was warm and dry. I worked sixteen hour days, cleaned up in a horse trough, banked the fire, slept in the wagon bed.

Buster had pulled the wagon into the repair barn. I had stabled him near. He didn't seem anxious for his partner or Ambrose or to return to camp either.

The army had a contract with a boarding house. Saul had been there. I ate breakfast and supper there. A few times I went upstairs with the black cook's daughter. The first time I used up Saul's credit. She was a yellow working-girl but her name wasn't Rose. It was Tildy. The army paid for my food. I had to pay for Tildy. I could afford her. My sergeant's pay was now twenty-three per month. My ten percent cut from the Copperhead bounties was regularly coming in. I didn't have to tap my Christmas money or savings. She didn't have the clap either.

"What's clap, Mom?"

"Augustus..."

"You tell her."

*She did. Again, both were embarrassed.*

*For a know-it-all Senior, Hayley wasn't as worldly as she let on.*

*I limited myself to two shots of whiskey, smoked a pipe after loving Tildy. I limit myself today too. Drinking and smoking, no Tildy. I yearn for Mandi, not Tildy.*

*No comment from the redfaced Peanut Gallery:*

I said goodby to Old Warhorse and Tildy the day I drove him from the shop. I saw Old Warhorse again but never Tildy.

That's the way with working-girls - you love them, leave them...and pay them. I think my order is wrong. They want their pay first.

War Horse gleamed! He was so proud! I instructed the B & O engineer and the tender on how to take care of him, hitched up Buster and drove back to camp.

The men seemed happy to get their armorer back, even if he was a sergeant. The happiest was Ambrose who got "his" horse and wagon back.

Buster did not seem as thrilled.

In mid-February I rode the cab with the engineer as 080 pulled our troop train to the wharfs of the Potomac. The steamboat "Louisiana" waited for us to board. We Bucktails were headed to Belle Plain, Virginia to "train" for the spring combat campaign.

The engineer, an older man of thirty, told me to look him up after the war. "The B & O can always use a clever mechanic," he said.

"If I survive," I answered.

"Oh, we'll survive," he said, including himself in the mix. "The Union can't afford to waste a good mechanic. They'll keep us back. Protect us. You'll see."

In the 1880s I worked on Warhorse again. Found a different engineer. The tender told me the first engineer had been killed years ago, at Chancellorsville.

"In the war?"

"Yeah. Is that important?"

I didn't answer. I recalled our conversation in 1863. He had gotten killed and I hadn't.

Keep us back, huh? Protect us?

They did not!

## Chapter 30

# THE RIVERBOAT

On the wharf I saw the same two men I saw at church in October. They wore dark suits. Watched us us intently. The sharp-eyed man smoked the same expensive cigarette. I went to ask where he bought them. They saw me coming and disappeared in the crowd. On purpose. This puzzled me. The sharp-eyed man had been so friendly at church.

"ALL ABOARD!"

Major Wright's deep voice reminded me of the task at hand - supervising the loading of four companies of pack-laden Bucktails aboard the steamboat Louisiana, along with Captain Jonas' cavalry unit. Ambrose drove the armorer's wagon aboard, stabled Buster with the other beasts, joined the three of us topside.

Stickwalker, Saul and I were leaning on the gunwale looking south. I was between them, grousing about it being too crowded to be with the soldiers seeing Alexandria opposite us when the railing between Saul and I splintered. A couple of seconds later I heard the shot.

Saul tackled me. "Git down!" he yelled. "Let him think he got ya. He didn't, did he?"

I was confused. "Who got me?" I didn't think he had.

"Red Reb, that's who!"

I checked my left hand. It was bloody from splinters but still intact.

Boom! Stickwalker, using Saul's Hawken, shot at smoke trailing a thousand yards away. There was a bluff overlooking the river, just south of D.C.

Boom! Stickwalker had loaded another soldier's Enfield, sent another ball Red Reb's way.

I had never seen Stickwalker shoot a gun.

The red bandanna taunted us from the bluff. Then it disappeared.

Boom! Saul fired a third shot at the smoke. "Boat's swayin' too much for accurate shootin'," he said. "He's gunnin' fer ya, ya know." He looked at me.

"Why?"

"You're our fixer. He wants ya out of the way. Dead. Stay down! Let him think he got ya."

The boat rounded a bend. Away from the bluff and the shooter. I stood. Flexed my fingers. I was fine.

Saul examined the hole the bullet had made. Through the wood rail and metal stateroom, deep into a mattress. Missed us on deck, nobody yet in the stateroom to miss. Saul cut the bullet out of the mattress. "I was right," he said and held the bullet for us to see.

"A Sharps 50. I still think he pulls a mite left. Might be natural. Shoots right and pulls left. I'll bet he's left-handed, like Gus."

I recalled the smoker held his cigarette in his left. He and his friend skedaddled when I approached. A suspicion began to form...

We went to Belle Plain, Virginia to train for the Chancellorsville spring campaign. It was only thirty miles as the crow flies but only a bird or balloon could get there that way. We had to go by boat - a roundabout day-and-a-half long trek. We wound down the Potomac River, turned up Potomac Creek until we ran aground. Barges took us the rest of the way.

Actually the distance between D. C., the Federal Capital, and Richmond, the Confederate Capital, was only one hundred miles. But a brutal one hundred miles for any soldier. Between the cities were six rivers. All ran west to east and dumped into the southern Chesapeake. Swamps in between. Real Stickwalker country. Except for Belle Plain the area was all low tidewater. Once all the bridges were blown each army had to use pontoons. The "landed" army had the advantage. The "landing" army(us, usually) was...fodder.

The first two years of the war the big battles were fought near the capitals. We were each trying to capture the other's flag. It was most frustrating for the Union. We'd get close, the scrap would get bloody and bitter, we'd skedaddle. That's why the President kept firing our commanders.

Anyway, Belle Plain was our destination, a piney woods plateau higher than the surrounding swamp where we could safely train. We brought supplies and built everything: Mess hall, commissary, stock barns, officers quarters, our quarters, latrines and parade grounds. Last to be built - our quarters. No majestic white pines here. Short, stubby, gummy red things were called pines here. I believe I felled every one. It was cold, wet, uncomfortable. We slept in rubber blankets under tents of canvas. In the beginning, Ambrose, Saul and I slept under the wagon. Stickwalker made a dry shelter, slept on and under pine boughs. Buster and his partner had it better. They slept in the stock barn.

Once camp was set up we went to battle drill. Here the bugler made the calls.

Saul got stubborn again. During lunch break the men gathered around him, a natural, reluctant and utterly honest leader. "Mark my words," he said. "Cold food, drillin' all the while - real shit's comin'."

While we had practiced marching on the way to D. C., this was more intense. **Real shi**t per Saul. For example: Battle march was different from "Marchin' to Georgia." The bugler called and we marched four abreast, staying precisely eighteen inches from the column in front. Colonel Shannon was overseeing and he was an ass. He'd get after Major Wright and Captain Stone and they'd get after us. I was a sergeant, approved of the emphasis on teamwork, disapproved of precision. It might look good on the parade ground but, in battle, really? They got rid of me by making me replace our triangular broadhead bayonets with eighteen-inch saber-bayonets. That meant changing the sockets on a thousand Enfields and sharpening that many blades. I went from Company armorer to Regiment armorer with that task.

Saul said he'd had enough of that "Napoleonic bullshit" during the Mexican war and wouldn't do it. "Marchin' **in** formation **to** a battle is alright. Marchin' that way **into** it is not. You got to learn to fight Injun style, and not bunch up." He looked around for support but Stickwalker had seen a rider cantering toward us and slunk off. Leaned

## The Legend of Augustus McBoone

against the open door of the armorer's shed. We both could see and hear.

Captain Jonas rode up. His whip was coiled on his saddle horn. Skin still clung to its leather end. Blood stained it. This is what Stickwalker saw. The men who had gathered around Saul had not.

Saul had seen the popinjay's approach. Jonas and Shannon were peas of the same pod. Arrogant rule-abiders who were more concerned with looking good during battle than winning it. Not so Wright and Stone. The popinjay resented Saul's scout status. Felt it gave him undue influence. Like now.

Saul pointed at me. "He does good work, Gus, but when you get your bayonet make sure it fits."

"Why?" asked Pink-Cheeks. "We're a sharpshooting outfit. We won't get close will we?"

Saul tolerated Pink-Cheeks. Called him an ass-kisser, which he was. Worse, he was the poorest marksman in the outfit. Couldn't hit a bull in the butt with a fiddle. Still our poorest shot was adequate as far as the Powers That Be were concerned.

"You **always** get close," said Saul. "When you smell Johnny's breath - and its rancid - he's scared. When it's not - watch out - he's enjoyin' it. When you hear Fix Bayonets! Make sure yours is socketed. When you hear "Charge!" you run at 'em, yell like hell, spread out. Make your shots count. Aim, shoot, move, find cover, aim and shoot agin. You might get three off before they're on you. (Unless you got a repeater, which this g-d army don't have enough of). Then it's stick time. Might gut three there as well. Then it's melee` and your rifle becomes your club. You club the hell out of each other 'til the winner is the one still standin'. Have a pistol and a blade for close work. A 36 is puny for big men. I use my 44s. Always go for bone when you shoot. People don't die right off. Keep movin'! Take 'em as they come. The closest Johnny is the one that will kill you. If you're hit and can't hide, keep movin'! Crawl! Lots of time later for mendin'. The key to survival is movement. So move! Whoever said dyin' is honor is lyin'. What good is a dead man?"

He walked toward Jonas who wisely spurred his horse toward Shannon. He went into the swamp and Stickwalker followed. What Saul said he had said before. Still worth repeating. We wouldn't have had an outfit when we left Chancellorsville if it hadn't been for Saul.

*"Was he bad or good, Saul Poorbaugh?" This came from Hayley who was subdued now.*

"He was both," I said.

"He was more good than bad," said Brenda. "He might have been uncle to Spike and helped train him, but he saved our Grandpa."

I didn't correct Brenda. When she approved of me I was "Grandpa". When she disapproved, like when she was McB secretary, I was "Augustus." My correction would have been it was Jesse who trained Spike, not Saul. Saul was dead.

## Chapter 31

## HAWKS VERSUS HEROES

I learned by watching and doing - that included playing base-ball. On Sunday afternoon I turned the parade ground into a ball field. After two boat rides, there were ten companies at camp - nine infantry, one cavalry. The cavalry claimed superiority. They were good throwers and fielders, but off their horses couldn't run for beans. They called themselves the Heroes. (We called them the Bad Guys).

The nine infantry companies each had a team. Company B's name was the Buzzards, Company A (us, the Good Guys) were the Hawks.

We played nine innings or ninety minutes. The umpire kept track of score and time and would shoot his pistol to signify the end of a game. Three D's could stop play: Dark, Drunk or Down. The latter two were usually related. A single downed player was replaced by his unit. But if a whole team was sick and drunk at the same time, they were done. They could be up by 97 to 50 but if they couldn't take the field, the umpire could call a forfeit. The umpire was God. Otherwise known as Major Wright, he of the deep voice didn't have to yell. If you questioned or hit him he could shoot you with his Dragoon 44.

'Twas a dangerous game, base-ball.

I had never learned to play. I was always tinkering or logging or on the road with Dad. Town kids got to play and we had over twenty in Company A. But the team leaders, Pink-Cheeks and Darren, picked me to play. Why? Well, I was Sergeant McBoone and bigger and stronger than any others. Also, I had the equipment. I made the ball, bats and bases. I established the ball diamond by placing sand-filled feed sacks as bases ninety feet apart. I cut home and pitcher's plates out of a plank I fished out of Potomac Creek. I made the ball out of cord and cowhide and stitched with sinew. The bats I whittled out of forty-inch gunstock blanks. While Major Wright had the authority, I had the importance. Play? You're damned straight the two leaders better pick me to play!

The leaders were the best ball players. Company A's best were Pink-Cheeks Osbourne and Darren Chaffee. They had played together up north. After the draft, Darren showed up as Bronson's replacement. Even got his bucktail. Darren was a good ball player, a hunter and a fair shot. He was a decent soldier, Darren.

Scores were high. 37 to 23 were common. The runner had to be hit or tagged with the ball to be "out." Three outs and we changed "ups." I saw my first killing when the other team was up to bat. We'd had five deaths prior but I had yet to **see** a man die. This was different. And blue on blue.

We had an infielder named Shorty who could really "whale" the ball. Damn thing rose when Shorty threw it. I played first which was pretty safe for a rookie back then. I was always chasing after our infielder's wide throws (Pink-Cheeks, Shorty and Darren) but I had long legs and could run which meant I could put the ball back in play readily. I also had a strong left arm from throwing rocks at whatever so that was an added asset. I couldn't hit, relied on the better players for that. Still, I was Sarge. And I made the stuff.

We Hawks were on the field. The Heroes were at bat. It was near dark. The Heroes were under Captain Jonas who watched. Beneath all his big-eared dignity to play, I guess. The Heroes were leading 46 to 33. But we had next ups. If we could get 'em out quick and score 14 we would win. Yay!

*"Go Grandpa!"*

The pitcher threw underhanded to the batter back then. To a good hitter the ball looked like a pumpkin floating in there. Their opposing pitcher and best ball player was at bat. His name was "Pitch." He and Shorty were from the same town and used to play on the same team. They did not like each other. The soldiers and players were drinking from a large keg and the booze was starting to have its effect. Shorty and I were the only Hawks still sober.

Pitch was cocky, big-jawed, mouthy, proud of the way he'd turned out. And drunk. Scuttlebutt had it he joined to avoid marrying a gal he got in the family way. It came out during the ball game who...

Shorty was taciturn, not given to much talk. Pitch was bragging about busting cherries back home, naming the names of his conquests.

*"Players still say that, Grandpa!"*

*"Hayley!"*

*"They do, Mom. I've heard it. Now I know what it means. Tell whose cherry it was too."*

*I smiled. Hayley's innocence was coming to the fore. Lack of it too. I preferred innocence. Hated high school.*

*I recalled the situation in 1863. It was Shorty's sister Pitch was telling tales on:*

Pitch hit a one-hopper Shorty's way. The bat splintered. Shorty speared the ball with his left, transferred it to his right. He took his time, watching, aiming. Pitch took off for first.

He was slow, ran with a cavalryman's gait. Shorty threw...hard...the ball rose...

Whack!

I saw it all.

Brains and blood flew out of Pitch's head. He was gone before he hit the ground. His chin dug a furrow in the base path. Then, still.

He's out! said the deep-voiced umpire. He yelled for teammates to drag him away. He thought he was out cold, but I knew Pitch would be cold... forever. When his teammates saw the brains and blood they milled around. Major Wright saw what happened and shot his pistol. "Time!" he said. "Heroes win by forfeit."

My team, the Hawks, protested. The Heroes had batted one more time. We still had our ups! In answer the Major pointed to Pitch's body. Game over.

Shorty explained things to me. We were the only ones that knew he had thrown high on purpose. "She named her baby after me," he said. "But he was his, the sumbitch." We both took a cup of hooch that was offered.

## The Legend of Augustus McBoone

Pennsylvania Cavalry Troop Four buried Pitch in a latrine. Just dumped him in his dirty underwear. His uniform and boots were auctioned off and the money sent to his family. Shorty said his sister had no claim. I noticed Pitch's back was scabbed from where the lash had struck. Pitch had complained in Jonas' hearing and the Captain had him tied to a pole. Because he was their best ball player he got four lashes instead of twenty-four.

I examined the bat. It had been broken before, the gunstock made from pine. I had put some wood screws in it, but it was never solid. I threw it in the fire. The pine tar hissed and crackled. Before the next game I carved a replacement out of a white oak sapling, a hardwood. I stamped that bat with my McB brand, grain up, and ordered all players to hit with that brand on top. They all hit solid after that.

We marched for Charlottesville May second.

Games over.

## Chapter 32

# MY FIRST REBEL YELL

I played on Sunday. Other days I tinkered. My box of spare parts went down and got replaced. The Union's attitude toward the fourth "M" had started to change. "Gonna need more ammo, too," said Saul. Major Wright ordered sixty rounds per soldier, got forty. That change of attitude had not quite reached the commissary. Saul remained the skeptic: "They doubled the ammo 'cause we're goin' into battle soon."

Again, Saul was right.

Signs of spring were rampant. Turkeys gobbling, trees blooming, water rising...we marched four abreast and further south. Our objective? To join with General John Reynold's First Division and attack the Reb earthworks on the south bank of the Rappahannock River. On the way we overheard Pink-Cheeks and Darren discuss challenging General Doubleday's outfit to a game of base-ball and roasting a turkey over an open fire.

## The Legend of Augustus McBoone

"Shotguns work best for turkeys, if Pink-Cheeks is shootin'," said Saul. "Course Shorty could pick one off with a rock." He grinned. He knew.

We neared the rendezvous point with the First. The Fourth Pennsylvania was in front, we were next, Company B behind us and so on. Very organized, very alphabetical. Ahead we heard Captain Jonas snap his whip and exhort his troop to stay close together. Saul and Stickwalker moved into the trees, flanked the marchers. Stickwalker advised that I either join them or march behind the wagon. He spoke in French. Only I knew. Saul spoke American: "Shit's comin'."

I moved from the front of the wagon to the back wondering, how in hell did they know? Like Injun Joe and bloomers, they just **knew**.

Reb artillery always shot high. While shooting at us, the Rebs got lucky. Four canisters whined overhead and exploded above Company B. Two ranks of soldiers got mowed down just like that. We split and ran for cover. All that was left on that road was the rent bodies of eight Bucktails. Head count tally showed A still had 102. B down to 92.

We were close enough to the Rappahannock. We dug in, set up a perimeter.

The first time I heard the "Rebel Yell" I peed my pants. Literally. We've argued about it since - part wolf, part panther, part banshee - it was. Scared the hell and then some out of me. I waded into some dewy bushes, allowed their wetness to mingle and hide my fear.

I "guarded" a section of perimeter. There by choice, I had grown tired of fixing, wanted to roam the woods a little. The Bucktails were camped near Chancellorsville, Virginia. Bobby Lee territory. Pickin' a fight, we were. We had gone upstream, crossed the Rappahannock with the First Corps, then, when the attack came were given the job of skirmishers protecting General Howard's right flank. While crossing I had seen Jonas dismount and pee in the river. He did this with every crossing - symbolically telling the Rebs what he thought of their cause. Saul scoffed: "Hasn't drawn that saber yet, just his pecker," he said.

*I looked at Hayley and Brenda to see any embarrassment. There wasn't. Both had read this account before:*

We hadn't attacked. Made camp and waited. Waited too damn long if you ask me.

That scream unnerved me and any that heard it - except Saul and Stickwalker. It said the Reb's knew where we were and they wanted to scrap. At this point we were a green outfit. We'd been fired on, lost some boys but had not shot at the elephant (the Rebel Horde) so to speak.

## The Legend of Augustus McBoone

At daybreak, Captain Stone rode a circuit of our lines. "Sergeant," he said, "you **will** see battle today." I noticed his pants were dry. I wondered idly what he would do with his horse. Ambrose had pastured Buster, expected to skirmish beside me. "Where are Poorbaugh and Stickwalker?" he asked.

I gave him my "You know" look. He answered his own question and rode on.

He left and the scouts whistled they were coming in. My wide-eyed replacement Darren arrived. I strode into camp with our scouts. Saul's belt contained a blond scalp.

"We got that hooter," Saul said. "Pitched his smoothbore. Scrawny kid. Uniform's in tatters. No shoes. That boy's missin' his topknot. That'll teach 'em to yell on guard duty."

I could imagine **that** scene.

We brewed a pot of chicory. Stickwalker provided the root. It wasn't a bad substitute for coffee. We reviewed their scout. They found the Reb lines, scalped one sentry (the loudest). Saul said it was obvious we were expected. "That sentry was a scrawny private. No shoes, a crap gun, good knife. He never owned a slave! No coin. No money at all."

I reported this to the officers. Swapped the bloody topknot for a $5 gold piece. Colonel Shannon was there and grimaced at the brutality. "Is this necessary?" he asked. "This war is so damned inconvenient! Is my horse ready?"

"Inconvenient or not, Sir," I said, "Stickwalker recommends we advance and fast."

Colonel Shannon scoffed at the man who had fought in more battles than all of us put together: "What the hell does **he** know?"

Major Wright and Captain Stone exchanged glances. I saluted, pocketed the gold piece and left. On the way back I muttered, "It's your funeral."

A prophetic comment, that.

Companies A and B gathered for the attack. The plan was for us Bucktails to be frontline skirmishers, for us to hit 'em hard, soften 'em up so Howard's Brigade could pass us and finish the Reb host off.

"Fix Bayonets!" came the order from Major Wright.

"Holy Shit!" said Pink-Cheeks. "We **are** gonna get close."

We marched four abreast up the main, Colonel Shannon leading on his high horse. The other officers marched alongside us, sabers drawn. Our scouts disappeared into the woods. Reb artillerymen saw us coming, sent canisters. Again they shot high, a pattern. One round, however, glanced off the top of a nearby tree and sent grapes whirring our way. Shorty's head rolled in front of us.

"Holy shit!" yelled Pink-Cheeks again. There goes our best arm!"

He was thinking the Hawks were down to eight now. I was thinking our Bucktails were down to 102. We then left the road and marched cross-country. This was a mix of woods and fields. Harder going but a helluva lot safer. Colonel Shannon yelled from his high horse, trying to keep us close together. But the men followed their natural leaders, Saul and Stickwalker, who spread out and wove their way toward the enemy. The officers on foot followed our scouts. Ambrose and I followed them.

There was movement five hundred yards ahead. Their skirmishers advancing to meet us. Gray ghosts. Reb artillery stopped. Didn't want to kill their own. I saw a flash of red. He knelt behind a white oak. Aiming that Sharps. His spotter had a telescope peering at us from the other side of the oak. Red Reb shot. Boom! Made Mrs. Shannon a widow. The Colonel's riderless horse ran off. We answered with scattered rifle fire. I couldn't see any targets so I ran toward Red Reb and his spotter who stayed behind the tree. I noticed Saul trying to get a shot at him too. Slippery devil! I slid behind a close tree. Four hundred yards separated us now. Other Rebs were weaving closer. Saul warned us to take the closest but...My quarry stayed put. Minnie balls whistled by, two thunked into my tree. A minnie caught a nearby Bucktail. He folded, thrashed. I aimed left-handed from one side of my tree, shot, creased theirs. Bark flew. Too much smoke. Did I miss? As I reloaded another Bucktail ran toward the cover of my tree. Shooting a constant din now. The man grunted, clutched at his throat, gurgled, fell forward, sprayed me with blood. His bayonet just missed my head and stuck in the tree. His weight snapped the bayonet and he fell on me. I kicked him off. A helluva way to treat a fellow Bucktail but he was just a body in my way.

Both sides were headed for the cover of a stone fence. Their side had a wagon road. Open, twenty feet. For us it was two hundred yards to the fence. For them fifty yards more. We got there first. Only head and upper torso shots at us now. They spread out amongst the trees that grew across the road.

Stalemate.

Pink-Cheeks and Darren slid beside me. Reloaded their Enfields. One of the Rebs gobbled. They both peered over the edge. I yelled no! Two shots rang out and both kepis went flying. Branson's buddy "Catch" was on the opposite side of me, next to Ambrose. Catch had given Darren Branson's bucktail, had played on the same team up north, was a Hawk now. "There lay our two best hitters," he said. And started to cry. I was amazed that base-ball had such an impact on their lives. Realized it was probably the strain of battle that caused such shortsightedness.

Both hitters appeared to be sleeping but were very dead. On closer inspection Darren had a line of snot and blood running out his nose to one ear. Pink-Cheeks had a steaming groove across the top of his skull. Gray matter fell out.

I heard another sob. Ambrose and Pink-Cheeks had become friends since D. C. Would he tell Pink-Cheek's folks that their boy had fallen for a Reb trick?

Saul and Stickwalker crawled up. They both had gotten close. Stickwalker's stick tip was covered with blood. Saul's bayonet and bowie were too.

"Quit yer snivelin," said Saul to Catch and Ambrose.

Company A's survivors had beaten the Rebs to the stone wall. We crouched or sat. I was in the middle, the rest spread out seventy-five yards on each side.

"Gobble, Gobble, Gobble!" Saul speared Darren's kepi with a long stick. Gingerly he raised the cap up. The second it appeared over the edge there was a shot and the cap sent whirring away. "Snipers out there," said Saul. He drew his 44. "They got trees. We got the stone row and trees. Ours is better. They're gonna try to roust us outa here come dark."

The sun started down. Smoke drifted in like fog. Stickwalker slunk away. Captain Stone crawled up. "Hold this line!" he shouted. "Hold!" The situation is...Colonel Shannon is dead."

Saul interrupted. "Damn fool."

The Captain shrugged. He thought so too. He continued. "The situation **now** is Major Wright is in control."

Saul interrupted the Captain again. "The situation **now** is...they got help comin'. We don't."

"We don't?" asked Captain Stone.

"It's safe to look behind us. See anybody there?"

There weren't.

"God-damn that Howard!" This meant a lot. Captain Stone rarely swore.

Major Wright joined us. When he realized there were no reinforcements coming he swore too. This was more common as Major Wright could be a salty dog. He motioned for Sergeant Benjamin, another salty dog. There, crouched behind a stonewall near Chancellorsville at twilight, we held a council of war.

"They're in those trees across that road. Come night, they'll overrun us," said Saul.

"They'll **try** to overrun us," corrected the Captain.

Saul smiled.

"They'll be close and open in that road," observed the Captain.

"Yessir, they will," said Saul.

"Pass the word," said Captain Stone. "Volley fire. In threes."

Major Wright nodded. They all went to their stations. Passed the word.

It grew dark in the woods. No moon yet.

They sent scouts first. To see how many we were.

But we heard them coming.

A Reb head appeared over the wall. Saul smiled and waved. He pointed his pistol to shoot Saul. I stuck him. Right into his throat and out his head. Then I pulled him kicking over the wall. The first man I had ever killed that way. The men saw how

I did it and followed suit whenever a Reb head appeared. Then we heightened the wall with their bodies.

We waited. The moon rose.

They knew we had gotten their scouts.

Near midnight Stickwalker showed. We told him the plan. He held up a writhing burlap bag.

"When they come, before we shoot, let me throw this. A distraction," he explained. It wasn't long.

I had Darren's Enfield as an extra. Ambrose had Pink-Cheek's. I set Saul's third 44 and Dad's 36 beside me. Expected to use their double actions.

First we heard that infernal yell. Then the rustle of feet on the road. "They're comin'!"

Stickwalker's sack fell in amongst them. It, or they, **did** distract them. "Jesus Gawd Almighty!" we heard.

Captain Stone's cadence was next:

One-volley, two volley, three volley, Go!

Five volley, six volley, seven volley, Go!

Ambrose and I were part of volley's one and five.

Saul, our best cipherer, said, "You missed four," and stood.

I stood too and we opened up with our pistols as did the officers and remaining Bucktails who carried them.

Over one thousand bullets ripped into their charge. We wanted to finish them off but there were no targets. Most of the snakes slithered away. Stickwalker walked among the bodies pulling out his arrows. One rattler struck at him and he severed it in two.

He looked slow, but he wasn't, Stickwalker.

Our scouts guided us back to camp. Reb artillery had hit it after we left. Exhausted, I slept in a crater until I was awakened by a third Rebel yell. Saul, under a splintered tree, answered with the wolf howl he used to irritate Songbird. "Been wantin' to get that out since Halloween," he said. His howl must have irritated the Rebs too as their artillery opened up on the camp again. They had the range. Saul jumped in my hole. Captain Stone ordered Saul to be quiet, dammit! This was only the second time I had heard him swear.

"Just tryin' to make 'em waste shells," grumbled Saul.

But their bombardment had not been an entire waste.

The Rebs got lucky again. One Bucktail who had survived the day was not. "I can't keep 'em in!" he yelled. "I'm kilt. Damn you, Poorbaugh!" Then, silence.

We slept a couple hours. Then both scouts went to find that third hooter. I had just started our burial detail when I heard a shot from the river. Saul and Stickwalker returned with scalps but not the scalp of the hooter. They helped bury Shorty and the gutshot Bucktail from earlier. Saul complained about the unpredictability of this war. Take Shorty for instance. A canister got misdirected and cost Shorty his head. Saul liked to control his killing environment.

Sometimes war just got too wild.

Stickwalker handed me two products of their scout. They skirted the area where we met the Rebs and fought our first firefight yesterday. Found the body of a Reb Captain behind a creased white oak. Saul took the man's money, tobacco, bars and scalp, Stickwalker his Bible and telescope. "These are yours," he said.

I made a good shot. From 377 yards, aiming from my left side and using my left eye I nailed Red Reb's spotter. I opened his Bible. Found an

## The Legend of Augustus McBoone

inscription to "Gerald" from D. M. Brands dated October 24, 1862. The pastor also referenced Psalm 42. I recalled his history lesson on Psalms and him signing Bibles after service. Gerald had been with the sharp-eyed man at church and at the wharf! He had probably "spotted" Branson and Teddy, didn't expect to see me in Chancellorsville, didn't expect to be my first kill. Today his scalp and insignia would bring Saul fifteen dollars in specie. Out of that I earned a dollar fifty.

I was glad to rid the Rebels of Red Reb's spotter. Wished it had been Red Reb himself. He did damage, that Red Reb.

*"Grandpa! Does it bother you that you killed a fellow Christian?"*

*"It was kill or be killed, Hayley."*

*"I guess Uncle Josh is dealing with that in Germany. I don't get it, Grandpa."*

*"I'm almost 101. I still don't, Hayley:"*

Captain Stone stopped by. He made a point of thanking Stickwalker for distracting the enemy yesterday, ordered Saul and I to stop by the officer's tent later.

We thought we were in trouble. After burying the dead and reading Psalms 23 and 42, we went to the officer's tent. I had memorized 23, knew 42 had a deer in it. After my reading I resolved to memorize 42 as well.

Our men were grumbling. A third of us were dead. We had seen the elephant and held him off. Where were our reinforcements? They were to come and put Johnny away! When we got back to camp we found the Reb artillery had destroyed it. What the hell?

Officer's tent was a holed tarp over a table and chairs. The table was an old door supported by two sawhorses. Captain Stone thanked Saul for his role in decimating the enemy. Saul walked away with fifteen dollars in specie for his early morning work. His "howling" goof was not mentioned. I was ordered to stay.

I began the conversation. There were sixty-two Bucktails that wanted to know...what happened to our support?

For the second time that day Captain Stone swore. "That God-damn Hooker blinked! Let Bobby Lee get away. **We** outnumbered them and **still** lost. A lot of men never even **saw** the enemy. Howard hung us out to dry. Outgeneraled again!" He spat.

Then handed me two lieutenant's bars.

"Company A needs a lieutenant," he said. Didn't say why.

"I'd rather we won that battle, sir."

"Don't say that too loud, Gus. Apparently we're not supposed to win battles in this war." He spat again. He was mad!

The Brass did speak up. Got Hooker fired. Lincoln offered the lead to John Reynolds but he said no. Lincoln then ordered Meade.

None of us really knew Meade. He was at Chancellorsville. His folks didn't get to fight.

It took a while for word to filter down. We hoped he trusted his men, like General Reynolds.

I accepted the bars, saluted and turned to leave. But Captain Stone had one more bit of information.

"Red Reb shot Captain Jonas this morning."

"He dead?"

"Yep."

"How?"

He sighed. "Pissing. He pissed in the Rappahannock again. Ball broke his spine."

I left thinking... His spine? That's dead center! Red Reb always pulled left. **Always**. Even Colonel Shannon's heart shot was left of center.

Red Reb hadn't bought it at Chancellorsville. He would appear at our next battle - wherever that was.

I heard that Rebel yell again July first. At Gettysburg.

I did not pee my pants.

## Chapter 33

# A Bird's Eye View

We crossed the Rappahannock on a pontoon bridge, tails tucked between our legs. Our scouts cleared the heights but the Rebs were gone. I didn't ask if they found evidence of Red Reb's perch. I did see Captain Stone and Lieutenant Caulfield by Jonas' grave paying their respects. Neither really liked the man. Both would write to his widow, Millie. Lie about how brave he'd been.

All the officers and a few from the ranks received promotions after Chancellorsville. Because we fought, we did. The survivors anyway. I sewed everyone's bars. The last to receive his was Captain Stone. The most deserving had accosted General Howard and demanded to know where in hell their reinforcements were. Howard didn't have any explanation. After getting screamed at, he tried to savage Captain Stone's promotion. Word reached General Reynolds and he overruled Howard, gave Stone his promotion and an appropriate citation for bravery. Howard learned - don't mess with the influential Stones.

Company A's new officers were: Colonel Wright, Major Stone, Captain Caulfield, Lieutenant McBoone. Our Sergeant was Joss Benjamin, our Corporal, Ambrose Kuhl. Sergeant Benjamin never accepted a promotion, always wanted to be Sergeant. Regardless of my rank I would always be Armorer.

We had sixty-two first class men to support us. We had turned away the elephant but that battle cost us thirty-five men. Of these twenty-six were buried, nine were missing and presumed stinking in the woods.

"Grandpa!

"That's how details found the dead. By smell. Probably still do."

Within the support group were three members of our color guard. Ambrose would sing with them when needed.

One hundred two Company A Bucktails (First Class Men and Officers) left Belle Plain. Sixty-five returned.

"Where did you learn that snake trick?" I asked Stickwalker. We were marching back to Belle Plain.

"Seminole War," he said. "Chief named Osceola was immune, like me. He preferred moccasins 'cause they're so aggressive. I caught some big rattlers too. Long as me. I was the only one strong enough to heave a bag of them."

"What kind did you use back there?"

"Copperheads, several rattlers. Found a den while digging chicory."

Saul chimed in, "Men are sayin' that Stonewall got shot at Chancellorsville. Their pickets done it. Might change things." This was Saul's conjecture.

He was right. The South lost a lot of gumption when they shot Stonewall Jackson.

By the time we got back to Belle Plain, the northern papers were jeering Hooker. The southern papers were cheering Bobby Lee and praying for the recovery of Jackson. The latter did not happen. Stonewall died of pneumonia May 10, 1863. His wife was with him.

I felt kinda bad for Fightin' Joe Hooker. He got blamed for losing Chancellorsville but it seems he wasn't conscious to win it. The same artillery that destroyed our camp got his headquarters as well. Took a direct hit and knocked him catawampus. By the time he came to we had left the field.

When he heard this Saul vowed to shoot the Reb artillerymen next time. Even if they were a mile away he would nail them.

Saul Poorbaugh was many things. A lot of 'em bad. But he kept his word.

We settled into soldier life. I fixed and guarded stuff. Drilled some. Men bitched a lot. I guarded a new thing - a balloon. Big sucker. I painted it blue and white to match the sky. I also reinforced the bottom of the basket with steel plate. The pilot invited me to go for a ride. Saul, who really didn't like heights, said you only die once, go ahead. So I went.

We drifted high then south toward Chancellorsville. Did you ever have a bird's eye view? I saw straight railroad tracks, winding rivers and roads. Saw the battlefield, dead horses, burnt houses, splintered wood, wagons loaded with bloated blue and gray. Some honkers split their V around us, came back together, flying north. I followed them with Gerald's telescope. Holy shit! Below the geese, I saw a moving mass of gray. Longstreet's and Elwell's Corps. Bobby Lee was heading north! Had thousands, hell, tens of thousands of soldiers. Where? D.C.?

What goes up fast comes down slow, believe me.

I told the Brass and we followed.

Caught up with them at Gettysburg.

## Chapter 34

# HIGH GROUND

It's been eight decades since I fought in battle. Yet the impact on my senses remains. As if they are forever stained. I can still **see** the Rebs charging, still **feel** that saber slash, still **hear** that piercing yell, still **taste** the puke of fear, still **smell** death, the **acridness** of it all.

Some claim a sixth sense, a consciousness, an **awareness** of things to come. Stickwalker has it. As did Injun Joe. It might have developed in the tribes over time. In the purebreds. Saul had predictions aplenty but he didn't **know**. Stickwalker knows. I do not. I'm glad.

For me and mine these past eight decades have been more good than bad. But bad is still out there...waiting.

"Grandpa! You're wandering. Muttering. Where is the bad. Where?"

"Don't go lookin', Hayley. It will find us. It always does."

*Back to Gettysburg:*

I've been there what, ten times? Twice during the war, once each decade after. In 1870, I got The Medal. In 1900, I got "evens" with the Sykes Gang and saw Huckleberry for the last time. In 1930, I saw Tom for the last time as well. In 1960, I will be 116. Probably dead. I'm already the last Bucktail.

"Grandpa! Stop talking about being dead!"

"Death is part of life, Hayley. We all die."

"But you're dwelling on it. More and more."

*Hayley is sulking. Her bottom lip sticks out when that happens. Had I been dwelling on my death? My purpose has been to give my take on what happened before I leave to meet Mandi. Hayley doesn't want to hear about that. She does want to hear about the past. I will dwell on that.*

*Silence from the Peanut Gallery.*

"You're right," I say. "Let's get back to Gettysburg, when I was your age. Hand me Longstreet's book. Let's see what he says compared to my recollections."

*Hayley gives me the book. Flops down between me and Brenda:*

Longstreet was the expert. He saw Gettysburg in its entirety. I saw it as a Bucktail. He was there for all three days. I was there one. He was a General, West Point-trained. I was a Lieutenant, McBoone-trained. He was a Rebel. I was a Yank.

Longstreet was Lee's segundo after Jackson was killed at Chancellorsville. He was more of a defensive fighter than Jackson, preferred to fight from higher ground. He advised Lee to **not** fight at Gettysburg, to choose **better ground**. He thought the Rebs should sneak around us, bar our progress south to D.C., find a site of their choosing and whip us. It had worked before.

Bobby Lee, anxious to make a statement and end a bloody war, overruled him. Longstreet bowed in submission to his iron-willed commander and put his forces to work.

They both lost.

Why?

We had the higher ground.

"Dutch" Longstreet was a hulking brute of a man. Looked more like a prize fighter than an academic. Always disheveled, he wore slippers to my medal ceremony and we got along right away. That was in 1870 and ahead of this story.

Remember when I saw the Reb Army from the air? It was Longstreet's First Corps and Elwell's

Second I saw. They were sneaking off to the west side of the Blue Ridge, using the range as a screen for an attack in Pennsylvania. But that took them the long way around, and I saw them. We took a direct route. They came from the west through Harper's Ferry. We came from the south through Frederick. Both towns are in Maryland.

Gettysburg was an accident. One of Saul's "unpredictable" events. General John Buford of our side, a cavalry guy, got there first and took the high ground. The Rebs trickled in from the north and west. The Yanks trickled in from the south and east. Buford didn't trickle. (Neither did we). Buford and his cavalry and six cannons beat Bobby Lee there and set up on Seminary Ridge west of Gettysburg. His job was to slow them up (as was ours), his hundreds against their thousands (us as well). He bloodied them up good and skedaddled to another series of higher ridges to the south. Those heights were Culp's Hill, Cemetery Ridge, Devils Den, Little Round Top and Big Round Top. To someone accustomed to really high hills these ridges did not look that high. But they were higher than the Reb's! Here they were, 70,000 strong, in the north, attacking, and the North held the best ground. And the most men - 80,000 strong.

The Yanks weren't all there yet. Just Buford at first, then Reynolds, then us. We were enough to hold the ground.

Cost us, though.

On the first day, three companies of us Bucktails were in the fields about a mile below Buford on Seminary Ridge. We kinda surrounded Mcpherson's Barn. Crouched in the woods to the south were the veteran shooters of Michigan's Iron Brigade. The Reb infantry with Red Reb advanced toward us about a mile west. They had to cross Willoughby's Run. Had some rail fence and scattered trees over there. Above them, along Herr Ridge, the Confederate artillery was taking aim.

Our job as skirmishers was to slow the Reb advance. In a messy way we got the job done. This is how messy it was: On the morning of July 1, 1863, sixty-five Bucktails of Company A answered the bugler's call. Twenty-four hours later only three of us could answer that call. And we three were walking wounded. Company A was...gone. The surgeon sent us home.

Back to Longstreet and his version of the battle:

It lasted three days. They won the field on the first day but we gave it to them. The Rebs exulted in Gettysburg but Longstreet knew their joy was short-lived. Their advance had been slowed and the Union held the best ground. On the second day there was stalemate but the Union still held the high ground. The third day was Friday, July 3, 1863, the day before Independence Day. Longstreet argued to sneak by us, to find better ground. Again, he was overruled. Pickett's men came from his First Corps. They charged **up** a mile hill into the waiting Union guns. When the smoke cleared Reb generals Garrett, Armistead and Kemper were killed. No colonels were left, not a one. He sent nine brigades. They called for more. But he didn't have any more to send! The Union prevailed. News accounts said the failure of Pickett's charge broke the back of the Confederacy. But, General Longstreet gave credit to us first-day fighters. Our sacrifice made it possible for the Union to possess and keep the high ground.

Dutch Longstreet was far ahead of his time. Developed a system of trench warfare that was followed in World War One. I lost a son and grandson in those trenches. I never blamed the engineer. I blame the g-d krauts!

He fought with Dad, Saul and Stickwalker in the Mexican war. Said the three tallest members of the American army were a menace to the Mex's. When we met he knew I was Angus' son. Sorry to hear he was dead. He told Grant there wasn't a Reb company that stood a chance against me and Saul and Stickwalker. For certain I had earned The Medal but where in hell were the other two? Was that giant **ever** a soldier?

He and President Grant were longtime friends. West Point, the Mexican War, shared political philosophies kept them together. The Civil war was an aberration. After it, he joined the GOP, became Railroad Commissioner. He heard about my later exploits with Old Warhorse at Blackwell and after the Johnstown Flood. He said, in his slippers, if I **ever** need his help to let him know. So when Angus and Caleb applied to West Point I did. His letters had impact. 'Course so did my Medal and the letters from Governor Stone and Senator Allen. (They were Major Stone and Lieutenant Allen when I stuck them in the belly of Tom's dead horse).

Longstreet died in1904, aged eighty-four. Angus and Caleb attended his service in D. C. Angus was a pallbearer. They spoke the same language those two - both generals, Point grads, excellent writers. Angus cried.

Longstreet gave Angus his book and Angus gave it to me. He also told Angus the back of the Confederacy was broken on Day 1 at Gettysburg. The day that Buford, Reynolds, Michigan's Iron Brigade, and us Bucktails saved the Union's high ground.

## Chapter 35

# McPherson's Barn

June 30th I got proof the Union would ultimately win the war. It was the end of the month and we got paid. I got $70, Union scrip. Four days as a sergeant, fifty-six as a lieutenant. Plus $10 for clothing and shoes. If the Union could afford to pay for shoes and the Confederates couldn't, the Union would prevail.

We had to convince the barefoot Johnny's though.

I stuffed my pay into my money belt and we quick-timed it to five miles south of Gettysburg. The next day we quick-timed it again and faced west. The Rebs were massing there.

We were part of General John Reynolds two corps that he led into position that First Day. We were frontline troops, skirmishers, located on a big field below our artillery at our back and theirs at our front. Each was a mile from us. We were in the middle. In Saul's words "cannon fodder."

We had the advantage as General John Buford's cavalry had gotten there first, had time to dig in and held the highest ground. That was the only advantage we had. Hoped it would be enough.

We were badly outnumbered. Stall tactics here.

Saul and Stickwalker came in from their scout and gave us officers the grim news. Buford's cavalry unit was less than a brigade and only had six artillery pieces. The Rebs had thirty-six at least. Reynolds had brought two infantry corps, about 2,000 men. We would end up spread before a Reb advance that easily totaled 5,000 and would later swell to 10,000. Initially that was 5-2 odds with the Rebs doubling that with reinforcements. We could match that with ours but they were coming and the enemy was already here. And "here" meant the Virginia Infantry was 1500 yards away, almost a mile, and their artillery on Herr Ridge was a mile.

As a cannonball or bullet flies - a mile is **not** very far.

Major Stone and Captain Caulfield spread us out. Three companies of the 149th hunkered down by McPherson's Barn. A couple of small non-Bucktail regiments, the 143rd and 150th, took positions on either side of us. General Reynolds rode down from conferring with General Buford. He seemed so calm, so reassuring, General Reynolds. He rode off to direct the Iron Brigade as they approached the woods. He knew our reinforcements were coming. Right now the odds were awful but...His hat flew off and he toppled off his horse. The shot came across Willoughby Creek, smoke rose from the Virginia Infantry. Then the triumphant wave of a red scarf. He was cheered.

General Reynolds was dead.

We wanted to avenge him right there but could not. The second after Red Reb's wave came the whistle of artillery fire from Herr Ridge. First, they were high. Then got close when I saw a solid shot bounce and roll just beyond the barn. Then it was enfilade. They found the range.

Colonel Wright and Captain Caulfield were directing from their horses. A canister exploded over their heads and Company A lost two officers and two horses right there. And when I say lost, I mean...gone. Colonel Wright was knocked silly. Captain Caulfield was really gone...only one leg and boot remained.

Another canister exploded above Buster and my wagon. Buster and his companion were ripped into horsemeat. Ambrose was knocked off the driver's bench and sent backwards into the wagon. The wagon turned over and spilled its contents and Ambrose underneath.

From Reynold's killing to Buster's, it all seemed to happen so...slow. But it was at most, two minutes. Then a really bizarre thing occurred. Our color guard - drums, fife, bugle - and three flagmen carrying the U. S., the Pennsylvania and the 149th Bucktail Regimental marched away from McPherson's Barn. They marched as a tight unit, did "Battle Hymn," and drew the Reb cannon fire away.

That brave act gave us Bucktails **time**. I saw that Saul was shooting at the Reb guns. He promised he would. Stickwalker had grabbed an Enfield. I was doing the same. Their individual acts gave me an idea.

"Bucktails!" I yelled. "I want volley fire at their cannons! We'll go by Company." In just seconds all rifles were pointed at Herr Ridge. "Company A - Go! Company B - Go! Company C - Go!" By the time C had shot off their volley, A was ready. We did four repetitions. In the same time as they sent sixty rounds at us we sent sixteen hundred at them. I don't know if we got anybody but their guns fell silent.

I had turned to yell thanks to the color guard when deer hair plastered my face and I heard another shot.

"Sniper!" yelled Saul. "Git Down!" He tackled me and dragged me into the barn. Like on the boat, he said "Play dead." When we got inside, he said "He didn't get ya, did he?"

"He shaved my tail." I said, wiping my face.

"I'm gettin' that sumbitch," said Saul. He joined Stickwalker who was pointing out the open window of the barn. "I see him!" said Stickwalker. "He's kneeling over a fence at 1,200 yards. See that leafy tree behind the sob?" "I see him too!" said Saul. He set the Hawken on the window ledge so only the barrel end showed. He had reloaded. Brought a milk stool with him and sat. He aimed the Hawken. Started talking to himself. I pulled out Gerald's telescope.

"Thinks he got Gus. Rollin' that smoke. Don't know yet he shoots left. Bet Reynolds is kilt left too. I'm shootin' into the wind. Gotta aim what, two feet high?" Stickwalker grunted his confirmation. Saul set the back trigger, breathed out slow, touched her off.

I looked through my scope. The Reb officer hung over that rail fence. One half of his red scarf was blowing our way.

I ran out the door to thank our Color Guard but could not find them...anywhere. I looked where I had seen them last. Like the Captain, they were...gone. A bloody mist hung in the air. Over a tangle of limbs and some tatter of instruments. The remnants of our three flags blew in the same direction as Red Reb's scarf.

## The Legend of Augustus McBoone

"The Rebs are edgin' closer," said Saul from the window. I heard another voice, a new voice, an older voice then. The Reb artillery had quit. Were they afraid of hitting their own? On Seminary Ridge Buford's men stayed dug in, almost out of cannon shells. Stickwalker slunk back into the shadows of the barn.

"I see you're a sharpshooting outfit," the voice said. "Great shot, soldier!"

I'm thinking, can he **see** that far? Saul emerged from the barn and nodded at the compliment.

An old-timer approached. Tall, crazy, full head of wavy gray hair. Carried an older Enfield and as much ammo as I. No bayonet though.

Major Stone got off his horse. Shooed it into the barn. The visitor saw he was a major, figured correctly for him to be in charge. In formal language he said, "I request permission to fall in with your regiment, Sir. I killed many redcoats at Lundy Lane. I want a crack at those Rebs who threaten my village and my life!"

The Major was incredulous. "You fought in 1812? What is your name, Sir?"

"John Burns. A better sharpshooter you'll not find in Gettysburg...except that man over there." He indicated Saul.

Major Stone appraised John Burns carefully. He knew we were gonna be smelling Johnny's breath soon. He also noted the absence of a bayonet. "We sure could use you but...We're too open here. Best you join the Iron Brigade and shoot from cover. They are the soldiers in the black hats, yonder."

"Yessir! And, thank you! I'll fight Injun style just like we did when we defeated the Brits. Damn them!"

He left. The men were gathering, checking their loads. Fixing bayonets. I didn't have to tell them. They **knew**. "He's a crazy old coot," one said.

"He's not so crazy." said Saul. "He's fightin' mad."

"He **can** shoot." added Stickwalker, emerging from the barn. "I saw him."

Major Stone asked, "At Lundy's?"

Stickwalker nodded. "I couldn't get close enough to kill him."

"How old is he? Seventy-five?"

"At least," said Stickwalker. "But he can still **see**."

John Burns entered the trees. I knew they'd take the extra gun. Especially outnumbered 5-2.

It didn't matter anyway. We heard the Rebel yell and knew they were coming.

## Chapter 36

# HUCKLEBERRY

They crossed Willoughby Creek. The whistle of cannon shot overhead reminded us of Buford's protections. He and his knew the value of support, knew the affect it had on the men. Those shells blew geysers of water and gaps in their line.

They kept coming. Kept yelling. "1,000 yards now," said Saul.

I turned to the men. My Bucktails. Not just my Company either, **my** soldiers. "Bucktails!" I yelled. "Volley in threes. Shoot at 500, 400 and 300 yards." They got ready, Companies A, B, C. The other two regiments sent runners - wanted to help. The more Rebs we killed the better our chances were. The more we delayed them the better our Union's chances were. I noticed their bayonets were fixed as well.

They weren't the marksmen we were, so I told them to volley at 200 yards, then all five of us would volley at 100. We'd really blister them at 100 yards. After that aim, shoot at will, charge.

Saul did a quick cipher. "We're sending 15,000 rounds. If we drop half of them and they drop half of us that's still 2,500 - 1,000. That's the same as 5-2."

"We'll do better," I said. I prayed I was right.

They shot. A couple of my men yelled they'd been hit. "Spread out!" I yelled. "Fight Injun style." The men spread. No bunches to shoot at now.

"750 yards," said Saul.

"Hold! Hold! Bucktails get ready!"

"550," said Saul.

I got Gerald's telescope out.

"500," said Saul. "Fire!" said I. "Fire! Fire!" Maybe 25% went down.

"400," said Saul. "Fire!" said I. "Fire! Fire!" Maybe 33% of those went down.

From 300 yards in, the smoke and din got so bad I put away the telescope and started shooting myself. At 100 yards I recall we really blistered them but it got smoky and they were running at us, coughing, cursing, yelling, firing. I heard my men grunt, cry, fall. When I saw two gray-clad men run at us out of the smoke, I yelled, "Charge!"

"Go get 'em, Grandpa!"

"It was a helluva mess, Hayley. Just like Saul predicted, a mess:"

Stickwalker led us, created an old-time phalanx. I kept to his left. Saul to his right. The remnants of the Bucktails, the 143rd and 150th followed. The Iron Brigade was still shooting from the woods. How many had we gotten? How many had they? There was no time to count. Couldn't see anyway. Just stick, club, yell, cough.

Those Rebs were used to Yanks running **from** them not **for** them. Nor were they used to a wild and silent giant taking two out at a time with a long stick. Then there was Saul and me, both long men with long bayonets. Saul clubbed with the heavy Hawken then pulled out a pistol. Shot low. Got bone. He was whooping! If they smelled his breath - it was not rancid. He was enjoying this.

My breath was. But I kept on. That smoke hung over us. Served as a screen. Where was their line? Balls whined by. That line has to shoot through the smoke. Couldn't see us either. I felt the shock of a bullet, then another, both glanced off my belt. Then, no shots toward us. Afraid of hitting their own. Not so Saul! I thought of pulling my own pistol but there wasn't time. A gangly Reb stumbled out of the smoke. Growled at me and charged. I stuck him, lifted him, shook him off. I lost count then of those I stuck or clubbed. A riderless horse ran through the melee`, eyes frenzied with fear. Behind him rode a Reb. He pointed his saber at me and spurred his horse. Saul screamed "Use yer pistol!" No time. As he went by I crouched, his saber flashed down, I felt its whack on my collarbone, my bayonet thrust missed his boot, impaled his horse. I pulled it low, disembowelled the horse. He turned to attack again. His mount's entrails got tangled in its feet. He went for his pistol as I went for mine. A whirling stick struck the Reb's head. His hat flew off. Then he fell. His horse fell too, kicking savagely, upending men. I shot it in the head. I shot at Reb's then 'til my gun went click. "I'm out," I yelled. Saul threw me his third 44. He was still shooting and yelling. Very purposeful with his shooting. Stickwalker lopped off heads with the big Green River.

The smoke started to rise. Shooting from the woods told me the Iron Brigade was still engaged. Probably at Reb cavalry. I think now the sight of us big three, especially Stickwalker, was enough to send the Rebs back to the creek. They were running. Back to their reinforcements. Out of the smoke.

There was still mopping up to do. Then we had to grab who we could and get the hell out of there.

I ran toward two wounded Yanks being menaced by a crazed Reb infantryman. Major Stone knocked his bayonet aside. The other Yank thrust at his bare foot. The Reb was a sergeant, older, didn't see me coming...in time. I stuck him in the back, cracked his spine, my point exited his chest. I heard him say, "Well, Gawd damn!" then I turned him away and shook him off. I dropped my rifle and pulled our two into a dead horse's belly. The Reb officer lay near, head oozing blood. The second Yank was a lieutenant with the 150th.

"Stay down!" I said. Kinda silly. They couldn't stand anyway. From the cover of the horse, I looked around. Saw piles of blue and gray. Mostly gray. Some were struggling, some still...as death. A couple of the strugglers yelled, "Mother! Mother!" Those that were still could not yell anymore. It seemed Saul, Stickwalker and I were the only ones still standing. A Reb and a Yank died before me, side by side, their heels drumming the earth. Stickwalker was pulling arrows from dead bodies. I hadn't seem him shoot. He also retrieved his stick.

Saul was being Saul, rolling over bodies, looking for booty. He'd found a ring and cut it off. "No coin on any of these poor bastards," he said, grumbling. Then a little Reb emerged from under a flag, aimed and shot Saul with his musket. At about the same time the kid got hit. Ambrose, emerging from the wagon, grabbed his rifle, saw movement, and shot.

Too late. The shot killed the kid but Saul carried that minnie ball in his hip for seventeen years. Saul remained standing. Indicated he was okay. Blood stained his buckskins.

I heard a cough. A Yank sat up. Looked around, confused. I had never seen this soldier. I went over. Knelt down. He'd been shot through. Lung shot. Blood bubbled out his front and back. He would soon be dead. I consoled him. Least I could do. Offered him my canteen.

"Where's Tom?" he said. Frothy blood blew out his lips.

"Who?" I noticed an accent.

"Tom," he repeated. "Where... Is... Tom?"

"Who are you?"

"Huckleberry. I was in those trees yonder. With the First Missourah. Saw Tom ride by. Ran after. Got into this...mess."

He had that figured right. He gulped water. A comfort only. It ran out both holes.

"I'm dyin', ain't I?"

I nodded. No sense in lying to the man. "Tom's a Reb?" I asked.

"An officer. We agreed to swap Bibles! But I cain't find him." It was getting harder to talk.

"I'll do it," I said. But Huckleberry's eyes just stared. He leaned against me. I laid him back. Closed his eyes.

The medics came around then. We took care of the wounded first. Both blue and gray. Weren't many. Maybe 10%. Filled three ambulances is all.

The dead wagons held more. I personally shouldered Huckleberry onto a Yank one. That hurt! Reminded me of my cut. Told the driver his Bible story. He nodded but there were so many! He would be dumped with the other privates in a limed pit.

Ambrose carried the Reb kid to a dead wagon. He had him wrapped in his Confederate flag. Unrolled him and kept the flag. The kid wouldn't be carrying it anymore. Stickwalker helped, hauling two at a time, one under each arm. He was cut some, he could have been shot. He was so impassive, Stickwalker! Already his wounds were starting to close.

Mine weren't.

Saul stood near. Leaning on his Hawken. The smoke was rising. The Rebs massing again across Willoughby creek.

## The Legend of Augustus McBoone

Time to go.

Buford had left already.

It was two miles to the hospital tents. We walked the whole way. Stickwalker carried Saul's Hawken. Saul found one of my ball bats, used it as a cane.

The three ambulances passed us. Their drivers urging their teams.

What Huckleberry described as a mess **was** a real mess. Pieces of men, animals, and entrails reminded me of a slaughterhouse. Piles of tack, splinters, metal and gunstock were everywhere. The smell of smoke and cordite hung in the evening air. Carrion birds were squawking, swallowing eyeballs they found.

On the way we talked some about Huckleberry. "He might become a haunt," said Saul, limping on his ball-bat cane.

He saw my frown.

He explained.

"An unsettled spirit. Like Blacksnake. They're all over battlefields, ya know."

I had heard of them. Had yet to be visited by one. "Dad told me of Blacksnake," I said. "He wails."

"He does!" agreed Hayley. "We've all heard him."

*If you stay in Steam Vally long enough you **will** hear Blacksnake. He wails until the last cat is killed. He was still wailing in 1945:*

We found the hospital tents below the hovering carrion birds. Already piles of limbs were growing outside, drawing flies. We could not smell decay... yet. The blood smelled acrid now.

"Eww, Grandpa!"

"I've said war is hell on earth, Hayley. We were the lucky ones, hurt but still walkin':"

We ducked into the Bucktail tent. I was covered with blood and gore - some mine. My tunic and shirt were slashed with bullet holes. My money belt was gone. I was getting woozy, starting to see double. Stickwalker made Saul and I sit. Polly Llewellyn came over. Sponged me off from a pan of bloody water. Stitched me up with sinew provided by Stickwalker. I grumbled something about losing my gold pieces. She smiled and held up her fat and grimy ring finger. She hadn't lost hers! I swallowed some tepid water. Started to feel better.

Colonel Llewellyn came by. Wanted to remove the ball from Saul's hip. He refused, saying he didn't want a woman looking at his bare hind end. Stickwalker and I grunted. Polly scoffed. Actually, Saul was thinking he would lose his leg. Colonel sighed, said, "Well, it's your funeral." (It was too, seventeen years later). So he cleaned out the wound, closed it with gauze soaked in whiskey. Saul thought it was a waste of whiskey. The surgeon suggested laudanum for pain. "I can handle the pain, Sir," he said.

Ambrose looked a sight too. Dirty and caked with the Reb kid's blood. He declined treatment, his wounds were superficial...he said.

We stood.

That was the qualifier for staying in the hospital. Those that could walk could not stay. We made the rounds. Found Colonel Wright, Major Stone and Lieutenant Allen of the 150th. There was only one other survivor of Company A, Sgt. Benjamin had lost both legs. A few from B and C were still alive. Colonel Wright was awake, claimed he didn't need laudanum...yet.

"We sent them running, Sir." I said. General Buford softened them up. We scared them, Sir."

"How?"

"The smoke. Confused them. We did our job, Sir."

He-of-the-voice-that-carried said, "Tell the rest of the men I said thanks."

"You have, Sir."

He seemed confused.

"We're it, us and the few men in this part of the tent."

Indeed, Companies A, B and C were **gone**. Those not dead were wounded. We shared the tent with the survivors of the 143rd and the 150th. The 149th didn't even have a bugler for "lights out" that evening.

Of the ninety-eight First Class men that left Wellsborough as Company A only three would ever return.

## Chapter 37

# What Goes Around...

John Burns came in. Litters of the Iron Brigade entered the next tent. They had repelled Rebs too but lost over half of their men. The First Missouri had lost all of theirs. Burns was walking wounded like me and Stickwalker. He eyed the latter quizzically.

"I saw you at Lundy Lane!"

Stickwalker nodded.

"They said, back then, that your kind live long. I didn't take stock in it 'til now."

Stickwalker just stood. Held out his huge hand which John Burns shook. He was a tall man for the day, a six-footer, small compared to the giant.

"This time we're on the same side," he said. Burns approached me. "Battle stories travel like echoes, even faster." He handed me two Bibles.

He continued. "Damnedest thing. This Reb officer came riding by, saber drawn. Had him in my sights. Then this private from the Missouri Boys yells "Tom! Tom!" He runs in front, forces me to hold up. Saw another officer. Blew him out of the saddle. Got smoky and busy in the woods after that. We were loading the dead wagon and the teamsters tell your story of the Missourian. On the way here I found the Yank's haversack and the Reb's horse. The Reb's saddlebag had a Bible. The haversack another. The inscriptions inside support the story. Rather odd is it not?"

I took the Bibles, read the inscriptions out loud. The Reb's Bible was "To Huck" from a Mrs. Watson. The Yank's was "To Tom" from Aunt Polly. Both had the same admonition: To read their Bible daily. Obviously the two ladies from Hannibal had gotten together. Then their boys had gone separate ways.

These things happen in war. Not that odd, I guess.

I could see the men as lads during better days, getting their ears pulled for mischief by their matrons. Mrs. Llewellyn heard us talk, walked to her husband, her eyes misty. "Our boys have done that," she said.

She wasn't the only person who heard. From the Reb corner came some moaning and "Huck? Where are ya Huck?" Mrs. Llewellyn rushed over, washed him off with the same bloody sponge. There was a huge gash on the top of his head. Stickwalker provided more sinew, Polly the sewing expertise.

"Lieutenant Sawyer, 4th Missourah Cav," he said.

I had heard a similar drawl a couple of times before. Mrs. Llewellyn motioned me over. "Lieutenant Sawyer, meet Lieutenant McBoone," she said. We shook. A few hours earlier we had tried to kill each other.

These things happen in war.

I handed Tom both Bibles, told him about Huck, walked away.

Tom Sawyer needed the time alone.

*I noticed Hayley and Brenda had misty eyes as well. I turned back to the journal:*

Meanwhile, John Burns joined the wounded of the Iron Brigade and Polly Llewellyn whispered to her husband. The Colonel motioned us over to his desk, a door supported by nail kegs. I couldn't help but recall the time when Captain Stone had reason to bust me. He didn't bust me and Colonel Llewellyn didn't either - The Colonel discharged me.

With his signature Ambrose, Saul and I were mustered out of the service. I read his papers to Saul. Company A was gone, it said. We were too shot-up to continue. Saul, who had been threatening desertion since Chancellorsville, whooped. Ambrose seemed dazed, confused. I stood there, my collarbone hurting, and thinking: These two had homes to return to. I did not. Mrs. Llewellyn blew me a kiss with her right hand. Held up the newly washed left. The ring gleamed. Stickwalker said it best: "What goes around comes around," was his comment.

As we were leaving we heard a commotion at the rear of the tent, where several wounded blacks were.

"You stop that! You stop that now!"

The orderly doing the hollering had a saw in one hand, a black foot in the other.

Another surgeon closed the unfortunate's wound.

The orderly called to the Colonel. "Get him the hell out of here! He's cutting off good limbs!"

I heard a familiar chuckle.

Out of the gloom emerged Junior Sykes. He saw me, said "You!" ran out the back door.

"Someone shoot that son of a bitch!" yelled the orderly.

Junior got away.

That night we rested on the back side of Cemetery Ridge. We could hear the Union forces digging in, making ready their fortifications. The Rebs would want it - it was the highest hill around. Although we had given up the field, our delay tactic worked, the Union reinforcements were coming in the night.

Tomorrow would be dicey, unpredictable. Saul was for leaving at first light. Stickwalker knew a way around Gettysburg, which the Rebs had occupied. We could hear them whooping it up. Temporary.

"What the hell they crowin' about?" said Saul. "They may have won the day...but we got the highest ground."

"Let's get out of here," said Ambrose.

The smartest thing he said during the whole damn war.

## Chapter 38

# OLD WARHORSE, AGAIN

I kept this journal hidden. Never shared it with the girls. 'Til now:

We got up around three, before the bombardment began, before the sun. It was Thursday, July 2nd. The stars were twinkling and I wondered about Stickwalker's prediction about it being humid that day.

We went by the hospital tent. Peeked in. The poor medical men had not slept, were still in fact - sawing. The pile of limbs outside had grown. The officers of Company A were sleeping. They were on laudanum now.

Colonel Llewellyn told me the officers were discussing a medal for me.

"Probably the laudanum talkin'," I said.

He shook his head. "This was **before** the laudanum."

Saul overheard and came over. "We're leavin'," he said. "Takin' him home."

Again I thought, "I don't have a home." Didn't say it though.

The Colonel gave us a tired smile. "They'll find you."

Never at a loss for words Saul said: "Have 'em send us our pay, would you?"

"Request went with your discharges last night. Polly insisted."

She knew when to stamp her foot, Mrs. Llewellyn.

Stickwalker led us to the train station. From the hospital we went east then north around Gettysburg, then east again. He knew hidden trails to his cabin in Paxton. On the way, Ambrose and Stickwalker caught a loose Yank horse, made Saul ride it and forded a creek. We heard the thumping of artillery in the distance. "Glad we're free of that shit," said Saul.

We got naked and washed off the gore in the creek. Stickwalker's cuts had already closed. He foraged, made poultices for me and Saul. Ambrose moved deliberately, figuring out his every move. "Shell-shock," said Saul. "He'll come around eventual." Stickwalker wasn't so sure. He had noticed a slowness while catching the horse. We rinsed our clothes, spread them on the creek bank to dry. Stickwalker examined our wounds, pronounced us hale but not hearty. Hale enough to travel, I guess. We dressed, Saul proved he was feeling better by mounting the horse himself. I looked at my reflection in the water.

A hairy, full-bearded eighteen going on twenty-eight, stood there. I had grown. I was now a full two inches taller than the six-and-a-half foot tall scout. My belt was a third notch beyond Camp Curtin. "Thickenin' to manhood" according to Saul.

We rested at Stickwalker's cabin, ate on his front porch. It was humid but cooler under the awning of his wraparound. He gave us money. "For the horse," he said. I don't know how much he gave Ambrose and Saul, never asked. I had enough for **three** horses. The Yank horse was blind in one eye. Not worth a lot. "He'll probably eat him," said Saul.

We shook, said our see-you-laters at the train station, none knowing when that "later" would be. To my mind that seemed more like a greeting than a benediction, which proved true. The engine pulling us was B & O's 080 - Old Warhorse. The pilot was different from the engineer at D.C. I didn't say anything, wondered where he was. Figured he'd been assigned to a different engine.

## The Legend of Augustus McBoone

ALL ABOARD!

The conductor this time:

We weren't alone either. We joined Millie Jonas and her son, now three, for the trip north. She was a widow, had gotten two special letters from Captain Stone and Lieutenant Caulfield from Company A. I told her they had both been promoted but Caulfield was killed at Gettysburg. I left a lot out of course. I did not tell her how Major Caulfield had died nor her husband. I did not tell her what a martinet he had been, that we despised the man. She noticed my lieutenant's bars. "Seems you rose the most, Augustus. When you were on this train last you were a private." I answered I was lucky and Saul opined that I was good. I did notice she called me Augustus. She whispered she would be in her sleeper later. She had large brown doe-like eyes, reminded me of Peggy Sue.

This I told Saul after she left. "She's a doe alright," he said. "A doe in heat."

I knocked on her door later. She answered in her nightgown. Her son lay asleep on a pile of pillows in a corner. We sat on the bed and whispered. She borrowed ten dollars. Said she'd pay me back when she got her widow's pension. Then we kissed. I raised her nightgown, discovered she wasn't wearing bloomers. I couldn't tell. **How** could Injun Joe tell?

Millie and her son were still sleeping when I eased out the cabin door.

WILLIAMSPORT! The conductor said.

Saul and I got off there.

Millie, her son and Ambrose went on to Troy.

"Did you ever tell Grandma?" This was Brenda.

"No. She suspected. Never said."

"You had a one-night stand when you were my age, Grandpa?"

"Is that what you call it now, Hayley?" I'm thinking, **What** are we teaching these kids? She knows about one-night stands but has to ask her mom about clap and backdoor?

But Wicked Girl wasn't done. "Did she ever pay you back, Grandpa? Was she worth ten dollars?"

"She paid me, Hayley:"

I let the matter drop there. Hayley seemed disappointed to learn that I had been repaid. For this eighteen-year old - even if she totally forgot - yeah, Millie Jonas was worth ten dollars.

## Chapter 39

# OVERNIGHT AT THE LADY

You can tell how busy a town is by its early morning activity. In my experience, a boom town **never** sleeps.

We breakfasted near the train station. Two bloodied returning soldiers. Saul limped, I grimaced.

It was Friday, July 3rd, 1863. Factory men were at the restaurant smoking and eating, drinking coffee in preparation for the twelve-hour shift that began at six A.M. These were all older men, the younger having gone to the woods or war. There was no evident class structure here. Laborers, foremen and owners sat together, dependent on each other later, not at breakfast.

We came in carrying heavy packs and Saul his Hawken. We groaned and sat. Ordered steak, eggs, taters and coffee, gallons of coffee. The owner told us whatever we ate was "on the house." We thrilled the waitress by us each giving her a silver dollar.

## The Legend of Augustus McBoone

The locals peppered us with questions: How's it going at Gettysburg? There's been no word since the wires were cut. And, You're Bucktails, aren't you?

We answered truthfully. Like Stickwalker said "Truth never gets you in trouble. Lying always does." "We should do okay at Gettysburg," I said, "thanks to Buford securing the best ground. Once the Union gets all there the lines will hold again. As for Company A Bucktails, well, we're it. Us and one other on his way to Troy. Out of a thousand Bucktails in the 149th, maybe two hundred fifty have survived... so far."

It's a cliche I know, but you could have heard a pin drop in that restaurant.

Saul, never one to dismiss his audience, said more. "We sent those Rebs back to their lines, halted Bobby Lee's advance. There was Buford's cavalry, us Bucktails, the Iron Brigade, the 143rd and 150th. They hit us hard, us Bucktails most. We hit back. Lieutenant McBoone here, led the way."

They applauded. I said that Saul was just opposite me. How can you tell about an unrecorded giant leading the phalanx? So, I didn't. I colored up but was so bearded and red from the outdoors they could not see my embarrassment. Then the shift whistle blew and the men scattered.

A well-dressed man, obviously a millowner, approached. "My son, Bill Allen, is with the 150th. A lieutenant. Do you know him?"

"Lieutenant Allen?" said Saul turning to me. "Isn't he one of the men you pulled into the horse?"

I nodded. Correctly deducing the dad's question I said, "Your son's okay. Shot in the leg. He'll be home soon."

"Thank God!" he said. "I'll tell Clara. You men need a lift?"

He drove us to the smith's. Then drove off to tell his wife their son was coming home! I got down first. Overheard Saul say, "Gus saved your boy. They're puttin' him up for a medal." Mr. Allen waved and said "What goes around **will** come around."

Saul bought a wagon and a two-horse team. Bob and Dick were their names. Twins, born from a purebred Belgian mare and a sneaky neighbor stallion. We never knew him but he sure was big! Bob was brown. Dick was black. Green-broke to pulling, young and spirited they were. Saul brandished the ball bat he used as a cane then asked me to work the team. It hurt but I took a whole hour showing them I was Boss.

Saul never said what he paid for the combo. The smith threw in a sack of grain. The wagon was sturdy and dirty. Oak, it had hauled coal from the Bloss Mines. It needed a new hickory tongue. A piece of red oak had been scabbed on. The bed had a couple of rotten boards. I told Saul what he and Jesse had to do. He just grunted. I told him what he would have to do with the team, too. I would not be around to train them. Those two would need a really firm hand. He and Jesse were strong but impatient. I'd hate to see prime horseflesh wind up in their pot. Again, Saul just grunted.

"Since I wasn't gonna be around to train the team what **was** I gonna do?" he asked.

"Hunt and trap," I said. "I know how to log. And tinker. I can always do that."

"We'll help," said Saul.

"I'm goin' to the Big Woods. Fifty miles away, at least."

"We been there. We'll help."

That ended that discussion

We watered the horses at Trout Run and south of Buttonwood where an artesian spring crossed the road. We made Buttonwood late that afternoon. Saul was anxious to get home to his wives, especially Songbird, who, he knew, would have no truck with Jesse.

Ike McFee was cutting hay when we drove by The Lady's. He invited us in. Saul spoke up, said "No, Gus will be down later. Did they have room for the horses?"

Ike said there was plenty of room and they'd see me later for supper.

On the way to the Poorbaugh cabin I asked, "Why can't you put up the horses?"

"Cause they're yours!" he said, laughing. "The team **and** the wagon. A getting-started present from me and Stickwalker and the Bucktails. They that lived, chipped in."

I knew better than to object. That gift was the blessing that got me teamstering.

I misted up. Before only Dad, Ike and The Lady and the Glovers had ever given me anything.

He saw my emotion and said, "You earned it Gus! You saved our asses in that battle."

I objected. "You saved mine! You and Stickwalker."

"The point is…You were there. For all of us. Not yourself. You saw the elephant and didn't panic. Soldiers never forget that, Gus."

I swallowed hard.

A raucous reunion awaited Saul. His wives and daughters were all glad to see him...alive. They shot off guns to alert Jesse who came in from a hunt. Except for the knives and Saul's limp they **were** identical. Saul had gotten off the wagon gingerly. He favored his hip, kept my bat. He insisted the wound was just a scratch. Songbird, more insistent, replaced his bloody poultice with another. While the other women repaired my shirt and tunic with sinew, Songbird replaced my poultice and rebandaged my shoulder.

"Can't have Lieutenant McBoone not presentable for Lady Louisa," chortled Saul. He beamed after some private get-reacquainted time with Songbird.

I left after hugging Saul. Jesse walked with me to the wagon. He reminded me of a panther - smooth and fast. Saul's carnal twin. According to Saul, worse. Too mean for war. He liked me, I could tell.

"You keep an eye," he warned. "I was dressin' out a big cinnamon bear when I heard the shootin'. Fact is, I **found** this bear yestiddy. Neck broke. Twisted. Marking his territory when this other critter ambled by. He shoulda let it go. Just amblin'. Instead the big dummy attacks. Gets kilt. Then this critter scales Bear Moutain, the steep side, with ease. I could feel it lookin' down at me from the laurel. Tell Ike. Thing walks on two legs. Has twenty-four inch feet.

I interrupted. "Another giant, like Stickwalker?"

"Naw, it's a critter. Has red-brown fur. Stickwalker has six toes. This thing has four."

*"Did you ever see it, Grandpa?"*

*"So far, only it's tracks, Hayley. Injun Joe saw him."*

That evening I shared supper with Ike and Lady Louisa in her dining room. Kinda formal. I brushed my uniform. My right sleeve was blood-stained. It's never come out.

She served chicken.

We talked, drank cider, I talked some more.

Maybe it was the cider. Didn't have the same affect as whiskey. I think it was the security of the Lady's. I knew I wouldn't have to face sabers or grapeshot anymore. I was safe.

I talked, though. Told about my days as a Bucktail, about Stickwalker and Saul, the places I'd been, the things I'd seen. I told about Red Reb and Pastor Brands and Huckleberry and Sykes Junior.

"You haven't heard the last of the Sykes Gang, I fear." said Ike. "Nor have I. When I learned of Seagreaves and Angus I prepared for them to come here. Instead they went west. I heard they joined Quantrell. Junior must have gotten caught. Joined up to avoid jail."

"Why didn't I ever see you?" asked Louisa.

"I think it pained Dad to come this way. There was you and Jacob Miller and the hanging of Elmer Sykes."

Louisa changed the subject, asked me my plans. "I want to make something of myself." I said. "To hunt and trap, to be a market hunter like the Poorbaugh's or Injun Joe." They listened. Ike smoked a pipe, such sweet-smelling tobacco! The Lady remarked that Angus had done a "good job" with me. They were so glad he had "straightened out" and the parts they had played in that.

I slept upstairs in the biggest bedroom I had ever been in. Ike aired it, opened six tall windows. I kept them open. Listened to the Steam Valley night sounds: Blockhouse riffles, a great-horned owl, peepers, a rabbit's scream. It stormed that night. The curtains blew in. I swear to God I heard Blacksnake wail.

I slept warm and dry and secure - by the bed- on the floor. More comfortable there. After Blacksnake wailed I thought it unfair that I should be sleeping in a bed while Huckleberry slept in a trench, in an unmarked grave.

I awoke at the crack of dawn. Found Ike and the Lady already up. I ate a huge breakfast and Ike helped me with my team.

I offered to help with cleanup like in the Army. Got a firm NO!

Ike gave me a sack of oats and another of corn for the horses. Also, a tarp for the wagon. I knew I had made a favorable impression when he said, "You don't have to go Augustus."

"I **do** have to Mr. McFee. I have to make it on my own." Whatever "it" was.

"Well don't stay a stranger, like your dad. Stay in touch."

"I will," I said.

I promised them all I would.

Like Saul, I kept my promises.

## Chapter 40

# Whatcha' Cookin'?

I turned north. Steam Valley's fog unrolled like a scroll. I drove by the lane to the Tom Ross place. I couldn't see his homestead. I heard him chopping kindling for heating his breakfast.

"Poor man," said Louisa. "He's all alone. Wife died last Christmas. Kids have gone to war or west."

It was Saturday, July 4th. Independence Day. Bob and Dick were frisky. Anxious to go. I let them.

We got through Fallbrook as the fog was lifting, over the mountain to Bloss by noon. Fed and watered the horses in the Tioga River north of town. Got behind a parade in Mansfield.

They had firecrackers. I shied from them. Bob and Dick wondered why. I heard "Battle Hymn" as we passed the Underground Railroad House. It took me back, that song. I thought of the Cause and our Great Republic and how I knew what the "grapes of wrath" were and how I could still feel that "terrible swift sword." Glad it wasn't God wielding it.

"*Grandpa!*"

The news had travelled north faster than I. The Union had "broken the back" of the Confederacy. Longstreet had lost more than half his men at Pickett's charge.

I heard "Our boys are comin' home!"

I wanted to say…maybe five percent. If you're lucky.

Then someone else called "Soldier!"

I ran the team around the parade. In front of a confused bunch of watchers. I kept going. I didn't want to be the bearer of sad news. Let Ambrose do that. If he has any mind left.

One more day is not gonna hurt.

On Sunday let them find out about the Glories and Ghosts of War, of the Cause, of our Great Experiment, of our Great Win.

Of it's Costs.

I made Lawrenceville early that evening. There too I could hear firecrackers but it was in the distance.

I decided to camp by a large sycamore along the bank of the Tioga River.

A fat yellow rattler sunned itself on a rock near the river. It was suppertime, I was hungry, so I pulled a Stickwalker, killed and skinned that snake. I cut the meat into sections, got out my fry pan and lard, started a cook fire. While the fire grew to hot coals I unhitched the team, took them to water, gave them some grain and picketed them out. They munched on grass, quite content. I filled the pan with snake. It sizzled, browned up nice. I looked around for the snake's mate. They travelled in pairs, rattlers. Hunted after dark. Were especially active this time of year. I wasn't anxious to sleep on the ground that night. Thought it best to sleep in the wagon. I'd pull up Ike's tarp, in case it rained.

A gal came walking down the road. Approached me and my fire. I noticed she was young, had curly brown hair, big blue eyes, freckles and was right pert if ya know what I mean. She spoke first, "Whatcha' cookin'?"

I grabbed my extra plate and fork, panned her out a big piece.

She thought it tasted good. Then told what she was really getting at, why she was really there. (I thought she might be interested in me). "Did **you** steal one of my chickens?"

## The Legend of Augustus McBoone

I grinned, showed her the snake skin.

"Eww!" she squealed.

I'll **never** forget that.

# Comments about

# BEAR HOLLOW

"Very good writing...impressive research, strong characterizations."
- Hilary Hemingway, Director Hemingway First Novel Contest

"Bear Hollow makes terrific reading and it'll look great on the big screen - or even a lot of little ones."
- Hy Cohen, Hy Cohen Literary Agency

"Rod Cochran has created a rich, evocative novel here, with some wonderful hunting sequences that are really quite compelling."
- Leslie Schnurr, Editor In Chief, Delacorte Press

"There is some great writing in this novel and both the concept and execution are solid."
- Paul D. McCarthy, Senior Editor, Simon & Schuster

"Rod Cochran, into timber and writing, represents Pennsylvania well."
- Napoleon St. Cyr, Small Pond Magazine

"The story is certainly a dramatic one... Cochran gives us a sense of place."
- Jonathan Galassi, Editor in Chief, Farrar, Staus & Giroux

"I am very familiar with this area of the country, having grown up in western Pennsylvania, and I thought the geographical context of the book was excellent."
- Harry Helm, Editor, Bantam/Doubleday/Dell

"Bear Hollow does have some polish."
Joseph M. Fox, Senior Editor, Random House

"I read the book with much interest."
Thomas Dunne, Publisher, Thomas Dunne Books, St. Martin's Press

"...a touching, old fashioned sort of story."
Meaghan Dowling, Assistant Editor, Harper Collins

Recognition for

# Bear Hollow

Finalist, Hemingway First Novel Contest

Winner, Willamette Writers Kay Snow Writing Award

Winner, West Branch Christian Writers Fiction Prize

Excerpt, "The Cherry Tree," published in the New England Literary Journal Small Pond

Excerpt, "Farm Girls," published in the Willamette Writer

Excerpts, "The Cloak of Many Colors," "Old Ebenezer," "The Drive," "The Game," published in the Pennsylvania Reader.

Reviewed by Jim Collins, Columnist for the Bradford Era

## The Legend of Augustus McBoone

Reviewed by Gayle Morrow,
Columnist for Wellsboro Gazette

Reviewed by Michael Capuzzo,
Publisher of Mountain Home Magazine

# To Order signed copies from the Author:

Phone: (814) 367-5228

Postal Orders:	Send Payment and/or Order to
The Rod Cochran Agency, Inc.
P. O. Box 157
Westfield, PA 16950

E-Mail:	rodcochran@gmail.com

Name_____

Address_____

City_____State_____Zip_____

Phone_____Fax_____

E-Mail_____

Payment:	Check	Money Order

Costs:	Bear Hollow	21.95
The Legend of Augustus McBoone	27.95
A Temple in Nod	12.95

Shipping, Handling, Sales Tax: Include $5.00 for the first book, $1.00 for each additional book.

CPSIA information can be obtained
at www.ICGtesting.com
Printed in the USA
BVHW01s1924261117
500979BV00004B/6/P

9 781495 813924